KENDALL CARLSSON

SEVEN BY SEVEN

First published by Kendall Carlsson 2021
Copyright © Kendall Carlsson 2021

A catalogue record for this
book is available from the
National Library of Australia

Carlsson, Kendall
Seven by Seven / by Kendall Carlsson
Paperback ISBN 9780645183207
Ebook ISBN 9780645183214

Cover & text design by Cathy Larsen Design

Prologue

The natural world could never be completely conquered. This she knew.

Most people did not share this point of view. Fools.

They were relentless in their pursuit of a single goal – domination. They swarmed across the surface of the earth to ensure no place remained untamed. They would suffer no impediment. Every resource was by right theirs to seize and utilise as they saw fit. With technology and vast arsenals at their disposal, nothing could stop them.

Later, she would struggle to remember, though now, in this place, she alone knew the absolute truth of how much was yet truly wild. Unconquered layers of nature. Other places.

Nobody else could perceive this, not at this moment. She was the only one here.

Perhaps not. She was moving, not of her own volition. A pull that could not be resisted. She was caught in a rip yet there was no water.

She knew the destination. A shadowy place, her arrival therein anxiously awaited. They were always waiting.

She perceived an impossibly deep rumble. Some would assume a distant volcano or waterfall of epic proportions. She knew otherwise and wished she did not.

In moments, her journey would end. She would have company, unseen and unwanted.

The white-haired man would be there too. That smooth, pale face with large eyes of ice blue, unblinking, piercing her with unwavering intensity.

She felt an abrupt jolt. She had just been trying to remember something – or forget. Things were amiss though in a different way now. Her head ached.

There was a bright light, and voices all around. People singing.

1

Witek

A machete swung; a young woman fell. She had been trying to flee.

Witek Zabrewski squeezed his eyes shut. Had the grille outside his window not been malfunctioning, he would have known nothing of what was transpiring outside the bus.

He forced himself to look again. He had to. The victim was a stranger. The next might not be.

Witek felt his heartbeat quicken as he spied two more figures on the pavement. Two men, circling. A shopping trolley stood between them. Gardening tools were raised, now repurposed as weapons. He would never learn which man prevailed as the scene slipped from view.

Witek clenched a fist and ran his knuckles across his brow. This was not the new beginning he sought. Yet even here, on the far side of the world, he was fated to have his footsteps dogged by violence and death.

Other passengers were oblivious to the bloodshed. Only an armoured car was visible through the front windshield, leading their convoy as it picked its way through the town.

Their supervisor, a stern, ageing sergeant seated at the front, had told his charges the bus would have its thick metal window grilles closed whenever the convoy passed through urban areas. He had also said rumours of rampant anarchy outside the capital were conflated. Witek had learned he had to see something in order to consider it truth.

Their escort fell back, soon coming into view through the grille. Witek frowned as he watched the vehicle match their speed on the bus's flank. A trooper, barely older than himself, emerged from a hole in the armoured car's roof. He swayed, aiming his marksman rifle at something to the rear.

Witek's comrades on the bus continued singing. He shook his head and exhaled. Little more than schoolchildren.

"...Awesome Aussie After, isn't it real fun? Maybe I'll just blow my head off with a gun..."

If only they knew. Witek pressed his head to the window. Two young men on trail bikes, unhelmeted, were closing from behind, each holding a length of rubber adorned with sharp metal protrusions all along its length. Road spikes.

"...back there in detention wasn't time well spent, shipped off to a farm – this is how we'll pay our rent..."

Witek opened his mouth to speak to Vlad, who danced in his seat beside him, singing along with the others about the "Awesome Aussie After". Apparently, that's what they were calling this new life. All 24 passengers – more in the bus behind them – had been essentially marooned in Australia after a deadly new pandemic caught the world completely off-guard and society crumbled.

The sergeant locked eyes with Witek before he could so much as utter a word and shook his head. This was unfair. His friend had a right to know of the impending danger. Yet Witek complied.

"This old man in blue here, thinks he is our boss. Tells us what to do but we just don't give a toss..."

The silver-haired sergeant eyed the other passengers, his expression cold. Most people called these guys "Blues" – the security force of the new Australian Ministry of Home Defence. Witek wondered how the officer's duties compared to his own during his time in national service. The time he had ruined his own life.

Witek turned back to the action on the street. It could be no worse than the experiences he tried to forget.

Three denim-clad skinheads waving makeshift weapons emerged from a building and ran out onto the street, the largest man pointing a large hooked blade at the convoy. The other two hurled spiked bats. The escort vehicle's armour plating served its purpose though its driver swerved about, almost losing control.

The pursuing trail bike riders were of more concern. They were the ones who could bring this convoy to a halt.

Witek had hated the boring confinement of the "protected accommodation" blocks back in the heavily militarised capital, Canberra. Mere hours ago, he was glad they were being sent west. Now he was having second thoughts.

Witek thought of his kinsmen in Poland and Lithuania, who last century had been forced into a dreadful journey of their own after their homelands were annexed by the Soviets. Most fell to elemental and human brutality in the gulag of Siberia's far northeast, their remains perhaps encased within the infamous Road of Bones.

"Awesome Aussie farmers, what will they be like? Give us too much crap

and we'll make 'em take a hike…"

Witek glanced at the singers: mainly backpackers from other nations, a few Australians too, twenty-somethings, some still in their teens. Circumstances deprived them of self-determination, but they had full bellies, warm seats and armour all about them. This was better than traversing 1940s taiga, shivering and starved – it was hard to imagine the life those poor souls endured. While he was not the political prisoner of a despotic regime, Witek owed it to them to remain cool and resolute no matter what confronted him.

He hoped this Australian "emergency government" had the strength to maintain order as he watched the escort trooper open fire, silenced shots inaudible over the din within the bus. The riders drew closer and Witek did not blink. One fell from his seat, his road spike contraption writhing as it struck the pavement. The other veered off down a side street.

Several heartbeats later, the scene was clear. Witek rubbed his forehead with the back of his hand.

His comrades continued to sing.

A sharp elbow brought his attention back inside. "Come on, Witek. For once, join in."

Vlad could usually lighten his serious temperament. His friend ran a hand through his blond hair before proceeding to fist pump the air with such enthusiasm, Witek thought his friend might bounce out of his seat. He could have almost passed for a beach-dwelling Aussie.

The pair had met while fruit picking, not long after each had arrived in Australia on working visas. Ever since, they had travelled together, drunk vodka together and chased the ladies together.

Well, admittedly the more gregarious Vlad had been much more proactive and successful with the latter pursuit. While more restrained, Witek could not help but turn his head should a fair female pass by, albeit more discreetly than most men. No one would ever accuse him of being a flirt.

"Why watch the boring scenery out there? Come, join in before the song ends. I could add a melody of my own."

Vlad reached into his pack and withdrew his koncovka. The instrument's elder wood was ornately carved and Witek appreciated its physical beauty and the traditional melodies Vlad played, but this was not some pleasant evening by a campfire.

"Put that away. Work on something when we arrive. I have a headache."

They bumped over a level railway crossing and Witek gripped his seat. He spotted the second rider, crossing the same tracks around 100 metres away, where it sped along a parallel street, undeterred by sporadic fire from the escort trooper. Glancing ahead, Witek saw a curve in the road. Their routes would intersect; the rider, road spikes still in hand, would reach that place first.

Bricks rained from a rooftop onto the armoured car. The rifleman was struck. Dropping his weapon, he collapsed back within the vehicle.

Sunlight reflected from something small and metallic in the air closing low and fast behind the trail bike. Moments later, the young rider tumbled onto the asphalt. Buildings obscured his fate.

Witek took a deep breath in and held it, eyes darting about the streetscape.

The singers' tune was building to its crescendo.

Seven by Seven

"Awesome Aussie After, we're all vibing out. This lame bus trip, it makes us scream and shout. Hey!"

Witek did not feel part of this group. Nor did he deserve to be. Vlad winked at him and put away the koncovka. Witek inclined his head, grateful his friend recognised when he needed a bit of space.

The armoured grilles opened unexpectedly, revealing a bright, sunny, empty rural landscape. Witek released his grip on the seat and exhaled as he felt the bus gather speed.

He and the Blues alone knew what had transpired in that town. The uniformed men appeared completely calm and unaffected, making Witek wonder how familiar such action had become to these troopers.

The image of a swinging machete kept replaying in his mind and Witek knew he had to file it among the other memories he bore with forced stoicism. The landscape, now devoid of threats, offered little distraction so he forced himself to focus on the interior of the bus.

Witek glanced around at the other passengers. Though some had been accommodated in different blocks, there were familiar faces. Many had bonded quickly, with similar stories of having been fortunate enough to reach the capital, a designated "safe zone" with food, water, power, shelter and law enforcement. Areas with this designation were deemed free of contagion too, or so the authorities claimed.

The more silent people on the bus stood out most prominently. Closest to the Blues was a large, broad-shouldered, round-faced guy who wore his hair in a short military style, much like Witek's. He did not care to be festive and watched the way ahead. Looking past

Vlad, across the aisle, Witek noticed a slim guy staring silently at his own hands, fidgeting. In front of him was an equally serious girl, sitting motionless, lost in thought. She was slightly on the tall side but her long, sandy-blonde hair, despite being much fairer, was worn in two long braids, just like Marcelina.

The blonde must have felt his eyes on her as she turned, frowning, meeting his gaze with her own large, dark eyes. The freckles sprinkled across her nose and cheekbones, as well as the bronze hue of her skin, hinted at someone who had spent much time outdoors. He stiffened, realising he was staring. Giving a curt nod and flushing slightly, he turned back to the window to brood about his cousin.

Marcelina was somewhere in this land, having sought work "out west". Witek knew that might be anywhere in the continent's vast interior. Everyone else on the bus had been disconnected from loved ones when the pandemic escalated, but some weeks after arriving in Canberra, Witek had been surprised by unexpected contact. Despite no access to the failed communication networks, he always kept his Marektek smartphone charged just in case.

Marcelina had called late one evening, her anxious voice speaking rapidly in Polish, telling Witek to shut up and listen. He had contained a torrent of questions and remained silent. There had been a commotion in the background. Marcelina had said she was "still here" and had stolen a guard's phone. Something was going on, people were coming. Gunshots. She had paused to catch her breath. She said they were already in the yard. Another pause, then, her voice confused, "These people are not —" Disconnection. Silence.

Witek had no callback number, no phone service, no idea where she was. There was the question of Marcelina's final words, regarding *what* exactly these people were or were not.

Most troubling was a whisper that people sent out to work on farms would sometimes disappear. Someone knew someone whose roommate had heard a guard say this. Normally Witek would dismiss such gossip. Thinking how Marcelina's panicked words were somehow connected had twisted his insides ever since.

He had a duty to try to find her and took vague comfort from the fact he had a better chance now he was no longer confined within the capital.

A proximity alarm beeped inside the bus as the escort vehicle moved to retake its position in front. Several passengers voiced echoes, mocking the alarm.

"Safety features on everything these days, so my father always said," Vlad observed. "Hashtag nanny states."

Witek nodded to his friend. "Yes, Vlad. Nobody takes personal responsibility for anything anymore… and look where that got the world."

Outside, the rolling hills were painted in hues of light brown with swathes of yellow gold in places. Though the farms here were comparatively vast, the canola crops reminded Witek of home. Other hills were bare, brown, crowned by boulders. He wondered whether he would ever see beauty in this land.

Witek's attention was drawn back inside as a voice blurted out on the speakers. "All right, keep it down now, people."

The officer up front stroked his moustache, curtly clapped his hands twice and continued.

"I am Sergeant Booth. We are between safe zones. We expect no trouble ahead but please be vigilant and keep the noise down."

Witek noted the complete lack of acknowledgement of the trouble behind them.

"Later, we will disembark at a checkpoint, then continue directly to your place of work within the Northern Riverlands Ag Zone. Your farm overseer will give further instructions."

Witek was aware that some supervisors had historically treated backpacker labourers on farms less fairly than others.

"Is anything unclear?" Sergeant Booth dusted the front of his navy-blue uniform.

"Will we sleep in a town?" someone near the front asked.

"No," Booth replied. "There are towns servicing each zone, but all workers are to remain on their assigned farms."

Vlad nudged Witek. "Are these guys even soldiers or what?"

"Probably not. Ex-cops? I heard some were recruited from private security firms. I can handle a rifle. Should I volunteer? The job might have advantages. I might learn more about what is really going on."

"Ha, very funny, Witek. Even you are not grumpy and serious enough to qualify for that uniform. See how they get less and less friendly every week? Hope these Blues do not turn into a bunch of reds."

Witek nodded and scrunched his face at the thought of a full-blown totalitarian regime seizing control here.

"I have a question — will there be a beach there?" someone drawled from the row behind. This drew laughter; even a couple of Booth's men sniggered until their sergeant flashed the troopers a brief glare.

He exhaled audibly. "No. The ocean is hundreds of kilometres away, but who knows? If you're a good boy, your overseer may let you build a sandpit."

More laughter.

"Maybe I was wrong," whispered Vlad. "That sounded like humour from the sergeant. Quick, Witek, go and sign up."

The bus brakes squeaked as the convoy slowed.

The dark-eyed blonde spoke next. "Is this agricultural area a designated safe zone?"

"Yes," Booth replied. "This ag zone is part of our jurisdiction and therefore is monitored and protected. The work you will be doing is crucial for maintaining our food security –"

Booth cut off his explanation as he noticed his men murmuring to the driver, pointing at an intersection ahead. There was no time to close the window grilles. Everyone leaned to one side and peered outside as the convoy made a slow left turn. Several crows scattered as the vehicles drew near. Everyone on board was silent.

Adorning the signpost were three severed human heads.

2

Phuong

"Don't worry, Foo. They said we'll soon be there. I'm sure Duc's fine."

"Thanks, Sam. Though I still don't get why they made him take the other bus."

Tran Thi Phuong continued pushing back the cuticles of her nails, unconsciously moving from finger to finger, changing hands, all the while staring blankly at the back of the armoured bus in front of their own. Samantha's attempts at reassurance were not helping much, though Phuong appreciated the gesture.

"It does feel weird, Foo. I can't remember a school bus trip ever in our whole lives where Duc wasn't sitting right there across the aisle on his phone."

Phuong glanced across the aisle at the stranger sleeping where her brother normally would have chosen to sit and sighed. While Duc was physically slim, like her, she always felt more secure in his presence.

"We're going the wrong way, Sam. I thought this farming trip might bring us closer to Sydney. Have we ever been this far west?"

"Don't think so. I have no idea where we even are. The land of freaks and killers, that's for sure. Not gonna be easy to get home now."

"Mm," Phuong replied, looking at her feet.

"Still worried about everyone? Remember Foo, Protea Place has survived lockdowns before and they'll pull through this one too. After the last one, my baba got more into the community garden than ever. She'll be feeding the whole neighbourhood by now."

Phuong leaned back and looked through the window grilles. The open landscape in no way resembled the tiny sliver of green space nestled between two apartment blocks in Protea Place. She knew that little garden would not yield enough to sustain even a few families for very long, assuming they had survived the pathogen that had run rampant in the coastal cities.

"Yes, Sam. I am sure they are eating better than us."

"So, back there. Have you ever seen anything like it?"

"Only on the loading screen of one of Duc's games. 'Tyrant's Castle' I think it was."

"Don't think that was a mad king's work. Drugs for sure. Reckon it was bullblood?"

Phuong winced, remembering the grisly task of the troopers who were ordered to get out and remove the heads from the sign.

"Probably. No sane person would do that. They'd have to be on something."

"Well, they reckon full-blown bullblood rage gives you heart failure, so hopefully whoever did that won't be coming after us."

"I hope so, Sam."

Phuong glanced about outside. There was no sign of anything moving aside from their convoy. The undulating landscape closer to the capital lay behind them, having given way to flatter country. There was little to see aside from dry, untended pastures.

As the bus entered a dip in the road, Phuong saw a buckled floodway sign, snapped depth indicator pole and several shrubs in disarray.

Concerned voices murmured about her.

"What the…" Samantha began.

A truck had overturned and come to rest in a dry creek bed several metres off the roadside. Bits of metal, broken crates and other debris were all strewn about the gully. Something resembling a large white letter Z had been spray painted on the side of the truck's cabin.

"Can you see anyone, Foo?"

"Nothing moving. No bodies as far as I can see. Maybe they got out alive."

"I sure as hell wouldn't want to be stuck out here alone," said Samantha, twirling a strand of hair.

The convoy moved up and out of the dip and Phuong could see they were approaching a natural gap in a range of tooth-like hills. A railway joined the highway, running parallel, both routes taking advantage of the easiest path through the terrain.

Minutes later, they had passed through the gap and the convoy began to slow. People started chattering.

"Relax, everyone," said the uniformed officer at the front. "It's just our pit stop."

Phuong spotted the Blues' checkpoint — a gated compound surrounded by a high fence. Concrete barricades placed on the highway forced traffic into a choke point. Guards were waving through an armoured road train heading the other way, presumably transporting goods back to the capital. Their own convoy held position to let it pass. Phuong could not see what supplies the truck was hauling but armed Blues were riding shotgun on each trailer so she deduced the cargo was sufficiently important.

A guard in the tower by the compound's main gate waved them forward. Inside were small modern portable structures and a much older timber railway building on a decaying platform, flaking paintwork suggesting it had not seen service in decades, perhaps only still standing by virtue of heritage status protection. At one end of this building a workshop was attached, two troopers tinkering with a large drone within.

A small solar array had been installed to power the facility and at the end of the platform, old grain silos rose high above all else, several derelict rail carriages coupled together along their base. Several more stretched along the railway outside the compound too, all rusty and covered with graffiti. Phuong spied a guard ambling lazily high up on a catwalk linking the silos.

As their convoy stopped in the yard, passengers from the bus in front spilled out, swinging arms, stretching legs and loosening stiff joints. An officer appeared to address them as they stood in neat lines, as if at a school assembly. A couple of small drones buzzed among them for a while.

The sergeant in charge of Phuong's bus, Selvin, was leaning out the door, observing.

Phuong turned to Samantha. "Can you make anything out?"

"Apart from the school assembly, not much. We're not refuelling or anything. Why stop here?"

"I don't know. To swap supplies? Look."

A pair of Blues exited a portable building carrying some metal chests. Phuong craned her neck as they approached. The lids were closed and locked but she could make out little more before they were loaded into a storage compartment somewhere in the side of their bus.

"What do you think happened to him?" Samantha pointed to a trooper being helped out of an armoured car and placed on a stretcher.

Phuong shrugged, watching the young man writhing, his eyes squeezed shut.

Their friend Jacko appeared beside them, standing in the aisle. "Hey, hey, ladies. I spy Duc."

Phuong sat up straight. "Hey, Jacko. Really? Where?"

Jacko pointed.

Her brother was striding their way. He was a little taller and lankier than Phuong, his face thin and angular, while hers was more heart-shaped. Sergeant Selvin blocked his approach.

"Hey kid, stick with your own crew."

Phuong jumped to her feet. "Wait, he's my brother. Can I please get out?"

Selvin eyed her for several seconds. "Now, we can't have you lot running about our compound all at once..."

The sergeant was distracted by a senior officer on the railway platform, signalling.

"Hmm. Boss man says it's your turn. All right, I'll allow your family reunion. Maybe someday you can do a little favour for me in return."

His lingering leer left Phuong feeling more than a little uncomfortable and she averted her eyes, grateful when he turned to swing himself back out of the bus.

"Everybody out now please," Selvin called over his shoulder.

The sergeant strutted over to the railway platform, saluted the senior officer rather casually, and entered the old building.

Phuong hurried out with the others. Duc was waiting just outside the door, face lined with anxiety.

"Foo, are you OK?"

"Yes. Yes, I'm fine. We all are. Have you been told anything?"

"Not much. Just that this ag zone is close now. Our sergeant said about an hour to go."

Samantha spoke up. "So… you guys saw…"

Duc nodded. "I was on the wrong side of the bus so didn't see much. A guy called Chad said it looked like it just happened. Fresh. He saw blood dripping when the Blues took them off the sign."

"Whoever did it was probably still nearby," said Jacko. "What if they followed us?"

Phuong stopped, shuddered and looked back, the others watching her gaze. Perhaps a maniac was still on the highway, hidden in the heat haze or staring down from the rocky hills encircling the outpost to the east and north.

Duc mused, "Bullblood? Random local nutter? There's talk of people going completely feral outside the safe zones."

The sergeant on the other bus shouted something, then a tall guy hollered over to Duc, "We're heading out. All aboard, bud."

"OMG, you're kidding, right?" Duc grumbled, holding up an arm.

"It's fine. We're all OK and can catch up when we arrive," said Phuong.

Duc gave her a hug, waved to the others then spun on his heel to jog back to his bus. Phuong watched him go, stretched and looked about the compound.

Selvin had not yet returned and was still up at the railway building, enjoying a conversation over radio peppered with intermittent laughter. Phuong winced at the sound.

"Oh, he's so gross," said Jacko, coming to her side to watch the officers on the platform. "Can smell his nasty aftershave a mile off. Such a sleaze."

"After we reach the farm, hopefully we won't see him again," said Phuong. "Hey, I wonder what kinds of drones these Blues are using."

Phuong had worked with agricultural drones used for monitoring and enhancing crop performance. The big ag companies utilised new high-efficiency solar technologies to power many of their UAVs, some of which could stay aloft virtually indefinitely. The drone in the workshop had a V-shaped flying wing design, which Phuong knew were used for a range of different applications, from data communications to surveillance.

Before she could investigate further, Jacko nudged her. "Eww. He's coming back."

Selvin had finished his radio conversation and with the assistance of two other Blues was now herding everyone together.

"Time to check in, people. Form two lines for your scans. Spread out, stand on the marks."

Phuong was unsure whether the chalk marks on the concrete

were set so far apart as a social distancing measure or simply designed to allow a clearer look at each individual. The Blues seemed unconcerned about disease prevention given the cramped seating aboard the buses. Even protected accommodation had not afforded anyone much personal space. No trooper even wore a mask, nor had anyone in her group been given one.

Small drones hovered momentarily in front of each person in turn, checking temperatures and scanning faces. If they were building a face database, Phuong wondered why the Blues were using drones.

When it was her turn, she irritably glared at the lens. She was an Australian citizen inside her own country yet it seemed everyone was being logged, regardless of citizenship. The drone hovered in place, rocking a little from side to side then moved on to Jacko, who poked his tongue out at the pesky machine and danced on the spot.

A trooper strode forth, grabbing her friend by the shoulders from behind and barked into his ear. "Keep still. Eyes front."

Jacko rolled his eyes but remained motionless. The drone merely lingered in front of him a little longer before continuing down the line.

"Fascists," she heard Samantha mutter.

"Jeez, what can I say? Some men just can't keep their hands off me," said Jacko, dusting himself off.

The trooper did not acknowledge either comment as he marched to the front, clasped his hands behind his back and glared at the next person being scanned.

Soon the scans were done. If the Blues had issues with anyone, they said nothing. The UAVs buzzed up and over the bus, out of sight.

Selvin ushered everyone back on board. Phuong waved to the other bus as it idled by the main gate, waiting for other vehicles to take their positions in the convoy. She could not see Duc.

Soon everyone was seated and they rolled out, the guards at the highway barricade waving them through.

Sergeant Selvin sat sideways, leering at various female passengers.

"Don't make eye contact," whispered Samantha. "Just look at the land."

"I know. When we arrive, we'll stick together, buddy up with other workers and make sure we're good friends with the farmers."

"Sounds like a plan."

Phuong felt Selvin's eyes linger. She pointed to the right, raising her voice. "Look, that might've been be a nice place to live back in the day. I hope our farm is like that."

They passed the entrance to a long driveway, towering silver-green aloe plants growing scrappily on each side. The driveway then crossed the railway, where a sign leaned sideways, the words "GIVE WAY TO TRAINS" still discernible despite a peppering of bullet holes. Long grass growing between the railway sleepers suggested the sign had been rendered obsolete.

A second gateway, old timbers now collapsing, lay beyond the crossing. The driveway became a once-grand avenue, trees now half-dead, leading to some old farm buildings halfway up the jagged hills.

"Dread to think who lives there now," said Samantha.

The railway remained parallel to the highway and they passed a couple more disused grain silos, painted top to bottom with huge murals. Though faded from exposure, Phuong could see these works of art depicted scenes of early settlers and farm animals.

She turned to Samantha. "Wonder how the artist got up there?"

"Abseiled down from the top?" Samantha ventured.

A guy with floppy hair seated behind them interrupted. "Actually, they most likely used a boom lift. Probably the telescopic kind."

"Umm, alright thanks, Harry."

Phuong knew her friend did not like know-alls but did not like to sound ignorant either and was unsurprised when Samantha leaned close to her ear and whispered, "Boom lift?"

"One of those cherry picker things," Phuong murmured.

Samantha nodded. "Do they go that high?"

Another interruption. "Some operate at well over fifty metres and it's 'Harrison' by the way."

Samantha whirled, standing to lean over the seat and glare down at him. "Well, Foo, it's a good thing we didn't forget to bring our HARRY-fucking-paedia."

"I can't help being more informed than some," he muttered, turning away.

"Fun fact — no one gives a flying fig tree," said Samantha.

Phuong pulled her friend back down before she became too fiery.

"Look how flat the plain is out there, Sam. Bit different to Sydney or Canberra."

Phuong had never seen so much open space. The only trees visible were growing along roadside verges and fence lines. There was nothing but brown dead weeds and dust in the paddocks.

There were several more silos along the railway, spectacularly painted with unique imagery, each perhaps the work of a different artist.

"Is this our ag zone?" asked Sam.

"Surely not. Can't see anyone around, no machinery moving, no irrigation. Looks like it was once dry-area grain farmland but no winter crops have been planted."

Phuong noted some silos and farm gates bore relatively new signage, overtly displaying the logo of the Lucky Dragons Corporation, one of several multinational big ag companies that had steadily acquired many smaller holdings in Australia, mainly producing large-scale crops exclusively for export.

They passed tiny ghost towns, their decaying buildings mainly constructed from fibro or weatherboard, with corrugated iron roofing. Some structures, like the big old pubs, looked like they had been there over a hundred years, perhaps surviving due to heritage listing more than customer support. Phuong did not know anyone among her peers who saw much historic value in dusty old pubs.

There were small public parks too, their once manicured lawns now overgrown, seating benches half-obscured by long dry grass and weeds. Full of snakes, she suspected.

One of these abandoned villages served as another small depot for the Blues. The convoy slowed but passed by without stopping, a handful of morose-looking guards waving them on.

As they passed another pair of silos, painted as a war memorial and covered top to bottom with poppy flowers, another range of hills loomed ahead. These rose higher than the rocky range near the Blues' checkpoint.

Phuong was surprised when they entered through a forested area, skirting the base of a prominent hill. The sun had dropped low in the sky, treetops lit with golden hues. A welcome contrast to the dusty plain behind.

Five minutes later they slowed, as the trees began to thin out revealing more farmland.

They reached a crossroad. Up front, Selvin stood and waved to the other bus. Phuong saw it was making a right turn, crossing the railway onto an unsealed side road that disappeared northward into the trees. Along with its escort vehicle, the first bus stirred up red dust as it left the asphalt.

Their own driver tooted the horn and turned left, accelerating down a long straight sealed road stretching in the opposite direction.

Fear shot through Phuong's chest and she gasped. Duc was heading someplace else. She was being separated from her brother.

"Wait, where are they going?" she heard Jacko call out.

Selvin turned to them. "Oh, just off to their farm. And you? You'll soon be enjoying your own new home too. The overseer just can't wait to meet you."

As his eyes flicked in her direction, Phuong did not like the way the sergeant was smirking.

3

Sienna

The bus stopped abruptly, wheels crunching on the gravel road, passengers lurching forward. Dust swirled about outside while uncertain voices within expressed statements of confusion, peppered with a few expletives. Sienna remained silent, large dark eyes darting in all directions, peering through the grilles. The late-afternoon sunlight revealed native woodland on both sides of the road.

As the dust began to disperse, Sienna saw they had stopped on a small concrete causeway where the road crossed a dry gully littered with lumpy rocks. Sergeant Booth nodded to one of his men, who adjusted his rifle and raised it as the door opened. The trooper leaned outside, scanning the bushland before disembarking to meet the armoured car in front. Booth took a rifle then joined his men, who were pointing ahead.

A short distance in front of the escort vehicle a massive gnarled dead tree had fallen, completely blocking the road. Its top branches disappeared into the scrubby understorey on the right, while a mess of twisted roots was unearthed to the left. There was no way any vehicle could skirt around the obstacle.

Booth cursed and waved them back. The bus and its escort could only reverse. Booth stayed put, rubbing his chin. Sienna was still unsure what she thought of the man. There was little warmth about him.

She disliked authoritarian types and despised the Blues' "do as we say, without question" attitude. Most of all, she hated them for taking her parents and brother away with no explanation other than, "Your government needs these people. You will be provided for." Stopped on the road and forcibly separated.

They had been travelling using false names and false records. Her travelling name was "Sindy Mason" – easy enough to remember, her family presenting themselves as unrelated people sharing a vehicle.

Her family disliked the present government. Before the pandemic, they had claimed power with ease, following public dissatisfaction with ineffective previous political parties but also by their tactic of fielding sports stars and well-liked celebrities as candidates. Sienna considered herself savvy enough to have recognised that high-quality political credentials were not traits most sought after by much of the voting public.

Sienna looked at the troopers' uniforms. There had been men like this on every corner in Canberra. She wondered if this was what it was like living under less democratic regimes – those her parents suspected had been manipulating affairs here at home. She wondered if any celebrity puppet politicians were still even in parliament.

Sienna maintained her false name, secure among the lost and orphaned, another faceless solitary refugee fleeing civil strife. However, she still felt hunted without entirely understanding why.

Now, out here with this bunch of randoms, Sienna was to pay for the privilege of months of detention with forced exile at a work camp in the middle of nowhere.

Sienna admitted it was a very pretty part of nowhere, especially given the absence of people. Life went on, oblivious to humanity's crises. She had seen great mobs of kangaroos in the abandoned pastures and the ever-present crows were thriving. Outside, hundreds of tiny bugs were lit by shafts of sunlight filtering through the trees, their airborne dance resembling a miniature dogfight.

Aboard the bus, tired, restless voices were mumbling. Chad, the big American guy with two-toned hair, paced the aisle. He walked to the front, where a trooper glared, sternly demanding he get back. Chad stopped but refused to retreat, pausing by Sienna's seat, gripping a metal rail that ran along the ceiling with long, muscular arms. He swung in place for a bit, staring defiantly at the trooper. Sienna liked those arms, slightly bronzed from the sun but, unlike many of her fellow Aussies, not covered with an excessive mess of tattoos. She gratefully noted he used antiperspirant and wondered how he had been able to obtain the scarce luxury item.

Before she could think up any small talk as a means of introduction, the American dropped with a thud and pointed towards Booth.

"Hey man, check it out," he announced, to nobody in particular.

Booth and his men stood with weapons raised. Sienna could hear the motorbikes before she saw them and they soon came into view, stopping beyond the fallen tree.

"Two trail bikes and a quad," Chad observed.

The rider of the quad bike dismounted, hands raised, and vaulted over the fallen tree. He was quite tall and wore a great coat, dark blue-grey, neatly tailored with large buttons that caught the sunlight. Almost like a uniform but no insignia were visible. Weapons were lowered as he approached Booth, stopping metres away. A discussion began.

"Wish I could hear," she murmured after observing the conversation for several moments.

"Yeah. Think it's getting heated," Chad noted.

Arms gesticulated. The tall man turned his head towards the bus, a few more words were exchanged, then they all strode onto the causeway.

Booth returned to the bus and leaned in. "OK, everybody out. Collect your gear."

One of the Blues had already opened a storage chamber from which he hauled all the personal belongings brought from protected accommodation and dumped them in a heap.

As Sienna jumped outside, she caught scents of dry grass and dust. The smells of the Australian Outback were unmistakable.

Booth addressed the group once all were assembled.

"OK, everybody. You've arrived. That is Acting Overseer Kilo —" Booth narrowed his eyes at the tall man as he spoke the odd-sounding title "— and he will take things from here. You are all fully aware what a mess the world has become. Remember, your efforts on this farm will help keep things working. Your government thanks you for your service. Come on, troopers."

Booth nodded at Kilo, then hurried aboard the bus.

"And there he goes..." observed Chad.

"Doesn't mess about with words. Dude says his piece and he's gone, just like that," Sienna agreed.

"I'm mister military man, straight to the point," mocked Vlad, one of the backpackers, holding his forefinger over his top lip.

"Ex-police, most likely," said Vlad's uptight-looking friend as he hoisted a large pack onto his back.

"Finally, Witek," said Vlad, whose long hair was sandy blond, much like her own. He cheerfully addressed the group.

"I've been telling my friend here for weeks these guys are definitely ex-cops."

Sienna wondered which country they called home. Somewhere within continental Europe.

The serious guy gave his friend a look and simply said, "Well, Vlad…"

He did not bother to continue, instead turning from the group to fuss about with a strap on his pack.

"That moustache does look like a cop's," said Chad.

Sienna tilted her head. "How does a cop moustache differ from a military moustache?"

Vlad repeated his Booth impersonation. "Your government thanks you for – Hey, does this mean we're all now officially citizens of, er, whatever's left of Australia? Where are our Aussie passports?"

"Nice of him to let us know s where the other bus went," said Karmen, a girl around her own height, who was blessed with long, healthy, shiny brown hair.

The Blues' vehicles roared to life in unison and began to depart. Sienna noted even the escort had difficulty turning around with so many obstacles about. The bus required a long careful reverse and a five-point turn.

Kilo took a couple of steps forward as the convoy departed. His eyes were concealed behind dark sunglasses, face clean shaven and young looking but somewhat gaunt. Sienna could not guess his age.

The vehicles accelerated and soon vanished in their own clouds of dust. Only once the noise of their engines faded did Kilo address the group.

"So, it would appear you are my guests." He spoke with a somewhat cultivated Australian accent.

He gestured at the road. "They say we have an important duty – to feed what's left of civilisation. In return, they offer us protection, watching over us with their drones. A 'safe zone' they call it. What a joke. If you have not already figured this out, get used to the fact that nowhere is safe in this world now."

Kilo scanned the group silently for a few moments then went on. "As far as I am concerned, you are all free. You do not have to stay here, do not have to work for the Blues nor serve any government. You can simply walk away – now or whenever you please. However, I suspect you all have an inkling of the kind of lawlessness that exists out there."

Chad spoke up, "We know… today we saw…"

He stopped and took a deep breath through gritted teeth.

Kilo regarded him for a moment. "American. Texan?"

Chad's face lightened again. "Why yes, sir. Wharton County, Texas."

Kilo nodded. "Welcome. Any news from home?"

Chad shook his head slowly. Kilo glanced at the other faces assembled. "Anyone?"

A murmur and more shaking of heads.

The brief silence was broken by an ocker voice. "Look, mate, we've been stuck in a building for months. Us Aussies haven't heard shit about what's going on in our own backyards, let alone these poor bastards."

Kilo turned his head momentarily in the direction of the rough-spoken girl, who'd seated herself on a large rock beside the road with a friend. Sienna had heard the pair's loud voices aboard the bus, their language coloured by expletives.

Kilo did not respond, instead turning back to the group assembled on the road. "In any case, welcome. I can see most of you are very far from home. Exiled out here at the ends of the earth."

Sienna thought of her mother's words – *information is everything.* "And where exactly are we?"

She had a reasonable idea, but despite being well-travelled, had never visited this part of the country.

"Is there a town nearby?" she added, hoping for a clearer picture.

"Budgieweir is the nearest town you may have heard of."

Sienna recognised the name but knew little aside from that the area had produced rice and other crops for decades.

Kilo elaborated, confirming her assumption. "It was built as a central hub to service the irrigation scheme, which has kept the area productive for over a hundred years. Population has taken a massive hit, just like everywhere else I gather."

"The Big V?" asked Chad.

Vlad interjected. "Wait, is that what we're calling this virus now? I thought it was Hainan duck flu or something."

Kilo rubbed his chin. "I am not sure if there is an official name or if it is a type of influenza. There may not even be a viral pathogen involved. It might be bacterial or some kind of parasite. I really do not know. I hoped you might have brought more information from Canberra."

"Most do think it's a virus but nobody confirmed that in lockdown. We were screened for symptoms when we first arrived in Canberra and had temperature scans this afternoon," Sienna explained.

Kilo nodded curtly and scanned the group. "Yes, good. That is what the Blues said. I was told you are all clear."

Sienna then realised that Kilo had remained standing well back from the group, over ten metres away. A cautious man. Sensible. Perhaps well practised in social distancing from having lived through previous pandemics.

"If it's got any of us, we just haven't figured out we're supposed to be dead yet," said Vlad.

Vlad's serious friend spoke up again. "What he means is this thing acts fast. Much faster than something like influenza or coronavirus. Kills the infected person very quickly. We would have all died in lockdown months ago, living so close to each other."

A strong guy, who looked like a soldier, spoke up. "You sneeze constantly for a whole day. Everyone nearby gets infected. You get a fever. Airways full of blood. You choke up, cannot breathe. Two days later, you are dead. I overheard some guards saying this."

"Yes. This is consistent with what I have heard," said Kilo. "Respiratory droplets are at least one form of transmission. Anyway, remember it is virulent enough to have spread worldwide in under two weeks. I have heard of no new cases in this area for a while but we can never be complacent. The Blues claim they are controlling all roads into this ag zone and restricting movement in and out of Budgieweir. Let us hope they are truly watching for signs of infection."

Kilo scanned the group again. Sienna sensed he was looking for something else. Perhaps someone.

A large flock of galahs passed overhead, their noisy chattering drowning out any attempt at further conversation. Kilo glanced up, his mouth drawn into a line, brow creasing.

When the birds moved on, he continued. "It is late. If you choose to live and work on my land, I assume you will want to reach your lodgings while it is still light. Grab your gear, climb over that tree and follow the road. After a couple of kilometres, you will reach some sheds. We will meet there. Let us see who arrives first."

Kilo turned on his heel and strode swiftly back to the fallen tree, which Sienna could clearly see was a massive eucalypt.

"Wait, what about the other..." Vlad called out.

Kilo held up his hand, twisted it as if to wave, and departed without turning. As he started his quad bike and sped away with his escort, Sienna realised the overseer's companions had remained in the background, silent and helmeted.

Chad came up beside her, already having shouldered his pack. "A challenge. Race you? Anyone?"

The brash girl seated on the rock spoke up again, "Get stuffed, mate. Why should we rush off to his place just cos he says so?"

"Nobody's making you go, Jazlyn," said a big guy with an impressive mane of hair. "He said you can walk away. Walk back to Canberra."

"Maybe we will, Iosefa," said Jazlyn's friend.

"Fine, Chaylarna, good luck with that," said the big guy. "Try to keep your head on your shoulders."

"Don't listen to any of 'em, Chay," said Jazlyn. "Let's just hang here for a while, until we decide what we want to do."

"Night will come soon," said Vlad.

Sienna glanced at the group, which numbered around twenty. Aside from the two defiant Australian girls – Jazlyn and her friend Chaylarna – everyone was gathering their gear and preparing to move out. Sienna gathered the two girls were immature but probably not stupid.

"Bet they join us in the end," she said to Chad.

He nodded. "I'll definitely beat those two."

Chad started jogging at a brisk pace and vaulted the fallen tree.

Sienna and several others followed the American. Sienna noted his competitiveness. In different circumstances she may have raced ahead to challenge him but settled for a fast march, to better take in her surroundings.

To the right of the dusty road, the woodland continued, thick with undergrowth in some places, sparse elsewhere, particularly where the land rose gently. Catching glimpses of hilltops, Sienna could see they were now on the west side of the final range of hills they had passed on their journey. To the left, the forest thinned, the land flat, open, with overgrown but otherwise empty fields, all bathed in orange light.

She paused to watch the sun vanish over the horizon as two group members jogged past, ignoring her as they puffed rhythmically by. Sienna planted her feet and stood straight, closing her eyes, taking a moment to enjoy a small breeze that sprang up and caressed her face.

She felt a pleasant rush of goose bumps on her spine. Enjoying the sensation, Sienna nurtured it, deliberately channelling the energy down her arms, letting it wash over her before it faded. The feeling was strong in this environment, enhanced almost.

She knew that for regular people, this was something only induced by external stimuli — an awe-inspiring vista, a singer's incredible vocal performance or an epic movie scene. However, Sienna could bring this sensation on at will with no trigger whatsoever.

The rest of her family could not do this. As children, her brother Craig had teased her about having the world's most useless superpower. People on social media would no doubt puzzle, discuss, debate and troll her about this trait if they knew, so she had spent her life keeping it to herself.

There was a dark side to this ability too, a chill born of fear that lurked in nightmares, associated with a shadowy place she had learned to push to the farthest recess of her consciousness, at least during waking hours.

Sienna opened her eyes. She fingered her medallion, feeling the lines of the smiling cat etched into the metal on its front face. It was a precious thing — her mother had made it years ago as a birthday gift. She had never taken it off since the family had left their home for the last time.

She sighed, not wanting worrying thoughts of loved ones to ruin this brief sense of connection to the land, and took note of the birds. Crows cawed somewhere in the distance. Something chirruped in a tree, perhaps a galah or parrot of some kind. She heard the distinctive whistle-song and chattering of a willy wagtail and spotted it chasing insects out in the fields.

Footsteps crunching up the gravel road grabbed her attention. This group would soon pass by, hopefully giving her no more than an odd look or muttered remark behind her back. Even among this diverse group, no doubt some would judge her as "a little bit different" and Sienna was most comfortable being invisible, unless she had something to say.

She started as Vlad unexpectedly clapped her on the shoulder and swung in beside her. He was carrying a woodwind instrument, some kind of flute perhaps.

"Tired already?" He looked out at the western horizon, audibly inhaling the country air deeply then pretending to sneeze.

Vlad's friend did not stop to join them and marched on, thoughts directed elsewhere. Sienna watched the grim young man pass by.

"What's up with the serious dude… your mate there. Witold, right? Think that's the name I read on his pack."

"Witek. He says only his family call him 'Witold' and prefers the common nickname for a quite common Polish first name. Just as I am Vladimir."

He bowed theatrically.

"However, you may call me 'Vlad', my lady."

"Well then, Vlad. Serious question – are we making the right decision? Doing what the Blues demand and choosing to work out here?"

"Witek and I have already spent very much time on farms in this country. This kind of work is not so bad but the Blues – we do not care for them. Witek saw murderous bandits attack our convoy in a town back there and that sergeant kept it hushed."

"Ah. I felt something was up before we even saw, well, what we saw next. Blues probably wanted to prevent panic but…"

"If this farm is terrible, remember the boss man here said we could leave anytime we wish, no?"

"Yeah. So said every freaky cult leader who ever lived. Keep your guard up, Vlad."

"Aha," he replied. "Hashtag streetwise. This is good. I like this. One who is both clever and cautious will live longer."

Sienna nodded. "Don't get me wrong. I'm keen to check out the place but with both eyes open. I feel… I almost feel as if there's more to… Never mind. We're all going to be pretty edgy for a bit."

"And it would be my greatest pleasure to watch your back at all times."

Sienna narrowed her eyes, regarding him for a moment, then decided Vlad projected more the playful flirt kind of vibes than those of a sleazebag.

He winked and swaggered away after his friend, adding to the birdsong a melody of his own. Some kind of traditional music issued from his instrument, unfamiliar, but not unpleasant to her ears, apt for an evening like this.

Sienna smiled and turned back to the horizon for a few last moments, giving the two friends time to move on. She preferred solitary travel. Her father was the same. Whether bushwalking, swimming or driving out on the open highway, her dad said he preferred to steer clear of human traffic.

Hearing chatter from another approaching group, Sienna set off, quickening her pace to enjoy her last moments of solace.

She thought about the man in charge. Kilo seemed very well-spoken, an intellectual type perhaps. If he had been wearing some kind of silly hat, the brimless type that served no practical purpose, she would be worried. She noted how cult leaders and oddball mystic healers had a penchant for things like silly hats and too much facial hair. While he did not fit that stereotype, Kilo did not look like a regular Aussie farmer.

A commotion of birds took to the sky, squawking. Sienna halted, having a distinct feeling of being watched. She always sensed when eyes were upon her and often enough, they were. She stood a little taller than her peers. That alone was enough to make her feel self-conscious. She loathed the inevitable turning of heads when she entered a room.

No offending eyes were present. She saw naught but the thick scrubland. It was unsettling. She felt her sensitivity to the natural world amplified. This land was simultaneously beautiful and threatening. Definite vibes of something abnormal in the bush piqued her curiosity but common sense urged her to move. The light was steadily fading so she hurried onward.

Minutes later a rusty metal arch fixed over an old cattle grid swung into view. Letters forming the name "Kirilia" adorned the arch – an ageing property entrance. A newer gate was to its side, much wider to accommodate large vehicles.

Kirilia. The name struck Sienna as unusual for an Australian farm. It did not sound derived from an indigenous language, was not a native wildlife reference nor had any historic context, as was often the case with rural property names. She would have thought little of something typical, like "Carinya," "Emu Downs" or "Oxley Springs".

She chose to enter the property via the old gate, under the archway, leaping across the cattle grid into the red dust beyond.

Junk was piled along the fence lines stretching from both sides of the gateways, comprised of old rusty metal, sheets of corrugated iron, old car doors and broken farm machinery.

There was newer material in the barricade too, including a couple of large signs displaying the familiar logo of the Lucky Dragons Corporation: two jovial sinuous Eastern-style dragons twisted around each other — a gold one gripping a sheaf of grain in one clawed hand, an ingot of precious metal in its other, and a silver dragon bearing a pearl and a crayfish. Sienna understood these represented the corporation's considerable investments in land and marine-based industries, but it had more recently come to the forefront of the tech sector.

Beyond the barricade, a heap of combustible trash was smouldering, throwing off heat from the embers. Sienna strode past, making for what looked like equipment sheds and other farm outbuildings.

She caught a whiff of food cooking, something fragrant and spicy. People gathered ahead. Someone flicked on electric lighting in a large shed. Kilo was there, speaking with Chad and some others, including a lean wiry young man with long black hair, his dusty clothing suggesting one of the trail bike riders. Vlad and a few others wandered about as best they could in the gathering gloom.

A stocky older-looking man stood alone, leaning casually against the entrance to another shed, smoking as he watched her approach the group. The bandanna tied about his head, thin moustache and machete at his waist gave him the look of a pirate, the kind of character Sienna imagined one would meet on some nameless island in the Moluccas. Following her nose, Sienna guessed there were cooking facilities within.

As she approached Kilo, shaking off her pack, he nodded. "Welcome…"

"Sindy."

Kilo glanced from her to the darkened gates. "Anyone else?"

"More are coming," she said with a nod.

As if on cue, she heard voices back near the gates.

"You are the tenth to arrive," Kilo observed.

Stragglers shuffled into the shed in small groups, dragging their feet and yawning. Jazlyn and Chaylarna were not among them.

"Twenty-two in total," Kilo's long-haired assistant noted.

Kilo inclined his head then introduced the young man. "This is Agus… and he is Rocky."

The older man by the kitchen shed door removed his cigarette, grinned widely, revealing a prominent gold tooth, and in a croaky voice simply said, "Rocky, yesss."

"They have worked here for years," Kilo continued, "and will show you around in the morning. The first twelve to have arrived will be accommodated in the old shearers' quarters, over there. There are beds with clean linen in the cupboards. The rest will have to make do setting up your own gear in this shed for now. The water in the quarters is solar heated. There may even be enough towels in the cupboards for everyone."

"Might need to clear out the bugs," Agus added, smiling.

"He is right," Kilo went on. "Those rooms have been unoccupied for some time. Dust gathers fast here. Clear out any cobwebs and beware of redbacks."

"Ugh, I hate spiders," said a colourfully dressed young man, with an exaggerated shudder. "Australia is full of things that want to bite, kill and eat you."

Kilo forced a smile. "Well, Riku, you will be glad to know we get brown snakes in summer. None lately, but as we are coming out of winter it pays to be vigilant."

Sienna decided it was time to address what was on everyone's mind. "We had companions on another bus —"

"And family," interrupted Duc, a slim, twitchy guy Sienna knew only by name.

"When they drove off a different way, the blue guy told us they'd been billeted elsewhere," said Chad. "He would not elaborate."

Kilo raised his eyebrows. "Booth did not speak to me of other buses. Farms closer to Budgieweir have had teams of workers producing crops for some time. The Blues demand more productivity from the zone. This means they expect those of us farming here on the fringes to become fully operational without delay. Which way did your friends go?"

"South at the crossroad, where we turned onto the dirt track that brought us here," Sienna explained.

"The road south runs dead straight for many kilometres, to Wilgah, then on further still, right down to the river near Yarrantree Weir."

"I doubt those names mean much to anyone here," Vlad remarked.

"Apologies," Kilo continued, "Wilgah is an old village a half hour's drive away. The weir is where one of the canals that irrigate the zone takes on river water. The road to Wilgah follows the old stock and coach route that ran right through this land in the 1800s. That route went far to the north as well, following the line of these hills. It is still a dirt track in that direction, but I digress. Your friends could be on any farm between here and the river, assuming they did not turn down a side road leading elsewhere."

Sienna saw Duc's shoulders visibly slump as he turned and wandered away.

A squealing door distracted them. A young man with short neat hair emerged from the kitchen shed with a large cooking pot and Rocky ducked inside to retrieve another. Both were placed on a long portable table beside some bowls and cutlery.

"Dinner is served," said the young man who had brought the first pot. He flashed a cheerful, toothy grin.

"This is Putu," said Kilo.

The group crowded around the table. Sienna's mouth was watering from the wonderful smell. It was some kind of curry or stew, comprised of brown gravy and chunky vegetables. She tried to identify the spices. A hint of lemongrass. Yes, as Putu stirred the pot's contents, she spied its distinctive stalk, no doubt having been pounded a bit to help release its tasty flavour. The second pot was filled with steaming white rice.

"It is a vegetarian curry," Kilo announced. "We had no idea about your individual dietary preferences or restrictions. Hopefully this is acceptable."

He frowned at the table. "If there are not enough bowls for everyone…"

"It is OK. Some of us have our own," said Witek, producing an enamel bowl and his own metal utensils.

"Good," Kilo nodded. "Now, rule number one: We eat first. Those Blues will only get their hands on what we do not need to survive. Welcome to Kirilia."

"Works for me, man," said Chad. Grunts of assent echoed about.

"A bit on the spicy side for me, but compliments to the chef – it tastes amazing," remarked Vlad.

Sienna thanked Putu as he served her portion. She watched the gravy soak into the rice and inhaled. There was no hint of anything amiss and she enjoyed the delectable aromas. Her gut told her these people were genuinely hospitable. She now doubted they would all pass out from hidden toxins and later find themselves dressed in cult robes.

Chad moved to her side. "Seems to me we just checked into a post-apocalyptic bed and breakfast, with gourmet dinners from professional chefs."

"Hope they have a good stash of spices," said Sienna.

Witek was standing nearby, sniffing at his meal. Before starting, he turned to Kilo. "You are the acting overseer, no? Where is the usual one?"

"Several months ago, before the Blues locked down the area, the farm was attacked. The boss suffered serious chest trauma and was taken away. Now, after all this time, I am not entirely sure if or when he will return. You are stuck with me, for now."

Sienna recalled Kilo having referred to Kirilia as "my land". He seemed well and truly at home. Over time he must have gotten comfortable with the idea of being permanently in charge.

Sensing uncertainty in the group, Kilo continued. "There have been no further raids, but we must always be vigilant. We do not know how thoroughly the Blues' surveillance drones watch over this area or if they will rush to save us should an incoming threat be detected. We could always radio for help, but again... will there be a response? Will the Blues in Budgieweir even listen?"

Not the most inspiring pep talk but she noted the man was a realist.

"I understand this sounds grim, especially with you all having just left the security of the capital. If it puts your minds at ease, know it has been nothing but peaceful for months. Even so, we have slowly improved security by ourselves. You may have noticed our crude barricade. Not much, I know. We can work together on far better ways to protect our perimeter. We will discuss this in the morning. Enough chatter from me. Enjoy your meals while they are still hot."

A disquiet fell over the group as they tucked into dinner. Sienna was aware of how tired and hungry she was, but decided to live in the moment, thoroughly enjoy her food and worry about tomorrow when it arrived. She closed her eyes, preparing to savour the first mouthful.

The silence was broken by a long scream of agony, somewhere out in the hills. Sienna dropped her bowl as chills rippled through her body.

4

Harrison

The sound of dogs barking woke Harrison Fletcher. He cursed, a thin sliver of orange sunlight on the wall suggesting it was still early. He was not ready to be roused. Half the night he had struggled to get comfortable in this extremely basic accommodation – a bedroll on a dirt floor in a long narrow shed.

Heavy old benches, a rusty vice and tool racks on the walls suggested an ageing workshop. Hanging hideously in the undisturbed corners were things he called "spider guoals" – old cobwebs matted into a mass made of congealed dust, old egg sacs and long-dead bugs.

Looking down at him cheerfully from the nearest tool rack was a familiar image – Kozzie the Koala, symbol of Aussie Kozzie Industries, for whom he had worked in tech support. He knew there was nothing "Aussie" at all about this subsidiary of a large foreign corporation. Even so, consumers had let the company thrive, with its mass-produced imported range of *"everything your home needs"* undercutting what few genuinely Australian competitors remained with their *"krazy Kozzie prices"*.

He hated that koala and its presence did nothing to improve

his mood. He considered it an idiotic logo for a dumbed-down population, becoming ever more stupid, fattening their arses in front of the television as they were spoon-fed a diet of ever more low-brow reality shows. At least he had been able to profit at their expense, but nevertheless despised the fools for their inability to pay attention to what was really going on in the world as they blithely choked on their own ignorance into lives of debt and poverty.

The barking ceased when their host shouted a few harsh words. Harrison closed his eyes and rolled over. One of the German backpackers was snoring loudly on that side so, huffing, he shifted again, opting to lie on his back and stare at the corrugated iron ceiling.

The structure offered little insulation from the cold. While not as chilly as winter nights in the capital, with its higher altitude, this inland river country, far from the sea, still was uncomfortable.

This was not the improvement in circumstances Harrison had been promised. His task was to be shipped out with this lot and keep an eye on things in the Northern Riverland Ag Zone, reporting observations on request. Satisfactory intel meant better lodgings in the part of Canberra reserved for government personnel.

Unfortunately, there was nothing scandalous to report about anyone in this stinking bunch of sleepyheads. He feared the restless night was the first of many to come.

Harrison heard the song of a pied butcher bird greeting the sunrise with its distinctive melody. A magpie lark, known as "peewees" to some, joined the morning birdsong. He had no desire to lie about any longer and figured he might as well get up and scout the property. Fumbling for his glasses, he brushed his hair out of his eyes then put them on, yawning as he stood.

He shuddered a little and grabbed his black Urtaxx hoodie, the metal band's distinctive sheep skull insignia staring from the back with hollow eyes. Suitably insulated, he put on his boots and picked his way around the sleepers.

Harrison swore under his breath as he nearly tripped over a pair of shoes next to Jacko. He was one of those obnoxious cool kids from Sydney who considered themselves too good to listen to the benefits of Harrison's wisdom.

He decided to call it "Small Sydney Syndrome" – that city had long been Australia's largest – until its sprawl was restricted by the difficult terrain encircling it. Melbourne, his home, had no such constraints on its flanks. With backing from successive governments spewing the "growth is good" mantra, it had swelled into a supercity, engulfing all the once quaint surrounding towns like an insatiable amoeba.

Harrison stepped outside and looked around at the quiet empty landscape, frowning. He missed the city, but the Melbourne life he knew had ceased to be. For all its cosmopolitan glory, it was now likely the worst place in the country. He had heard how the plague and supply shortages reduced it from prosperous metropolis to anarchic maelstrom. Even in the city's affluent "inner ring" his parents and friends could not have held out for long.

At least the authorities in the capital had maintained order and a defensive perimeter and Harrison was fortunate to have been working there that week everything hit the proverbial fan.

Thinking of boundaries, Harrison decided to take an early stroll and passed some machinery sheds as he made for the perimeter fence. He noted a hint of frost on the brown grass. They were coming out of the short winter of the Australian interior, if one could call it that. Melbourne, with its perpetually grey skies, at least attempted to look wintry for much of the year, but even there each summer was becoming undeniably longer and hotter.

Various birds wheeled about in vast flocks. He spied two black and white magpie larks, confidently territorial in spite of their size. The pair were chasing some kind of brown hawk or eagle who had offended them with its presence. The larks took turns swooping and harassing the larger bird as it tried to go about its business in peace.

Leaning on a fence post, Harrison paused to peer through the shrubbery growing on the other side along strip of land marking this farm's border. He saw no sign of agricultural activity in the neighbouring property and wondered how many farms in the zone had been abandoned.

Without warning a hideous dog charged right at him from out of the shrubs. It was technically a bitch, squat, ugly and white, with pink piggy eyes. Harrison nearly fell back onto his arse as it reared up against the fence. Sniffing out excitement, two equally beastly companions emerged and closed fast, keen to investigate.

As he hastily backed away from the fence, hoping there were no breaches in the barbed wire, Harrison heard their host roughly address his dogs again from somewhere near the farm's rather plain-looking main entrance. On arrival he had noticed the metal gate was adorned with just a small faded yellow sign with lettering in painted black italics, which simply read "Farm 1469".

Deciding to watch their host from afar, he hurried back to the shed area. Striding around a corner, Harrison slammed into the back of a powerfully built young man, who stood a full head taller than himself.

"Apologies, err…" Harrison offered his hand.

"Junior," a deep voice replied, the man slowly turning to accept his hand with a crushing grip, meeting his eye with a serious, unsmiling expression. Only a fool would mess with this guy – perhaps the perfect person to get on-side while stuck in this place.

"Englishman?" said Junior, studying him.

"Well, originally yes. Norfolk. Though I moved to Melbourne as a kid."

"Zimbabwe," said Junior, releasing Harrison's hand and turning back to the gate.

Harrison discreetly rotated his wrist and twirled his fingers behind his back, making sure everything was still intact, then stepped up beside Junior.

Their host was feeding his dogs. The savage pack occupied a very long pen, the narrow strip of boundary land where Harrison's presence was clearly unwelcome. He was grateful this dog run's fences were higher than those typically used on farms. It seemed to encircle the entire perimeter. An effective deterrent to anyone trying to get into the property – or out. Despite all the open space, he felt trapped.

"Not exactly the prettiest pets," Harrison observed.

"Pig dogs," Junior replied, his eyes fixed on the gate. "A man I worked for hunted pigs out in the bush with dogs that looked just like these."

Harrison saw variations in coat, colour and ear shape. All appeared equally mean and unruly.

"I won't be wandering near their turf again anytime soon," he muttered.

A female voice distracted them. "Jon-Jon, come back to bed."

Harrison spotted one of their host's concubines in a doorway of the property's main house, clad in apparently nothing more than a short silk cerise robe, long dark hair spilling rather messily over one shoulder, arms tightly folded.

Unbothered by the morning chill, the overseer was dressed in a durable-looking labourer's shirt, its large popped collar boasting some fashion logo. Harrison wondered if the guy intended to look "on trend" for his new guests. He might have missed the mark as he wore the shirt tightly tucked into unfashionably short shorts. The outfit was completed by knee-length socks and an oversized tool belt, from which a long, large wrench brushed against a bare thigh.

Harrison had expected a regular rural Aussie bloke. When they were greeted by this Jon-Jon and his entourage of clinging exotic female companions, he realised they would in fact be working for some kind of self-styled outback pimp.

Sergeant Selvin was already acquainted with the man, having greeted him with a hug. While he had been introduced as "Overseer Jon", some bimbo from the man's harem had spoken up, giggling, "He prefers to be called 'Jon-Jon'."

Presently, the overseer was shouting. "When the dogs have all had breakfast, I will come back in for mine." After a brief pause, "Coffee too. Thank you."

The cerise-robed woman scurried back indoors.

"Well, I could handle a double-shot caramel latte right now," said Harrison.

Junior remained silent but Harrison tried again. "Addressing a grown man as 'Jon-Jon' — I'm not entirely comfortable with that."

Junior spoke up. "Maybe we just call him 'Sir' or 'Boss' or something like that."

"Yes. Good thinking. He looks like the type who would get off on being reminded he's in charge."

Junior nodded slowly, still eyeing the perimeter. "Overseer? Or prison warden?"

"We'll find out soon enough, I'm sure."

Harrison watched Jon-Jon finish with the dogs, dusting off his light-blue shirt before striding in their direction.

"Good morning, Sir," Harrison called and Junior nodded a greeting to the man.

Harrison could now see the marking on the collar was the ubiquitous logo of the Lucky Dragons Corporation.

Jon-Jon smiled broadly, flashing his white perfect teeth.

"Ah. Good to see people up bright and early. Wondering about this?"

He traced the stitching of his collar with his index finger.

"I was farming this land long before the Lucky D's... *acquisition*. My father and grandfather before that. Part of the deal was subcontracting me as a kind of proxy overseer. I keep my house and some new techie gear was thrown in too. I am not a fully fledged employee hence blue shirt, not white. But I know this land better than anyone and believe they understand that's the most efficient way to run the place.

"With this crisis, the Lucky D's employees have their hands full with work on their other farms. Business in Budgieweir too. So,

I've kept farming with little interference, playing my small part in feeding what's left of our great nation.

"Anyway, I need coffee. At eight o'clock, we will meet on my lawn there. Make sure everyone's awake by then, will you?"

Not awaiting a reply, Jon-Jon strode off to the tidy garden surrounding his house. Another woman appeared at the threshold, kissed him and drew him inside. Harrison noted her teal robe did little to hide her long slender legs.

He realised he had been leering as Junior clapped him hard on the shoulder.

"I am worried about Amahle in this place."

"Your girlfriend?"

"Fiancée."

"We should check on the girls' dorm, make sure they're OK. See if anyone's awake."

Junior nodded, his features otherwise expressionless, then set off with great strides.

Harrison hurried after him to the other dormitory – a renovated fibreboard building, substantially more civilised than their rough lodgings.

"Somebody's up," he observed, indicating long human shadows extending from behind the building, fluidly shifting over the red dirt.

Rounding the corner, they joined a small crowd who had risen to watch two people demonstrating their athleticism, facing each other and leaping about in the air. Their bodies were lithe, sinewy and extraordinarily flexible.

"Maybe some kind of traditional dance," Junior commented.

"Yes. Oh wait, I believe it is *kalaripayattu*. It's a form of martial art."

Junior nodded his assent, watching the unique attack forms.

Someone in the crowd muttered, "Oh hello, Mr Knowledge has crashed the party."

This was followed by giggling – those annoying Sydney girls, of course. Harrison flushed with anger but refrained from turning to face them, instead choosing to scratch the left side of his head with his middle finger, keeping his eyes fixed on the two combatants.

"Oh, look out ladies, it might have head lice too." More shrill laughter.

The mocking comments were not voiced by a female, nor was the voice Australian. While Harrison suspected every nation had its share of arseholes, of course this one just had to be one of his own former countrymen.

Harrison recalled this big British prick back in Canberra. He wore his long hair in a man bun and always drew attention to himself, playing loud music and games on his phone during dinner, hitting on those pretty twins from Germany and going out of his way to rile up others. Solidly built and over six feet tall, nobody had challenged his behaviour.

Bullies of his father's time were primal in their torment, shoving around those they considered weaker or a bit different. While Harrison considered the underlying reasons no excuse, he concluded old-school bullies were motivated by an inferiority complex brought on by an awareness of their own limited cerebral capacity and/or lower socioeconomic status.

His generation, however, utilised subtler, less physical forms of cruelty. He knew there was an element of scum within every social class. With most tech now offline, at least keyboard warriors and online trolls could no longer harass others. However, the common sniping tactic of making snide remarks just within earshot was still an option for wankers like this guy.

"Amahle," exclaimed Junior, leaving Harrison's side and rushing away to join a tall young woman at the dorm entrance. Her physique was equally as athletic as Junior's and their fine forms were an unwelcome reminder of Harrison's lack of height and fitness. The couple disappeared inside the dorm.

Turning back to the bout, Harrison noticed a young man on the sidelines, observing the action. Fine. If knowledge was his forte, he would use it to gain allies.

"Excuse me," said Harrison, speaking low so as not to encourage further mockery. "Are the three of you by chance from Kerala?"

"Why yes. How did you know?" the young man replied, smiling.

"I recognised the *kalaripayattu*. I understand it is one of the oldest forms of martial arts, from long before many of the other famous styles, right?"

"Yes, this is true. The technique was brought from India to China and taught to the monks there, then gradually was adapted through East Asia over many centuries into the common styles we see today."

"I recall seeing a lot of weapons training with this style?" Harrison ventured.

"Oh yes. The three of us have trained since we were children. Weapons included. I don't know if we will be allowed to carry any here. Certainly not in Canberra. Yet we still train as much as we can."

"I am Harrison, by the way."

"Arjun," he replied, smiling, then indicating the combatants, "He is Aditya and she is Aradhya."

Harrison took a moment to repeat them in his head a few times. Aradhya was the girl. Arjun had a moustache.

"My turn." Arjun approached the other two.

Some onlookers began to disperse, including the obnoxious individuals. Harrison heard the Brit muttering about wanting breakfast. He glared at their backs as they ambled away.

He checked the time on his phone and noted the low battery level. He would need to find a power source. During lockdown, Harrison had complaints from people unable to fully utilise their personal electronic devices. Those more innovative found ways to make up for the lack of connectivity with far-flung peers. Plenty of apps still allowed social interaction or gaming with other devices in nu-tooth range.

Harrison watched the trio continue training. Becoming acquainted with fit, skilful people could prove beneficial. He knew he was no warrior. People capable of watching his back could prove the key to survival should things get ugly.

He informed everyone present that the overseer would like them to assemble at eight but pointedly did not seek out those who had wandered off.

Junior and Amahle reappeared. Harrison nodded, checking his watch. It was nearly time.

The group ambled to the designated area. Their overseer had not yet emerged so he approached Junior and introduced himself to Amahle who shook his hand. Standing so close, Harrison felt shorter still as he noticed the slender woman's chin was at his eye level.

Heads turned when Jon-Jon appeared, three slim ladies tottering along at his heels. No longer clad in colourful nightwear, Jon-Jon's harem had donned fresh outfits, apparently designed with the sole purpose of revealing a generous amount of flesh but no practical function suited to farm life. Harrison wondered if the women had duties besides pandering to Jon-Jon's needs and completing household chores.

One lady moved with a lopsided gait as she struggled with a sack.

Jon-Jon eyed the group.

"Good morning. Glad to see almost everyone here on time. I assume from your healthy complexions, long-overdue haircuts and lean, fit physiques that most of you are backpackers from abroad." The overseer smirked. "No man buns? Glad to see some bad trends die."

Harrison realised who was absent — pity those arseholes missed the meeting memo. It was equally amusing observing that Jon-Jon, with his ridiculous tight little shorts and skanky entourage, was by no means fashion incarnate.

Heads were turning, Jon-Jon's, then the rest of the group. Rushing footsteps crunched on gravel.

"Should I take back my last comment?" said Jon-Jon.

As Harrison's flustered-looking tormentors joined the assembly, he seized the chance to strike back and addressed Jon-Jon, pretending to cup the back of his own floppy hair into a bun.

"Unfortunately, Sir, there's always someone who prefers to party like it's still 2016."

Jon-Jon turned to Harrison, laughed and clapped his hands once with a sigh. Perfect. Harrison felt the baleful glare of the big British bastard but did not turn to acknowledge his presence. It was more prudent to shut up. Having the boss on-side could only strengthen his position.

"Now, back to business."

Jon-Jon turned to the girl with the sack, impatiently summoning her to come forward and pointing at the ground beside him. The girl complied, dropping her burden.

"Careful with that," the overseer muttered. She lowered her head, retreating to the back of the group.

"I was not expecting to play host to so many. Therefore, I sincerely hope everybody likes brown rice. Full of energy, good for the heart."

Jon-Jon glanced down at the bag.

"We have a plentiful supply, thanks to our friends in blue. We even received a delivery of rice cookers, which will no doubt get a good workout. The electricity is still on."

Harrison knew this was not the case everywhere and wondered how many power stations, solar farms and other electricity infrastructure were still operational.

"To keep meals more interesting, I will put you to work upgrading my veggie patch. We have been granted water allocations for rice growing and if all goes well, will sow in mid to late spring. If anyone has experience flying drones or operating a rice skipper then come and see me."

Harrison had piloted drones in informal races, versing friends. He did not relish the thought of sweaty work on a farm, especially should he still be stuck here when the brutal Australian summer arrived. A drone operator might enjoy working from a comfortable chair in a cool, shaded control room.

Jon-Jon curled his fingers and whistled in the direction of his house. Another assistant emerged, bearing a pot. Breakfast.

"Go. Help her," he commanded the other three, who scuttled away to assist. Harrison wondered if any was actually the overseer's wife and about the time frame over which he "collected" them.

"Today's breakfast – congee. It may be bland to some of you but remember what I said about the energy content of rice. We should be grateful; I'm sure many poor bastards out there do not enjoy such luxuries. Come."

The ladies bustled about bringing bowls and metal spoons. Jon-Jon strode over to supervise, the hungry group following.

As Harrison moved to join them, a hand gripped him roughly above his hip.

"Doughy love handles."

Harrison pulled away.

"Love hand…? Sorry to disappoint you, Man Bun. I don't swing that way."

"This isn't over, Doughboy," came the cool reply.

Harrison bristled but was too taken aback to think of another witty response. He could not believe this wanker had manhandled him. An actual old-school bully.

The thug swaggered off to join the Sydney girls by the breakfast table. One of them – Foo? – was already speaking with Jon-Jon, who gave his undivided attention as she explained at length how she not only had significant experience working with drones but had already piloted a rice skipper on a property elsewhere.

This was too much. As if the insolence of this group was not bad enough, they now were snatching away the one half-decent job in this crappy little part of nowhere.

Composing himself, Harrison resolved to ensure things worked out for him in the end. He would get allies firmly in his corner: bribery, stroking egos, kissing the overseer's arse. He would manipulate anyone he could to further his goal of getting out of this shithole.

If the Blues wanted a spy, he would be their man, feeding them whatever information they requested. He would uncover and report dirty secrets, regardless of whether they were truth or his own fanciful fabrications.

Above all, Harrison would do whatever it took to destroy the lives of the big British bully and his bitchy entourage.

5

Witek

This bushland was alien to Witek, devoid of oak, spruce, hornbeam and birch. He recognised eucalypts, ubiquitous throughout Australia, but nothing else. The scrubby flora on this rocky hillside sprouted from patches of red-brown soil between rocks. The air was full of unfamiliar birdsong and carried scents unlike anything in the few damp remnant forests back home.

Even in a strange landscape, he felt calmer within than he had in months, picking his way along this rugged trail.

The cool morning air made his nostrils damp. "Hunter's nose", he called it, something he experienced many times when enjoying the outdoors back in Poland. After confinement in Canberra, with few opportunities to move about, Witek felt free.

The cool morning air was invigorating after his rough night. Witek had given up his room in the shearers' quarters, preferring the familiarity of his own camping gear. Glad to be back in his swag after months on overly soft mattresses, he had expected good rest. However, that bizarre screaming unsettled him such he could barely sleep.

When he did, he had been tormented by dreams. Witek recalled being on patrol, in uniform, armed, wandering around some empty town, searching. He was in Australia but the buildings resembled those back home. Marcelina was standing on the roof of a bus, a small dog beside her. Some kind of terrier. It began to bark as a handful of people appeared on the streets and started mindlessly ambling towards her, closing in on the bus while he watched from afar. Plague victims. In place of eyes were red sockets, blood streaming down their faces. They exhaled plumes of infectious yellow steam. As they neared the bus Witek raised his rifle to fire. The magazine was empty. He had no spare ammunition. He had forgotten to load the weapon. The small group surrounded the bus, heads tilted back, the toxic cloud rising from them. Marcelina opened her mouth to scream.

Witek had awoken to darkness and a fox call in the distance. The fox. A feral creature, not native to this continent. An outsider like himself. Yet the creature he heard was born to this land and would live out its days here. Far more qualified to call itself local.

He had risen early, woken by the snores of one of those brash Australian girls who must have belatedly decided that Kirilia was better than camping out on their own.

Staying in shape was important so he had devised a short custom workout, hoping exercise would clear his weary mind.

During a set of chin-ups, he had spotted Kilo speaking with his men, shotgun in hand. Witek had dropped from the shed's metal support beam and joined them. Correctly surmising they planned to investigate the scream, he had volunteered to help.

Kilo had agreed after brief consideration. "We will form a

scouting party. Find four other volunteers," he had instructed.

Witek soon found four curious or intrepid enough early risers to join. Vlad had not risen and Witek did not rouse him. His friend was not a morning person.

Rocky had meanwhile distributed crude blades – makeshift machetes fashioned from old farm implements with which to arm the group, "in case of trouble".

Now a party of seven trekked single file along the trail, which followed a spur of the high hill overlooking the farm. Kilo and Agus led the way. The path was flanked by steep slopes on each side and strewn with multi-hued boulders.

Kirilia shared its eastern boundary with Cooper Hill National Park, which was mainly comprised of the hills stretching north. Kilo promised Cooper Hill, which they were presently ascending, would offer scenic views in all directions.

"So, did someone named Cooper live 'round here or did they make barrels in the area?" said Chad, who had been the first to join the reconnaissance party.

Over his shoulder, Kilo replied, "My uncle told me it was an old survey error. Few people know they were to be called Copper Hills. There was even a small mine somewhere further north. Never produced much ore and did not last long. In any case, someone misspelled the word 'copper' on an official document and it was never corrected."

Witek spoke up, cautious to speak softly, not knowing what was out here. "So, your uncle... is he... ah...?"

Kilo shook his head without turning back.

"Sorry."

Kilo stopped and turned. The man wore sunglasses and his face was unreadable.

He simply lifted his arm, sweeping it slowly across the flat land behind them.

Witek and the others turned. He could see the cluster of sheds and outbuildings on the edge of the wooded area, where Kirilia bordered the national park, as well as the rooftops of the ageing two-storey main house, which boasted a slightly elevated position on the lower western slope of Cooper Hill. Witek imagined it would offer a superb vantage point for Kilo to watch over the farm.

The fields of Kirilia and other farms beyond painted a patchwork landscape, dotted with houses, sheds and grain storage bins, all contained within a wide valley bordered by another range of substantially lower hills on its western edge.

"This land has been in my family for generations," said Kilo. "I loved coming up here as a kid. My aunt and uncle were under pressure to sell Kirilia. So many family farms have been bought out by multinationals."

"Lucky Dragons," murmured Chad.

Kilo nodded. "The Dragons are one of many but yes, one of the largest. They have invested quite heavily in this area. Claim their big ag infrastructure makes farming more efficient."

"Just like our own Midwest."

"So I have heard. Many Australian freeholders were aggressively approached. After droughts, uncertain water rights for irrigators, too many tough years... some took the money and moved away. Others stayed on as overseers but with the farms getting bigger and more automated, regional employment crashed. Local kids bet their futures on the cities. Now this government in its infinite wisdom has seen it fit to send scores of workers back out here."

"If there are more of us than you need, then what are we supposed to do?" asked Witek.

He would walk away if he was unwanted. Alone he could keep a low profile. Perhaps embark upon a discreet search of the valley for Marcelina right away.

"I asked Booth that very question," Kilo replied. "He instructed me to follow the Overseers' Handbook, which is sketchy, at best. I assume they expect us to be creative enough to figure out how to make this whole supply scheme work on our own. Anyway, I am glad you opted in. You will be adequately occupied. We should press on."

An athletic young woman with frizzy hair loped past Witek and Chad. "So, boss, the plague... did it reach the farms around here?"

"Sameera, is it?"

"Correct."

"Budgieweir was hit hard."

"Oh shame," Sameera replied.

Kilo nodded. "Outlying villages were somewhat spared. People hunkered down. Once the infected were all dead, it gradually became safer to come out, though the Blues do not like us wandering about. Parts of the valley are restricted areas. While there are no formal curfews, the Blues will ask questions if we travel outside Kirilia for no clear reason."

Witek felt a tap on the shoulder and turned. It was Riku.

"Hang with us a moment," he whispered.

Chad was standing back beside Karmen, whose long ponytail cascaded up and over the large collar of her jacket.

Riku spoke fast in a low tone. "Hey, so you are wondering about the relatives too, right? Missing the whole story?"

Witek nodded. "This was his family's land; his folks are now gone. Why was he not placed in charge?"

"The boss Kilo said took a chest wound, the real overseer – his cousin?" Karmen suggested.

Witek shrugged. "Perhaps. We could just ask, no? I do not want to be pushy with questions. Not until we know the man better."

"I agree," whispered Riku. "He has an angry look about him. Better not risk causing offence."

Chad scratched a patch of stubble on his chin. "Never mind the resting bitch face. I want to know how he got that gun."

Witek noticed the blank looks from Riku and Karmen. "I understand. Pump action, right? A restricted firearm. Illegal in Australia, unless you are police or military. Maybe he was one of the Blues."

"That's right, man," Chad replied. "We're in Australia now. They don't have our Bill of Rights. There's no Second Amendment. Civilians here don't have the right to defend their life and liberty the way we do back in the States. Hell, I heard these guys ain't even got a constitutional right to free speech."

"There's been a lot less gun violence here though, fewer mass shootings," said Karmen.

Chad exhaled. "If some rabid psycho comes here wanting to put my head up on a signpost, I want to be packing some serious firepower. I won't just sit on the floor, squealing, hoping some blue guy will trouble himself to rock up and rescue me… or clean up the mess. Come on, this is the Awesome Aussie After."

Karmen rolled her eyes and sighed. "Fair point thought I hate to admit it. In Argentina, some say there are many more criminals with illegal firearms than good people with registered ones."

"I wonder if it is the same here," said Witek, raising his weapon to inspect its rusty blade. "If so, we will need more than these to defend ourselves. Forget the world as it was. It is unfortunate, but in these times, whoever has the best weapons will be in charge – or at least stay alive longer."

He hoped that Marcelina had somehow found herself a firearm. She had also learned to wield a rifle during national service.

"Well, we better hurry to join the one in charge here," said Riku. "Look ahead."

Kilo and Sameera had stopped and were watching Agus, who had scouted further ahead, as he ran back down from the summit.

"I hear something. Sounds like a brush cutter," said Chad. "Which means..."

"A drone," said Witek, scanning the sky as he jogged ahead.

"Wish we had one," said Riku. "It would be much easier to find whatever we are looking for than running around these hills all day."

"Assuming the screamer is still out here," said Karmen. "Alive or..."

They caught up with Kilo just as Agus arrived, panting "Do you hear that? It is getting louder. Somewhere over there."

"All I can see is hills and trees," said Sameera.

"As do I," said Kilo.

Witek scanned the wooded hills and rocky escarpments then saw movement.

"There, in the valley, is that..."

"Which valley? Where?" demanded Kilo.

"See the aerial on the high hill?" Witek continued.

"That's miles away," said Chad. "It can't be way over in one of those valleys. Sounds much closer."

"It is closer. See where the aerial is on the horizon? Look directly down from there – in this valley, below us. It is dark, hard to see against the trees."

"Yes," said Kilo. "I see it. Well spotted."

"Thank you," Witek replied, wondering if being a scout or spotter would be an enjoyable duty.

"Wait, it's moving to the right, towards that bump of a hill at the top of the valley," said Chad.

"That is called the Hump on maps, for obvious reasons," said Kilo. "My uncle called it 'Mt Camel' though."

"Patrol drone sent by the Blues?" asked Karmen.

"Perhaps," said Kilo. "These hills form the eastern edge of the zone. It may be a low-altitude border patrol. First time I have seen one but this makes sense. It is too difficult for vehicles in this terrain and patrolling the entire range on foot is unfeasible. If only we had one."

"If it is moving from hill to hill, it will come this way next, right?" said Riku

"This is possible," said Kilo.

"It looks small," said Sameera. "What kind of drone is it?"

"Do you think it is remote controlled or completely autonomous?" Riku speculated.

"Anything is possible," said Kilo. "Aside from the V-shaped overwatch drones you may have seen up high, I have no idea what surveillance method the Blues have implemented. The internet is down. They might have some wide-area network in the valley linking their drones. My technical expertise is somewhat limited."

"Are we even allowed up here?" asked Karmen.

She pointed to the plain to the east, beyond the peak of Cooper Hill, and Witek could see the highway that had brought them here.

"We had our faces scanned at the Blues' outpost back that way," Karmen continued. "Where is the official boundary line of this ag zone and what if we have crossed it? Will we be questioned? Should we go back down?"

"Or find cover," said Chad. "Better choose fast. That thing is coming right this way."

"Karmen is right," said Kilo. "We should fall back closer to Kirilia. We are doing nothing wrong but there is no need for others to concern themselves with where we choose to spend our time. Keep low and hurry."

The group hastily retraced their steps, half crouching.

Witek noted the large eucalypts grew only in the valleys and on lower ground. On the boulder-strewn upper reaches of these hills everyone was exposed. The only trees here were thin conifers resembling little Christmas trees, and small straggly shrubs with sparse foliage and puffs of yellow flowers.

"It's right on us," said Sameera.

The drone closed in then swung around the group in a wide arc, maintaining its distance.

"I hope it just flies away," said Riku. "Should we ignore it and keep going?"

Before anyone could respond, the drone buzzed closer. Kilo stopped and they turned to face the little machine. It hovered in place, occasionally zipping laterally in random directions, like a dragonfly.

"Lite Shot," said Karmen. "The police use this type back home."

"We have them in Poland also," said Witek. "Armed. Only .22 calibre."

"But accurate targeting," added Karmen. "I would not like to be hit."

Witek had once loaded a magazine into a similar drone. He knew most of the firearm and magazine were housed within protective casing along with the battery, motor and other hardware. He could see a small barrel protruding from the front. He felt uneasy about the way the drone stared right at him, weapon pointed at his head.

"Remote controlled?" asked Kilo.

"Can be programmed with security patrol mission parameters or manually controlled, if the operator is near enough," said Karmen.

Witek was about to speak up but Karmen continued, voicing his own intended words. "They classify these drones as semi-autonomous."

Witek smiled to himself. He wondered about Karmen's background.

"I see. Versatile," said Kilo.

Chad loudly addressed the machine. "Well, you just gonna stare at us all day?"

A male voice emerged from the drone as it rapidly closed in, a few metres closer to the group. "CLEAR THIS AREA IMMEDIATELY."

Kilo glanced sideways at Chad.

"Sorry, boss. Didn't mean to piss it off."

"That's a big deep voice for a little drone," said Sameera. "I presume that is a security patrol mode."

"I recall an optional warning timer can be set," Witek explained. "We should leave before it decides to clear the area using force."

The UAV dropped low, metres from Witek, as the group began steadily retreating down the hill.

"It really likes you," said Karmen.

The drone was clearly keeping pace with Witek.

"HOLD POSITION MARCELINA ZABREWSKI."

6

Phuong

"Don't get too close, Foo. He obviously likes you but is a total creep, just like Selvin," said Samantha, narrowed eyes fixed on Jon-Jon as he strode to his house.

"Ay. A creep wiv a thing for exotic women," said Christopher with a playful wink.

Samantha elbowed the British lad in the ribs. "Cut it out, Chris."

Phuong rolled her eyes. "Hmm. Born and bred in Western Sydney. Really exotic, mate. Look, Jon-Jon would have tried something by now."

"I still wouldn't trust him, Foo," said Samantha.

"Oh, don't worry, I don't trust him as far as I could kick him."

"You'll be right, love," said Christopher. "They're probably all lady-boys he's got there wiv him. I mean, look at the faggoty shorts he wears."

Phuong winced and looked at Jacko, who cleared his throat and rolled his eyes.

"You can't use words like that anymore, Chris. Not in this country," Samantha chided.

Jacko turned his head and held up his hand.

"Just havin' a laugh, Jackie-boy," said Christopher. "This is the end of the world. No point mopin' around."

"Jeez," Jacko muttered.

The British guy was an unapologetic lout and naturally Samantha had developed an instant crush on him. Phuong had been ever critical of Samantha's choice in men though had held her tongue this time, leaving her friend to go ahead and pursue a romantic entanglement if that was what she really wanted. They agreed having the big fella watching their backs made them feel more secure.

"I feel sorry for Jon-Jon's... wives," said Phuong. "I mean, their previous life must have been bad if their only alternative was to be bought by some old bloke and live with him in the middle of nowhere."

Christopher raised his eyebrows. "Fink he really bought 'em? Like an actual slave market?"

"I don't know how the financial arrangements work but I've seen this before," she replied. "Perhaps it's more noticeable in rural areas. Not sure if it's because the men are genuine pigs no self-respecting local lady would want, or just not enough women to go round out here, and the men get themselves a partner any way they can."

"I can't see any woman marrying Jon-Jon for love," said Samantha. "He's not fooling anyone with that slick hair and fake suave voice.

"Anyhow, Foo. What is it he needs done? I thought you said the rice skipper will work fine."

"It is fine, the seeding arm is calibrated and ready to plant our rice crop when Jon-Jon gives the word. First, he wants to sync the skipper with a mapping drone, which will scan the terrain in detail before we sow. This new tech is for maximising efficiency and cutting down on waste. He wants me to test drive the drone to make sure it works."

"Is he going to do *anything* himself?" asked Samantha. "I thought he was a lifelong farmer."

"Before we sow, he'll prep the rice fields with a leveller to get the bays ready for sowing. Blues gave him a fuel ration to run his retro machinery for that. I don't think he knows how to use the new gear though. Getting the actual sowing done right will be up to us."

Christopher scratched his ear. "How did they sow before all this high-tech stuff?"

"Aerial sowing into bays already filled with water or direct seeding with a ground-based machine, like a combine. These days, satellites can guide the sowing process — they should still work fine. Not like they can catch the Big V.

"The skipper seeds the rice using its arm — it stretches way out from the body so downdraft from the engines shouldn't be a problem.

"If you really want to break your back though, you can always go old school and sow it all by hand."

"Think that's why they sent so many of us, Foo?" asked Jacko. "In case all the machines break down? Like seriously, if one person with a skipper can plant all the rice, what's everyone else meant to do?"

"Apart from the pleasure of digging up Jon-Jon's veggie patch all day?" said Samantha.

"Exactly." Jacko rubbed his hip. "Oh my God, I'm aching all over.

Thought I'd have toned up a bit by now."

"Ha. Dig harder," said Christopher.

"Honestly," said Phuong, "I think someone thought it was time we made ourselves useful. Probably got sick of babysitting us in Canberra."

Jacko nodded. "Yeah. A government figuring out what's best for the people. Making us go wherever they say, because they know better, right? Never heard that before."

Phuong spotted Jon-Jon strutting their way. He paused to inspect his reflection in a window. Short in stature but wiry, the man was clean shaven aside from his small self-styled moustache, which curled a little on each side. He patted his wavy hair, which he wore short and neat around the edges.

Then he marched over, teeth flashing in abroad grin. "All set?"

Phuong nodded and without breaking stride, Jon-Jon turned sharply into the machinery shed, where the new gear was conspicuous next to the tractors and other equipment from yesteryear.

The rice skipper was essentially a large electric-powered UAV, which hovered no more than a couple of metres off the ground when in use. Phuong saw it resting in its charging bay, a red light indicating its battery was being replenished.

Jon-Jon had complained about intermittent interruptions to their electricity supply. However, yesterday he heard Budgieweir's solar farm had just received some Lucky Dragons specialist engineers, promising more-reliable power and fewer blackouts.

This rice skipper was an experimental prototype. Only a handful had been produced for testing purposes, but Phuong had heard these were fast-tracked into service because of the pandemic. It was purported to represent the pinnacle of the Lucky Dragons Corporation's agricultural technology. While its mastery was beyond Jon-Jon's ability, Phuong was confident she could remote pilot and plot courses for the machine.

Jon-Jon handed its control tablet to her and reached into a belt pouch, producing some keys. He unlocked a metal chest, which she recognised as one of those loaded at the Blues' outpost.

"Time to play with my new toy."

He produced a small green and white drone and gently set it down. Poking around in the box, Jon-Jon retrieved a small paper booklet, turning it over.

"Some kind of manual. Here. Might want to read it in your spare time."

"Everything needed to program and fly this drone is already on the skipper's control tablet," Phuong explained. "I have already launched the software but it wouldn't let me do much without drone synchronisation."

"You can fly it, then?"

"Think so."

Her fingers danced across the screen. It appeared user friendly and Phuong doubted she would gain more insight by poring through the manual.

A couple of blip sounds came from the drone.

"Syncing now," she said, watching diagnostic information fill the screen. "It has enough charge for… just under an hour in the air. More than enough for a test flight."

"Is this the same as those you've flown before?" Jon-Jon asked.

"Similar. It's pretty straightforward."

"If you are one hundred per cent confident you know what you're doing, take her up." Jon-Jon kept smiling but Phuong caught his eyes narrowing. "Be careful."

She nodded then looked back down, giving the controller her full attention. The drone whirred to life and she raised it from the bench, taking care while manoeuvring within the confines of the shed.

"Looks fine. Data is relayed to the skipper entirely through this app."

Jon-Jon walked outside. "Good. Bring her out."

She complied and they filed outside, though unlike the others, did not lift her gaze from the screen to watch the UAV.

"Remaining stable, despite the wind," she spoke aloud in monotone.

There was a reasonably stiff breeze but the drone merely rocked slightly, auto-stabilisers instantly correcting its position in response to gusts.

"Checking satellites…" she went on.

"Hopefully all are directly overhead," stated Jon-Jon.

"They're not. But we don't want them all there. Sufficient satellites above the horizon, yes, but at different points in the sky — that's more ideal. All overhead is not optimal. In any case, there are two GPS base stations nearby. They should correct any navigational inaccuracies."

Jon-Jon remained silent. Phuong hoped she had not angered him by exposing his lack of understanding.

She plotted a brief course around the farm.

"Looking good. There's more than enough charge for a circuit of the fields."

"If you say so," said the overseer.

Phuong took that as permission to proceed and guided the drone up and out. There was much of Farm 1469 she had not yet seen. Beyond the residences, garden and machinery sheds, it looked like ordinary flat paddocks with irrigation channels here and there. A very large water canal was said to be at the rear of the property, serving as the main water supply for all irrigated farms in the zone. The dog run was planted with trees and shrubs, perhaps intended as a wind-break, but it obscured her view of the world outside.

Phuong wondered if she should chance taking the drone further out, to scout the farms beyond, but Jon-Jon's eyes were fixed on her. The man had been squinting at the sky, following the drone's movements. She was surprised by his lack of interest in learning the software, evidently happy to possess the latest, best technology, just not bore himself with the tedium of its operation.

Something obscured the drone's camera momentarily. Something in the air, close by. A bird. She knew some species were territorial.

"What?"

She sensed the overseer's piercing gaze as he spoke.

"Nothing. Just a glitch, I think."

"You think," he said, without emotion.

"Fly it back, Foo," Sam whispered.

"Yes. Bring my drone back," said Jon-Jon.

"Yes. Right away." Phuong struggled to mouth the words.

There it was again. Something was passing close to the camera, too fast to make out any details. She realised she had not set the option to record and save camera footage. Otherwise, they could have later paused the video for a better look at…

Something was wrong. She increased the drone's speed but the image wobbled.

"What is happening?" Jon-Jon demanded.

"Foo?" said Samantha, sounding as stressed as she felt.

Phuong watched in horror as the camera feed went crazy. She had lost control. The overseer's new toy was spinning headlong for the ground. Then the feed was lost, replaced by an error message. She tried to make sense of the diagnostic data still on screen but it was all too confusing and she could not focus.

Phuong wanted to crawl away and hide. She wished she had never been so enthusiastic about volunteering to do something that might make a difference. She had failed. Failed the overseer, failed the farm, failed her friends, failed herself.

She wished Duc were here. They were a team. He could always set things straight; together everything had a way of working out.

Jon-Jon stared. No feigned warmth played upon his chiselled features. He slowly twisted one side of his moustache, awaiting an explanation. Phuong found no words.

"Find… my… drone," he said.

She nodded, not meeting his eyes, pretending to check the screen for something useful, anything.

Samantha put a hand on her shoulder. "Come on. We'll find it. Bring it back. Figure out the mishap. We'll work it out."

The overseer nodded once and stood, staring, hand on his tool belt, fingers stroking the handle of his wrench. The aura of barely repressed violence about him was terrifying. Phuong was grateful she was not alone with the man.

Her friends ushered her around the corner of the shed. Once out of sight of the overseer, tears came. Phuong fought to hold them back. She hurried into the fields, her friends consoling her.

"Don't worry, it isn't your fault, Foo," Jacko was saying. "New drones probably glitch all the time. It was probably a dud in the first place."

She nodded but felt wholly to blame, crushed by the burden of responsibility Jon-Jon had placed upon on her. She had a pretty good idea where the drone went down at least.

Eventually, she managed to speak between sniffles. "I had it under control. Everything was fine. I don't understand."

"If we can't work out what happened," said Samantha, "then we'll invent a good story."

"Even if it's complete bollocks," said Christopher. "We'll tell that wanker whatever he needs to hear and get him off your back."

"I just don't understand. The readings are all over the place."

"Don't stress about the techie stuff, Foo. I'll take that," said Samantha, relieving her of the tablet. "Now think back. What was the last thing you saw?"

"I flew it along the edge of the farm, just inside the boundary. There was a channel. I followed that. Oh, I hope it didn't go down in the water. It should be this way."

Phuong led them across flat land, broken by small earthen ridges separating each bay in the rice field.

"It's too warm out here and it's not even summer," Jacko complained.

Phuong silently agreed, feeling the bite of the inland sun. After some minutes they found the small channel, one of several that distributed water into their farm from the main canal.

She was startled by growling. Three of Jon-Jon's beasts were prowling among the trees and shrubs of the farm's perimeter, sniffing the air, raising heads to the sky to bark.

Jacko eyed them warily. "Aren't dogs like that banned?"

"They were," said Samantha.

"I may not be local but I reckon the people out here play by their own rules, even before this 'Aussie After' shite," Christopher suggested.

"Let's stay back," said Samantha. "We don't want to stir them up… or find out how high they jump."

Phuong ignored the dogs and strode faster along the channel bank. The only way out of this fix was to find the drone, though she dreaded what she would discover.

Her worst fears were realised when she sighted the wreckage. The UAV had hit a small concrete irrigation gate used for regulating water flow. Despite all the open space, full of soft crumbly dirt, it had plummeted into the one hard solid object in sight and was now a battered mess. The sensor array had taken the brunt of the impact. No wonder she had stopped receiving data.

Phuong was amazed it was even in one piece. Nothing indicated why it crashed. She could pilot drones and knew how to receive and interpret their data but as for their inner workings — the electronics and other physical components housed within — these were an enigma. Even if this required some simple repair, she had no idea where to start.

"How am I ever going to explain?" she said tearily, almost in a whisper.

The others stared dumbly at the wreckage.

It was Samantha who broke the silence. "We were swooped by a magpie while walking out here. The bird must have done the same thing to the drone."

"Oh my… that's gold," said Jacko. "Totally believable – it's the right time of year and everything."

Christopher played with his ear again. "Wait. You mean we're supposed to say some kind of crazy bird attacked and took down a drone. Bollocks. He'll never go for it."

"Magpies can be totally aggressive during nesting season – which is now," Jacko insisted. "Trust me, if you've ever been swooped by a magpie, you'll know exactly what I'm talking about."

"OK, I won't debate local wildlife wiv an indigenous Australian," the Brit conceded, "but how do we explain it crashing?"

"It could have pecked a vulnerable part," Samantha suggested.

Christopher sniggered. "Well, I wouldn't want me vulnerable parts pecked."

Jacko giggled and Samantha rolled her eyes.

Phuong took a few breaths. "This could work. It is plausible that a bird chased and swooped the drone. Eventually they collided. All kinds of aircraft can be damaged by bird-strike, why not drones too? It was just pure bad luck it tumbled straight down onto that concrete."

"See? This isn't your fault," said Samantha.

Phuong still felt responsible and wished she had just flown a simple lap of the sheds then landed the stupid thing right away.

"I just hope the overseer sees it that way," she said. "Would be easier if we had a dead bird to show him."

She glanced around. There was no conveniently deceased magpie in the vicinity nor any other type of bird for that matter.

Christopher picked up the wreckage and started walking. "Oh well, sooner we face the music, sooner this is over. Let's go wiv the bird story and be done wiv it."

Phuong wanted to run the other way, over the empty fields, leap the fences, cross into the next farm and just keep running. All the way to those hills. Duc's bus had gone that way.

The dogs still bayed and growled from their perimeter enclosure. There was no escaping this place. Head lowered, she followed Christopher.

The walk back would be over sooner than she would like. Phuong prayed someone or something would intervene so she need never return. She wished this were just a nightmare and she would wake to the hum of suburban Sydney life – or even the stuffy, silent yet secure ambience of their room in protected accommodation.

Her friends tried to distract her with small talk but their words were just empty sounds. Phuong's own thoughts and fears screamed far louder inside her head, drowning out all else. She tried not to visualise the overseer in a fit of rage.

As they reached the farm's outbuildings, Christopher's words drew her focus back to the present. "Hello. Looks like Jon-Jon has a special guest."

Phuong saw the German backpackers lounging around nearby. One acknowledged their approach.

"Hey guys. Visitors – Blues." He tilted his head at a blue-grey armoured car where Jon-Jon was receiving his guests, a pair of troopers.

"Why are they here?" asked Samantha. "We've hardly been here long enough to produce any crops for them."

The German guy scratched his chin. "Who knows? They've been joking around with the boss man. Social visit?"

The troopers had noticed their approach and were staring. Jon-Jon slowly turned. One trooper adjusted the strap that held the rifle across his back and folded his arms. The other...

"Eww, it's that Selvin," said Jacko, scrunching his nose.

The overseer curled his finger, beckoning.

Phuong felt like she wanted to be sick as she approached. She had to put on a brave face, take responsibility and explain herself.

Before anyone could begin to explain, Selvin made a "tsk-tsk" sound and shook his head. "Well, well, that *was* an expensive piece of government property."

The sergeant swaggered forward, thumbs in pockets. He gave Phuong the impression of an Old West gunslinger or an over-acting B-grade celebrity attempting to play such a part. His police pistol slung low at his side completed the caricature.

Selvin's dark features displayed no sign of anger but Phuong despised the obnoxious smirk that permanently twisted one side of his face. His black hair and sideburns were neatly manicured but despite the well-groomed countenance, his cocky arrogance ensured he was far less attractive and suave than he thought.

They waited for a question to emerge from the man's lips. Nothing was forthcoming. He just peered at them with dark narrow eyes.

Phuong fought for the right words but Christopher, cocky as ever, spoke first. "Well, Sir. It was a bird, Sir."

"A bird," said Selvin. "I thought it was a drone. A highly specialised agri-drone. Place it on the ground, please."

Christopher complied, with a flicker of a defiant scowl, and opened his mouth to speak again.

Samantha spoke up. "What he means is that we were attacked out there by a very aggressive bird. We assume that very same bird damaged the drone in such a way that it no longer responded to this tablet's control software."

Selvin eyed the wreckage. "You expect me to believe a bird did all this damage?"

"It's nesting season," said Jacko. "The magpies go crazy and over-react to everything."

Jon-Jon was yet to utter a word. He was just staring at Phuong, expressionless.

She could not let her friends do all the talking. She had been at the controls. Her explanation would need to be short and to the point. No rambling, slip-ups or highlighting the risk she took by extending the drone's maiden voyage a little too far.

"I saw something pass by a couple of times, really close to the camera. Before I could figure out what was going on, it must have already hit a critical component. The controls stopped working. What you see there is impact damage. We found the drone right where it fell and crashed into concrete."

"You have concrete in your fields?" Selvin asked the overseer.

Jon-Jon folded his arms. "Yes. There are several pre-cast concrete irrigation gates."

Selvin sighed. He glanced at Phuong, then back to Jon-Jon.

"Sometimes a second chance is a good thing. May I borrow your young lady? Horace has need for a pilot."

Jon-Jon unfolded his arms and spread his palms wide. "Why of course. Please, take her."

"Good," said Selvin. He faced Phuong, flicking a finger over his shoulder at the vehicle. "Get in. Please. The rest of you, well, if any of you knows how to fix that drone or knows of someone here who can, then do your best."

Selvin walked towards the car as the other trooper opened the door.

"Tell Horace I said we're overdue for a good session and it's his turn to provide the drinks," said Jon-Jon.

Selvin spoke back over his shoulder. "Hey. No parties in this zone. Not unless I'm invited."

"Ha-ha. Of course. Make sure his alfresco hot tub is cleaned out and ready for our visit."

Jon-Jon turning back to Phuong.

"Hurry along, young lady. Best not keep the gents in blue waiting. I think you will be very welcome at Horace's place."

"What about her things?" asked Samantha.

"I'm sure she can borrow anything she needs from one of Horace's girls. Now go."

Phuong scurried over to the Blues' vehicle where she was ushered into the back seat by Selvin. Up close, the overpowering scent of his cheap aftershave was sickening. She was speechless and felt herself shake the way Samantha's rabbits back home sometimes did.

She had no idea where she was going and what was in store. She had no supplies, no friends, no Duc. She did not like the sound of this Horace. These creeps had this buddy thing going on and Horace was surely every bit as gross as the others.

As the car departed, Phuong looked back. She saw Samantha and the others pleading with Jon-Jon. Maybe they could persuade him to let them join her; convince him they worked better as a team. Unfortunately, despite the mishap, Jon-Jon knew she was quite capable of controlling a drone without assistance. The overseer turned his back on the others and busied himself closing the two sets of gates, letting his dogs run back into the space between them.

Jon-Jon waved and blew a kiss as they turned onto the main road. Phuong looked the other way.

Selvin turned around from the front of the vehicle.

"Play your cards right and who knows? You may yet enjoy a prosperous life out here."

Phuong doubted his idea of a good life resembled her own in any way. She was essentially their prisoner now. As the vehicle sped through unknown country, she had no choice but to accept her fate.

7

Witek

"Is that thing gender confused, man?"

"No, Chad. I think it is seeking my cousin. If the AI and facial recognition functions are not so great it must be an older model."

The drone may have mispronounced their surname but Witek was aware of his familial resemblance to Marcelina. They had often been mistaken for siblings.

Kilo pumped his shotgun and raised it as the drone zipped laterally, adjusted his aim and fired. The shotgun blast echoed as the drone spun backwards through the air and tumbled out of sight down the slope.

"Good shot, boss," said Agus.

Kilo nodded. "Lite Shot, meet boar shot. I will not have some machine making demands."

"What now?" asked Riku. "Should we retrieve it, go up the hill, back down?"

"Wait," said Karmen. "Listen."

Witek looked down the hillside where she indicated and heard the buzzing resume though in inconsistent pulses, like a race car driver revving on a starting grid.

"My shot was inadequate," said Kilo.

The drone spiralled into view, weaving as it raced back at them. Something hit Witek's foot with force, and he heard the crack of gunfire.

Kilo cursed as his own weapon failed to reload.

"Off the path. Scatter. Get behind the rocks."

Witek immediately complied with the overseer's command and glanced about for hard cover. The ground sloped away with a steep gradient and he took care not to slip but his foot felt unharmed and he did not fall.

He swung behind the nearest boulder and ducked, taking a moment to feel his boot. Part of the heavy heel sole was missing.

Looking sideways, he saw the others take cover. Kilo had his back to a rock and was fumbling with his shotgun, while glancing about skyward. Riku and the girls ducked behind some woody vines that cascaded over a larger rock face like a waterfall of vegetation.

Chad was nearer, attempting to hide himself within the branches of a small conifer.

"We're too exposed, Witek, we need to move into better —"

With a whirr, the drone appeared high overhead, its movements awkward though did not appear critically damaged.

Kilo chanced another shot as the drone swooped then exhaled, missing.

Witek's heart raced faster as the crack of another .22 shot was accompanied by a ricochet from his own rock. The UAV circled out of sight.

"It really wants you, man," Chad said.

Witek nodded, leapt to his feet and moved further down the slope.

"I will try to draw it away," he called back. "Looks like a rock crevice down here."

"Wait, don't go. I'll bring it down next pass," Kilo yelled as he pumped the shotgun again.

"No. Take the others back. The woods look thicker below. I will circle back to the farm later."

"I'll come down and watch your six," Chad called out.

"If it gets me, you may be next."

Kilo was moving from cover to cover.

"Just hide over here. Do not go down there. It gets steeper and more dangerous."

Witek could not allow anyone else to be harmed because of him. Ignoring Kilo's protest, he made for the narrow crevice. It was flanked by small scrubby plants and the terrain promised better cover than the high ground near the trail.

Hearing a buzz, he glanced over his shoulder. Chad was still hesitating by the tree.

The drone hovered above the rock Witek had used for cover and rotated in place, scanning.

"Get into hard cover, Chad. Go," Witek shouted and waved at where the others had vanished.

The drone turned to face him and he waved his blade in the air.

Witek pointed his weapon at the UAV and shouted, *"Pierdolę cię!"*

He doubted the machine could understand his native tongue but he had its attention – it fired, the shot striking his blade with sufficient force for Witek to fumble and drop the weapon. The machine's targeting was off but too close for his liking. It closed in, swaying from side to side, like a predator preparing to strike.

Witek rushed into the crevice, not stopping to retrieve his weapon. Chancing a look over his shoulder, he almost lost his footing on loose pebbles and slid, struggling to balance and keep himself upright. The rocks on each side were high, double his height, but there was no cover directly overhead. Scraggly vines covered the rocks in parts but there was no foliar curtain thick enough for hiding.

Rounding a tight corner, Witek hit more scree and lost control of his slide. Ahead the gully opened onto a rock ledge atop a cliff face. He dug in his feet but had gained too much momentum. Desperate not to topple over, he clutched at a vine, only to strip away handfuls of leaves.

He saw another vine, leafless but woody, his last chance. Witek hooked his whole arm around it, jarring himself as he came to a sudden stop. Pebbles tumbled down the cliff.

Finding himself in the open, the only way to proceed was along the ledge, just wide enough to traverse. In different circumstances, the woodland vista would be lovely. Over the treetops he could see the railway and highway carving parallel lines through the vegetation a few kilometres away.

There was no safe way to descend the cliff, let alone while under fire, so he sprinted along the ledge, dodging potential tripping hazards. The damage to his boot had appeared minimal but Witek felt more off balance with every step.

The drone was still nearby, its sound muffled. He knew he must find cover before it could locate and target him again.

In his path was a narrow cleft in the ledge. Witek considered leaping across but slowed, noticing more thick woody vines cascading down from above, some spilling down into the cleft.

Then the little UAV reappeared, now whirling over the very woods he sought to reach, skimming the treetops. It bobbed from side to side, as if to mock him, daring him to make his next move.

Witek grabbed a thick vine and swung into the cleft. Its stone walls were a pebbly conglomerate and there were ample footholds. He realised the strange outback plant he was gripping produced a foul odour, reminiscent of road kill, but was grateful its woody tendrils supported his weight. The cleft became choked with vegetation on all sides and he hoped these plants remained just as sturdy further down, should he become trapped and need them to help him climb back up.

Witek gained secure footing on a protruding rock and paused, hearing the erratic engine close overhead. He hoped it could not navigate in confined spaces. Witek tested another vine and descended further as the drone's voice boomed.

"CLEAR THIS… HOLD POS… MARCE-MARC-MARRR…"

It fell silent; then it fell from the sky. Witek nearly lost his grip as the drone struck the rocky outcrop on which he had just paused, spun right past him and hit the ground. He hoped it would stay down this time. Hoping to disarm the fallen machine, he hurried to finish his descent, dropping the last metre. The only buzzing sound now came from insects.

Witek took a moment to catch his breath, snorted the snot out of each side of his wet nose, then regretted this because the stench was worse.

The small drone lay motionless on the dusty bottom of the cleft.

Witek crouched and methodically examined the thing. Its battered alloy hull had been breached in a few places by Kilo's boar shot and a few rotor blades were damaged. It had no insignia or anything indicating an owner.

The design was similar to those used by Polish national service personnel. The magazine ejection mechanism could not be too different. Yes, virtually the same. He withdrew the long clip and examined it. Only three bullets remained.

Pocketing the ammunition and magazine, he lifted the drone with both hands. True to its name, the Lite Shot was not particularly heavy. He hoped someone may be able to hack it and identify who set its mission parameters.

Witek shouldered his way through curtains of vines. The cleft was quiet, its dusty floor undisturbed by anything save footprints. He had been too fixed on the UAV to notice them before but now realised the dust was criss-crossed by spoor of many shapes and sizes. Paw pads with little claw marks suggested a fox or perhaps a small dog. Bird prints were here and there.

There were also boot prints, not particularly large, perhaps two-thirds the size of his own. Surely children could not have been playing out here. The prints were probably old. It was sheltered and still, perhaps rarely experiencing wind disturbance, potentially a pleasant campsite without that stench.

Witek scrunched his nostrils, making a conscious effort to breathe through his mouth as the air became even more foul. He realised he was mistaken about the vines being the source — there was an animal rotting in here. Passing sideways through another veil of foliage he nearly tripped... on a corpse.

Flies buzzed about a sickening mess. There were three human bodies here – or what was left of them. None of these people could have been last night's screamer. Decomposition had set in and some flesh had been stripped by predators. Body parts were scattered or missing altogether. Large deep-red coloured ants swarmed over and through the remains.

Witek held his breath, immediately thinking of pathogens. He did not care to linger here a moment longer but thought of Marcelina. She had been hunted in this area. He had to check each corpse. He had to be sure.

The three wore identical clothing, which remained in better condition than the flesh below – white uniforms, each prominently featuring the Lucky Dragons logo, on both breast pocket and popped collar. As far as he could tell given their condition, two of the corpses' heads sported short, neat black hair. Marcelina's hair was long and brown.

The third was missing a head altogether but the body appeared to belong to a male with a short, broad frame. Despite the decomposition, Witek saw a horrible wound. A hole had been blasted into the chest, obliterating uniform, flesh and bone. He observed no obvious cause of death for the others and given the present condition of their remains doubted he would ever learn.

Witek placed the drone on an untainted patch of earth and withdrew his phone – a Marektek, with excellent battery life. It was last charged in Canberra and he had not yet sought a power supply at Kirilia but ample power remained. He took a few photos and a short video clip of the macabre scene to examine at length later.

Desperate for air, he pulled his shirt over his nose, took a single breath and held it again. If there was pestilence in the air, he had probably already been exposed and figured his shirt was likely useless as a filter.

He prepared to leave then hesitated, noticing a new set of tracks – paw prints, large, well over 10cm. Australia had no large predators as far as he was aware, excluding of course the giant sharks in coastal waters and massive crocodiles lurking in rivers in tropical regions. These were clearly mammalian.

Witek had heard the continent was overrun with many non-indigenous feral species: boars, goats, foxes, cats… If these belonged to a feral cat, it must be massive. A large wild dog was more plausible. Witek photographed the spoor, placing his hand beside some of the marks to demonstrate their size.

While he first assumed these were plague victims, Witek's gut feeling was that these people had all been murdered. That ghastly chest wound supported this conclusion for one of them.

Remembering the bus trip, he wondered about banditry. He thought the Blues were supposed to keep such people away from this area. Terrain like this offered ample places for criminals to hide, even from drones.

Unless this was the lair of some massive beast. Witek did not savour the idea of becoming trapped, his way out blocked by… something. He pocketed his phone, grabbed the UAV and, pushing through two more veils of foliage, found his way outside, on level ground, amid gnarly eucalypts. Then he hurried away from the cliff wall, anxious to put distance between himself and the cleft.

Once free to take several deep breaths of untainted air, Witek got his bearings. Trees, shrubs and long grass grew everywhere.

Cooper Hill loomed above him. If he headed west, keeping the hill to his right, he should be able to circle back to Kirilia.

There was a light breeze, the only scent now that of grass. Down here were few landmarks of note so before setting off, Witek took one last photo of the cleft's location. Not that he ever wanted to return to that grisly place. When he reached Kirilia, he would offer to quarantine himself, lest he carry a pathogen.

A twig cracked behind him. If the others had descended this side of Cooper Hill, instead of sticking to the trail, they should be ahead, not behind him. Witek saw nothing in the grass or scrub. Several birds took to a treetop, squawking, making a fuss. Then the small flock moved to another tree, closer, becoming more vocal.

Someone – or something – was coming. Witek was alone, unarmed and encumbered by an awkward armful of drone. He remembered the rumour of workers disappearing in the Outback. Rational thought and instinct were in agreement about dealing with this unknown entity.

Witek ran.

8

Harrison

Harrison doubted having worked pre-apocalypse with Aussie Kozzie Industries would be of any use now. To survive, he would need to adapt, learn and explore this new world. Poking around that derelict building was as good a place as any to start.

Many of these old properties had more than one residential building. The main house on Farm 1469 was Jon-Jon's but there were two smaller fibro homes, perhaps once housing shearers and other labourers.

One was renovated, now serving as the comfortable dorm where most of the girls slept. The other fibro home had fallen into disrepair, with holes in its roof, the interior full of dust and cobwebs. It was partly in a good enough state for Jon-Jon to store junk.

Harrison realised it could be the perfect quiet place to sleep, undisturbed and unbothered. Jon-Jon did not mind his male workers sleeping outside the shed, as long as they stayed out of the female dorm.

That British bastard had taken to sleeping around a campfire under the stars, with some German backpackers and a couple of girls who sounded Australian. They spent a lot of time partying and recording clips of silly dance routines. How pointless. With no more internet the only views they would get were from those shared locally via nu-tooth.

Harrison had seen the rude blonde Sydney girl liked to head out there to join in and get cosy with the Brit. Dumb slut. He figured she would be the type stupid enough to marry a brute like that and spend her life getting slapped around. Girls like that never went for nice guys. Harrison once had a friend who was a nice guy, who was overlooked by every girl he ever fancied in favour of physically larger but not so charming men. It had always ended in tears for those girls.

Harrison had decided to rise early to explore the dilapidated fibro house. It was far from the campfire – tick. Two rooms with more than enough space for sleeping amid Jon-Jon's old junk – tick. It was much better than the tool shed – big tick.

It would be prudent to invite Junior and the two guys from Kerala to join him. Having them at his back would ensure he slept better.

Harrison began tidying a room to make his own. He found an old broom in a decaying cupboard and set about removing "spider guoals" and cobwebs still occupied, squishing a couple of redback spiders in the process. He did not relish the thought of a painful bite.

Harrison shifted some boxes to make more room and was surprised to find they had obscured a trapdoor. He leaned on his broom handle, gawping.

It was padlocked. A familiar stupid koala looked cheerfully up at him from the lock — it was an Aussie Kozzie electronic Smart-lok. This product, like many others sold by his former employer, he considered especially lame given the deliberate incorrect spelling of "lock". These products sold like hot cakes in spite of their dopey names. He had never gotten around to asking someone in Kozzie's marketing division if products with dumbed-down names outsold those with boring but correct names.

Harrison recalled something his parents said about this particular product line — a fault. The locks should have been recalled as there was an override that was not removed before distribution. This was of course hushed up at managerial level so the company could avoid the expense, hassle and embarrassment of refunding or replacing their locks. He remembered the override code — sometimes random details just stuck with him. All you had to do was hold down both 3 and 4 on the keypad while mashing 7 repeatedly...

The hack worked. Kozzie had proven useful after all. The lock clicked open and Harrison lifted the trapdoor, then looked over his shoulder. There was nobody around so he activated his phone's torchlight to look within. Old steep wooden stairs led down into a very small basement.

He knew he had to investigate and descended with care. There was a wine rack, laden with bottles of red, beckoning him to take one. Each was covered with thick dust. Some were ancient, with decaying corks, their contents ruined. Others remained intact, aged around 10 years, and Harrison hoped they would taste great. He wondered if Jon-Jon would notice a few missing.

Harrison felt a cobweb brush the nape of his neck and launched into an involuntary fit, slapping at his head and back with his free hand. He stumbled into a junk pile and fell over. After straightening his glasses on his nose, pushing himself back upright and picking up his phone, he shined the light around, trying to calm himself by examining the other items around him.

There were personal effects, power tools, ordinary tools, a stack of plates, painted cups made from porcelain or china on a shelf, a pile of tacky-looking jewellery and some very old toys.

In the midst of the mess, he found a drone. He wondered if the overseer knew it was there. The dust over everything indicated nobody had been in this cellar for some time.

Harrison had been wishing for a drone. This one would suffice, even if its design was somewhat obsolete. Apart from invaluable reconnaissance, he had also been fantasising about ways to use one as a weapon or means of sabotage.

He decided to leave the wine alone, for now, but removed the drone and controller from its box, crept back up and out of the cellar then closed and padlocked the trapdoor.

The dilapidated building still had power and Harrison left the drone and its controller in a dim corner to charge all day.

He waited until just after dark to return and sat in the gloom for a while, hearing distant chatter from other workers. Nobody seemed to be nearby. He had been thinking of this moment all day and could wait no longer. Without hesitation, he flew the drone up and out through a hole in the roof, hoping no one heard its departure.

Using darkness as cover, he piloted the UAV directly away. There was little to see beyond the light of the buildings but he could still make out the dark line of trees in the dog run and crossed over to the far side. He heard dogs begin to bark but pressed on awhile before descending, setting down the drone in an overgrown field with care.

Nothing was visible on the view screen and Harrison hoped the long grass would serve as a perfect hidden parking spot. He switched off the controller and concealed it among some old word quiz books, piled upon the floor beside overloaded shelving.

"Yes," he whispered to himself, anticipating better times ahead.

Over the following days, during his free time, he walked alone to the far side of the fields, discreetly bringing the controller. There, out of earshot, he could fly the drone back over the dog run to his position, where he had the privacy to make some modifications.

The overseer's tool belt inspired his first crude attempt at weaponising the drone. There was a very large shifter in one of the sheds, not unlike Jon-Jon's own wrench. The tool had a hole in the end of its handle, allowing it to hang from a rack. Harrison threaded through some wire, the other ends of which he twisted onto the drone's frame. The result was a drone carrying a heavy object, perhaps capable of bludgeoning attacks.

Harrison had to test his creation to ensure it could fly with a payload or perform standard manoeuvres with something swinging from its frame. He hoped, if pressed, he could dive bomb his preferred target with sufficient accuracy and force to inflict serious cranial damage...

Out in the fields, the test flights showed promise. His drone was not only capable of lifting the solid metal tool off the ground, but maintained airborne stability. The next task was testing the effectiveness of the weapon. Those ugly dogs were always skulking in their perimeter enclosure. At the back of the farm Harrison found some places where Jon-Jon's house had no clear line of sight to his position.

There he proceeded to chase and harass the dogs. While it seemed a vain struggle to strike one with the swinging wrench, the endeavour was entertaining. He had to be mindful lest a savage beast turn on the drone or worse, jump the fence and take him down.

With that in mind, he began using his new bedroom as a base of operations. The drone was parked over a kilometre away but he could still launch it perfectly well from the comfort of the old house. He took pains to sit where he had a clear view of anyone approaching the building's entrance. The other three workers had taken up his offer to find their own patch of floor space, but generally only spent time in there after dark, which suited Harrison fine.

Whenever he completed his daily share of garden work, he conducted drone recon outside the farm or more dive-bombing practice. If dogs were not present, there were plenty of thistles and other weeds that made excellent targets in the abandoned pastures of the farm next door.

He ensured he flew nowhere near other people. Nobody could ever find out about this — the sole activity he relished in this place.

Before long, a new opportunity came knocking. Harrison was flying his obstacle course, weaving between trees in the dog run. Some agitated dogs were visible on the controller's view screen. They were always barking at something somewhere and Jon-Jon never paid attention unless the commotion was near the gates.

Then he saw her — that ugly white bitch with small pink eyes. She was fearless, the one beast who would hold her ground. The one most likely to tear his throat out. He was now confident enough in his piloting to go for a kill.

Then Harrison glimpsed something else in the corner of the screen. Airborne, high above Jon-Jon's fields. A bird would make an interesting new target.

No, this was better. Another drone. An important agricultural drone. The kind he should have been appointed to commandeer, if that Sydney girl had not stolen the opportunity.

He held position, the UAV hovering among the trees, as he checked for potential witnesses. There was nobody. Like him, the operator would be watching a screen, not the drone itself. Harrison would have enjoyed mapping fields much more than sweating in the garden.

Remembering the magpie larks that he had observed harassing a hawk, an idea formed. Thinking of their repeated dive bomb tactic, he took his drone higher, carefully tracking his target from above.

It took just a few swoops. His target practice was worth every second. The mapping drone followed a nice, steady, safe and predictable straight line. Hah. Not so safe.

Harrison's target vanished. It took another ascent to get a broader perspective to realise his complete success. There it was, a motionless green and white wreck beside some concrete.

Victory. Harrison had shot her down. He wanted to zoom in close and gloat but knew everyone would be aware a mishap had occurred and rush to investigate. He flew low and fast, away from the crash site, over the perimeter fence, back to his grassy hiding place, killing his drone's engines before anyone could approach the area on foot.

He stashed the controller in its hiding place, realising he must find an alibi, just in case. Junior and Amahle were toiling in the garden. He brought them both water and joined them, wholly focused on tilling the earth, careful to pay no attention to the group of people near one of the far sheds who appeared rather distressed.

He could barely contain himself. What an adrenaline rush. Harrison made a conscious effort to toil harder and sweat, lest the flush of his true excitement give him away. He engrossed himself in work and before he knew it, the Blues arrived. He did not look up, nor clean the fog and salty sweat streaks from his glasses but could hear the overseer was unhappy.

Junior tapped him on the shoulder.

"Look. They're taking Foo away. What do you think they want with her?"

Junior was a clean and honest man. He must not be allowed to suspect anything. Feigning disinterest with a stretch, Harrison thought of a quick reply.

"Oh really? Well, she's apparently quite intelligent. They probably need to borrow her technical expertise for something."

Being downwind of Jon-Jon and the Blues, he caught snippets of their discussion. Its tone did not sound favourable for his nemeses.

What success. Harrison had never dreamed things would work out so well. Thinking of the luck and opportunity made him want to dance but he forced himself to turn back to the garden. The Sydney girl was not his main target but if removing her from the picture destabilised their group, it was a victory nevertheless.

Days passed and the girl did not return. Harrison overheard she was at the farm of one of Jon-Jon's sleazy mates. He had to contain his glee. Focus on work. No more test flights. He could not do anything that would raise the slightest suspicion.

Without her bestie, the horrid blonde Sydney girl was morose and sulky. If his win had broken the spirit of the others, it was icing on the cake. Yet he could not be complacent. With enemy morale down, it was time to plan his next move, strike again during the window of opportunity.

The blonde was closer than ever to the Brit, who looked cranky and ready to lash out at anyone who pissed him off. Harrison reminded himself to keep his distance. If he was suspected of involvement with the crash of Jon-Jon's precious drone, the Brit would not hesitate to run to the overseer. They would tear him limb from limb – or throw him to the dogs for that same outcome.

As he mulled over this, he became frustrated by his inability to conceive the next logical step in his revenge plot.

Harrison's thoughts were disrupted by singing. It was Junior and Amahle, just outside the old house. They did have quite lovely voices, he just wished they would sing something other than religious songs.

The first time he heard them, he worried they were "God's CHAPs", members of a popular worldwide religious movement, the Church of the Harmonious Prophets. This cult was founded by a teen idol-turned-Christian rock star, known simply as Zach, who caused a stir among the paparazzi when he began dating Aree, a pop singer who was Muslim. The two found common ground in music then decided to rewrite their respective religions into one, all to a soundtrack of catchy tunes.

Despite the inevitable outcry from followers of more orthodox branches of Christianity and Islam, Zach and Aree's charismatic personas drew hordes of followers and the CHAP thing took off.

Harrison, both metal head and unbeliever, detested their ear-worm tunes. Their lyrics attracted controversy, with subtle elements of bigotry directed at minority groups and "unenlightened" traditional cultures, as well as a general intolerance of other religions.

Of course, their cult was the only true path to salvation during the inevitable doomsday. The CHAPs were surely loving how their foreseen apocalypse actually eventuated, though Harrison hoped the pathogen nailed the pair and they bled to death from every orifice, painfully aware they were just as mortal as every other poor bastard who had been infected.

To Harrison's relief, Junior and Amahle proved to be just regular Christians. A little daily devotion was a small price to pay for having the big man from Zimbabwe close by. Harrison still had his wireless nu-tooth headphones, so could always drown the singing with a good dose of nu metal if it got irritating.

Thinking of the bigoted CHAPs gave him an idea. One member of the Sydney group was being excluded – Jacko was obviously equally upset about his friend being unexpectedly spirited away, but got no sympathy from the Brit, who continued to taunt and antagonise him with below-the-belt remarks. It was surely hard enough being a chubby, gay indigenous Australian without some loudmouth outsider with no concept of political correctness invading his clique.

Harrison did not give a damn about how people chose to swing, nor of their cultural background, just as long as they did not join scumbags like Christopher in a "let's bully Harry" session.

Aggressive action would not be the right tactic with Jacko. Instead, he could offer a sympathetic ear — support from an unexpected quarter could change the dynamic and the other two fuckers would soon find themselves alone, the last of their bitchy group. Divide and conquer.

Harrison could not remember Jacko ever directly hurling an abrasive comment his way. The worst he might have done was show a little amusement at comments spoken by the others. Harrison could not even recall a specific instance of that. Yes, get him on side, that would be the way.

There was a scent of something cooking. Amahle, Junior and Aditya were heading over to the outdoor food prep area so he hurried to join them. He hoped Jacko was cooking; he could perhaps pay him a compliment. Jacko gravitated towards that duty and had a bit of skill. Most others rostered on to cooking duties were clueless about culinary arts.

Harrison scanned the crowd. Jacko was not cooking. Two girls from the Philippines had made some sort of traditional boiled meat dish. He did, however, see Jacko serving himself. The despicable duo, Samantha and Christopher, were nowhere in sight. This was a perfect opportunity. Grabbing his meal allocation, Harrison wandered over to Jacko.

"A bit bland for my liking," Harrison said, as if to himself, then turned to Jacko. "That steak you cooked the other night was much, much better."

"Why thank you, Harry."

Harrison cringed on the inside but refrained from correcting his name.

"Must be your seasoning. Did you manage to find some herbs or something?"

Jacko looked amused.

"You do realise that was just salt and pepper?"

"Ah. Well. It was cooked to perfection anyway. Guess we're pretty lucky to still be able to enjoy steak at all. I'm guessing cows don't get the plague?"

"Apparently not," said Jacko. "One of Jon-Jon's friends killed and butchered the one we enjoyed eating and we're still OK."

Aditya chimed in, "Enjoyed? Not me. I am vegetarian."

Harrison looked at his bowl, filled with rice. Aditya had not partaken in the meaty main dish though was not missing out; the boiled pork really could have been spiced better to give it more of a flavour kick but Harrison knew Tala and Reyna probably had to make do with the ingredients on hand. He wondered how long it would be until simple things like salt and pepper became luxuries.

He looked out at the veggie patch, which Jon-Jon hoped would eventually become a market garden producing not only enough to feed them, but surplus for the capital. Harrison sighed. He suspected all of their diets would become more vegetarian soon enough.

Aditya continued. "I wonder what the overseer traded for the meat. Surely it is now a rare commodity."

"Oh, didn't you hear?" said Jacko, then hushed his voice to a near-whisper. "One of his mates has a whole herd of beef cattle. Jon-Jon loaned the guy one of his wives for a week."

"Wow. He really is trading in flesh then," said Harrison.

He had suspected this but now was the first time somebody confirmed the man's seedy business arrangements. He wondered if

Jacko had speculated about the true fate of Foo. Harrison avoided that subject, for fear of revealing his part in her expulsion.

"I always thought farmers out here were all a bunch of good old Aussie blokes," he added.

"Most people in these areas are not Australian at all," said Aditya. "You will see that many more are like us – from elsewhere. Before this pandemic, we moved around different farming areas. There were many seasonal jobs for workers from India and other countries."

Harrison nodded. It was true that the relaxed border policy before the pandemic, which was designed to stimulate economic growth, triggered a population boom. Therefore, the majority of people on the Australian continent were, like himself, actually born overseas.

"In remote areas, you'll still find people who've lived there for generations," said Jacko.

"More remote than this?"

Harrison was a city boy and to him this was the end of the earth. It was hard to conceive that people would live in the desolate wastes further north and west.

Jacko continued, "Go far enough, we might even find people who've been living continuously on Country for tens of thousands of years. Unless they were displaced – most of my mob were."

Harrison was informed enough to know this was a politically sensitive topic for many indigenous populations worldwide, even centuries after they were forcibly removed from their homelands by outsiders deciding what was best for them.

He hoped some of Jacko's family had found some way to preserve some of their culture and traditions but figured it prudent not to raise the issue. No good could come from delving into a potentially painful subject for somebody he was trying to keep happy and on side.

Therefore, he kept it simple and said, "Bloody governments."

This gained nods of agreement from everyone around. Being sent out here was not something optional.

He felt the firm grip of Junior's hand on his shoulder.

"Speaking of authority – look. Motorbikes. Visitors."

Harrison's heart sank. The Blues knew. All of his activities must have been detected by an overwatch drone high overhead. He had been totally absorbed with the action on-screen, forgetting to look away and check the sky for that distinctive V-shape. Jon-Jon had even told everyone the drones were there, seeking incoming threats, enabling the Blues to respond with rapid ground-based interception.

Harrison knew they had AdSoS panels – Advanced Solar Systems – fitted to the upper surface of their wings. One of the Lucky Dragons' recently acquired companies had researched and developed the AdSoS technology, enabling the Dragons to mass produce the panels for a whole new range of applications, selling them to anyone who could afford the cost of upgrading their existing gear.

What this all meant in practical terms was that overwatch drones were almost always airborne. Only landing for the occasional maintenance check, they were always watching.

Harrison squeezed his eyes shut and stretched back his neck. He had failed to watch for them and was caught out in the end.

9

Witek

On his first day in the bush, Witek had run without looking back. He had arrived at Kirilia's gates, unscathed, feeling foolish. Wired from the drone chase, he had overreacted to some non-existent threat. Not everything here was out to get you.

He had spent every day thereafter alone and unbothered.

The thought of making a home in this woodland was likely unappealing to most. Witek proved it was not impossible.

His offer to remain outside the farm was appreciated. Kilo had proposed a shelter shed in the stockyard for self-quarantine but Witek insisted on staying in the bush. He had rejected the offer to bring his camping gear and settled for some old blankets and was given an old .22 calibre rifle for protection.

Witek's bush shelter was unconventional. More defensive than a practical long-term shelter, he had erected a lofty platform, affixed to two near-horizontal branches in a massive gnarled eucalypt. His first ascent had been challenging but now his base was fully established, providing easy access to his elevated retreat. Rope, timbers, nails and even some shade cloth made all the difference, some materials scavenged, others from Kirilia.

Witek was glad to be free to explore – this woodland was rich in useful junk.

Days passed. He did not become ill. He was only visited by others delivering meals from a safe distance. He became steadily more relaxed in this environment.

This evening, however, something was different. It was very quiet. The chorus of insects was missing.

A pair of birds squawked in unison somewhere out in the woods. Witek did not move, save for his eyes. Scanning the prickly shrubs in the vicinity, he saw nothing. His wet nostrils only detected the scent of vegetation.

There was, however, an unfamiliar sound on the breeze. Unintelligible voices. Investigation would reveal their source. Perhaps someone was bringing more supplies.

He glanced up and around. There was enough light.

Witek wiped his nose and strode into the woods.

The chatter was somewhere to the southeast, odd, given Kirilia was north of his position.

After a few minutes, he paused to reassess the situation. The voices came from the north after all. The breeze kept shifting, confusing things. Then it became calm.

Witek was alone, surrounded by still, silent scrub. He figured poor sleep had made him imagine things.

Light was fading, faster than anticipated. He began to backtrack.

Something crunched in the foliage behind him. Witek whirled, rifle raised. He saw nothing. The noise had lasted only a second. All he heard now was his own rapid breathing.

He turned again, quickening his pace. The woods were darkening. Witek knew his treehouse was close. It was the most optimal vantage point – and firing position.

He heard a deep growl, back some distance. This noise was real. Something was out here after all and had returned.

Witek's tree was in sight. He ran for it.

The thing charged through the undergrowth. He did not need to turn his head to know it was closing fast.

Slinging his rifle, he leapt for the knotted rope, climbing as if back in boot camp, glad he had maintained his fitness. Another deep growl, from directly below now. Witek felt a sudden shift in the rope's tension but dared not stop climbing to look down.

Only when he had reached his platform did he prepare to make his stand.

The land below was very dark now. Too dark. Something circled the tree. A great shadow. A massive beast. In the gloom he could not make out any detail. Witek raised his rifle, taking aim at the middle of the shape.

Before he could fire, the shadow sped away into the woods.

10

Sienna

There was definitely something about these hills. Sienna was drawn to natural landscapes but had never felt a sense of connection so strong.

While a beach lover, family road trips taught her to appreciate the variety of topography the country had to offer. She was bursting to explore the national park and paused a moment, gazing into the scrub beyond the garden.

Kilo had led short forays into the bushland bordering Kirilia, each trip uneventful, save the first. Sienna was frustrated at not having been invited.

The farm had been peaceful since that first night and with no sign of bandits or more drones, this country was less ominous and more intriguing.

Days tending the vegetable garden kept her fit, active and productive. It was hot work despite winter having just finished. Exhausted each evening, Sienna slept soundly, without being troubled by anything fearful in her sleep.

Sienna liked her surroundings at Kirilia. The established garden was nestled into the hillside and encircled the two-storey home-stead. A small natural spring emerged from a place further up the slope, providing clean water. The property was apparently unique in that it was not wholly reliant on the area's irrigation scheme or infrequent rains. Kirilia's fruit trees, vegetables and ornamentals all somehow thrived on spring water alone.

With the real farming largely automated, Kilo invested much of his labour force in undertaking garden duties, which made the yard busier than Sienna would have liked. Therefore, she did not hear Chad approaching amid the general commotion but sensed some-body was behind her.

"Hey, Sindy." His greeting was cheerful. "Kilo said it's time to bring Witek his ration. Wanna join me?"

Sienna was a little slow to respond to her fake name, something she would need to work on. She must try to be more social – here was an opportunity it would be foolish to neglect, one where she could finally get out.

"Dude, funny you should ask."

"Huh? Why's that?"

"I think maybe you know," she said with a wink.

"Ah… OK." Chad looked confused. Perhaps he thought she was being flirty, knowing nothing of what she was anxious to discuss.

"Anyway, where's Kilo?"

"After we spoke, he walked up to the spring."

Sienna nodded. "Good. Think that's his chill-out spot. Come on, let's visit this mysterious Witek."

Sienna stabbed her pitchfork into the ground, wiped her brow and followed Chad down the hill. She admired the thoughtful mix of plants chosen for landscaping the garden. Its native grasses and shrubs were well-established and they shared their work space with myriad bird species.

Putu emerged from the kitchen shed, bearing food and water for them to deliver to Witek in his woodland hideaway. If the corpses he had encountered were plague-ridden, she believed he should be dead by now. Yet his quarantine was set at a full fortnight, as a precaution.

On their way to the gates, Sienna noticed Duc, the slim guy from Sydney, wandering aimlessly by the fire pit.

"Hey, bud," Chad called.

Duc lifted a hand from his pocket to wave before replacing it, turning away and moving off, looking at the ground.

"Feel sorry for the guy," said Chad. "He still had family and friends but they were all on that other bus."

"Yeah, being split up is not so great. I know how he feels. Honestly though, I needed my alone time even before all this."

It was not uncommon for people her age to worry about the future. Before this pandemic, many had watched parents struggle with the cost of living – a lasting comfortable lifestyle never assured. Australia's moniker as the so-called "lucky country" was a relic from the days of "boomers". Despite life's challenges, Sienna and her peers had never envisaged a future like this.

Chad waved to a pair of backpackers from Denmark sitting atop the barricade. "Gotta get this to Witek while it's hot."

Kilo had rostered on people to watch the main access points to the homestead and outbuildings. The whole homestead area was fenced off, separating its innermost buildings from fields and bushland. She had heard Kilo would not be satisfied until it was completely encircled by hard defences.

Sienna had already done guard duty at a simple post consisting of an old picnic table under some shady kurrajong trees overlooking the open fields and western access road. It had been boring and uneventful. She would have preferred assignment to a patrol along Kirilia's wilder eastern fringe.

Jumping the cattle grid beneath the arch, Sienna realised she had not returned to the south gate since arriving. Yesterday, she had walked westward along the long, straight, well-maintained gravel driveway, flanked by open fields, to Kirilia's main access gate, which Kilo kept locked. Beyond it was an unsealed road leading to neighbouring farms then on into the heart of the ag zone.

She saw more footprints than tyre tracks on this southern route. Their arrival was likely the most traffic it had seen in a while.

The Texan soon took her off the track and into the woods, where they were greeted by birdsong. Fragrances from the native foliage all about were pleasant and she hung back, twirling about, taking it all in before striding on to catch up.

Chad was not only easy on the eye but had a relaxed nature. Maybe it was just that Sienna was half-American herself but she felt more comfortable in his presence than with others.

"So, Sindy. What's on your mind? Keen to get to know our Polish friend?"

"Witek's the one person I have seen the least of, but heard the most about."

"Anything… interesting?"

"Yes. I have his pictures. Busted Vlad and Riku speaking about tracks in the dust somewhere out here. They figured I'd heard enough so they spilled the tea. Got them to nu-tooth everything."

"Oh… hey, what's the deal with this new nu-tooth logo? I still don't get the red squiggle inside the tooth – I know it's supposed to be a capital 'N' but it's like a small 'v' as well."

"It's a Greek letter 'nu' – kind of looks like a small 'v' for sure. Wonder if they deliberately extended the hook on its left side to make it more N-like."

"Uh, OK. Guess I learned something."

She tapped her wrist-phone. "Anyway, the pics. I think we know more than Kilo. He hasn't seen these, right?"

"From what I know, Witek told the boss he just ran past some dead guys while that drone was on his tail. That's why they agreed he oughta quarantine. Didn't mention the thing had already crashed and he took a closer look at the bodies. We've been keeping quiet about that. Don't want to let on what we're thinking."

"And you're thinking about those dead dudes. One might be the real overseer, right? I mean, Kilo's all nice and hospitable, but what if it's all a big act?"

"That's precisely it," said Chad. "We don't know anything about this guy. Is Kilo even his real name? That's not a name. What if his story about the family farm is all a load of horse shit? I mean sure, he knows this area well enough, but he could be just some despera-do who rode on in with his gang, killed the Lucky Dragons staff and took over."

"If you're right, think he fooled that Sergeant Booth with smooth talking?" asked Sienna.

"Dunno. Wish I could hear what they were arguing about."

Everything she knew about Kirilia was from Kilo. The man was direct in his conduct and well-spoken but kept to himself. Sienna suspected he had his secrets.

The other three, Kilo's "deputies", would hurry about their assigned tasks and were always polite to the newcomers though not too chatty.

"Here." Chad indicated a large eucalypt. "You're gonna love this guy's pad."

Sienna stopped, frowning. There was no sign of Witek. She did, however, have that feeling of being watched.

In the tree, Sienna spotted a platform. An old brown plaid tablecloth stretched above it at an awkward angle. The platform appeared angular as its supporting branches twisted away in different directions but looked sturdy, with minimal gaps between the boards. A knotted rope dangled down.

Her dad would have admired this. He loved the outdoors. Memories of her brother flooded back too. While his recreational time involved screens, when he did actually go outdoors as a younger boy, he had loved to climb.

"Hey, bud? Lunch." Chad squinted then turned back to Sienna. "Thought he'd be in his tree house."

"Which is why I am over here," said Witek, startling them from his sit spot beneath a shrub. "Cannot be predictable, no?"

"Smart move, dude," said Sienna, nodding.

"I've brought Sindy today," said Chad.

She waved. "Glad you don't look half-dead."

Witek faked a cough. "Argh, stay back. Ha. I am really fine, thank you."

It was good to see he was capable of humour.

"Seriously, should we be wearing proper masks?" she asked.

"Boss says we have none," said Chad.

Sienna waved at the tree. "You built that?"

"I had time on my hands. Materials too. Some collected, some traded with Rocky for cigars."

"Traded? You're supposed to be quarantined," said Sienna. "Are they taking this seriously?"

"I did not have the cigars with me. I told Vlad where they were stashed in my gear. Could you put my lunch between those rocks please? I am a little hungry."

Sienna had carried the food ration prepared by Putu – rice with finely chopped vegetables, served in some kind of paper, rolled into a neat cone shape to support the food. It had a pleasant spicy aroma.

"In this gap?" she asked.

"There's a sweet spot that holds those things perfectly upright," said Chad.

Placing the water by the rocks, Sienna carefully wedged the cone in place, taking care not to spill any rice.

"Thank you, now back away and I will take my lunch."

"Come on, man. You haven't even got a cold. Do we have to keep this up?" said Chad.

Witek retrieved his meal.

"Remember your first lunch drop last week? You said, 'Hell no, I am going nowhere near the guy' and made Vlad place the food. My fortnight is nearly done, Chad. Best to obey Mr Kilo until the end."

"So, anything to report?" asked Sienna. "I saw your photos.

Riku said you thought something chased you back to Kirilia, then you changed your mind."

"I was right the first time. It came back. Right here. Last night."

Chills shot through Sienna and she looked about the woodland though she could not sense any disturbing presence.

"Kilo knows," Witek continued, tapping a two-way radio on his belt. "There was nothing for days. No more screaming, just regular night sounds. Kangaroos thump about and there are sheep or goats in the area. I think a large bird is nesting nearby. An owl or something like that comes out at night to hunt. Nothing strange about any of that. Last night, though, that thing was not normal."

"Then what was it, man?" said Chad.

"I do not know. I ran and climbed and only looked back down when I was up there. I saw a shadow, very large, bigger than any kangaroo or goat. It growled but ran when I was about to shoot."

"What did Kilo say?" asked Sienna.

"Consider my quarantine somewhere safer. I insisted on staying."

"Dude, you're crazy."

"Maybe, Sindy. I think I have a better chance of killing it here. I recall other nights where I heard a dog in the distance, sounded like a large one. I think a huge hound may be living in the area."

Sienna wrapped her arms about herself. "When I was a kid, I read these old English folk tales about enormous black ghost dogs. Some of the scariest stories I've ever heard."

"I only believe in what is real. No enormous dog can reach me there."

"I couldn't even climb that rope, let alone the tree," said Sienna. "What if it isn't a dog though. Check your photos."

Witek shook his head. "My Marektek has excellent battery life but it does not last this long."

Instead, Sienna studied Witek's pictures on her wrist-phone and magnified an image of a massive paw print.

"No claw marks. Dogs can't retract their claws like a cat."

"Is there some kind of large native species with cat-like paws?" asked Witek.

"Drop bear?" said Chad. "No, they only lurk in trees. So… it's probably the rare southern chupacabra."

"Well, we do have our own modern cryptid legends," said Sienna. "There's all manner of beings in the folklore of indigenous Australians as well. Don't know if any have cat paws though."

She paced about, tapping her cat medallion with her thumb while staring at the ground.

"People swear they've seen big cats in remote areas. There are unsolved livestock maulings too. Some say circus animals escaped and made themselves at home in rugged places like this. There are even old stories of army mascots dumped in bushland when soldiers moved on."

Witek rubbed the back of his neck. "People believe this? What evidence is there? Everyone has a camera."

"That's just it." said Sienna. "I love thinking these stories are real but there's never decent proof. Stuff I saw online was always either a good fake or not clear enough to show a big cat was really there."

"These stories been told around here?" asked Chad.

"I don't know this area's history and we can't search mailings online anymore. So, until we get a proper look…"

Sienna shrugged then paced a very wide circle around Witek,

studying his tree. "Most cats can climb."

"I felt a pull on the rope but when I reached the top, this thing did not even try. The shadow remained on the ground, then fled. What kind of animal can recognise a rifle?"

Sienna returned her gaze to the ground. "No footprints. The ground's too hard. Nothing's even stirred up the leaves."

"I only saw tracks near the bodies, nothing here."

"Probably followed its nose there," Sienna suggested.

"Hey, do you think we could lure it with bait?" asked Witek.

"Tell me you're not considering that," said Chad. "We'd be encouraging it. I don't think we need some cranky old lion mascot sniffing round our yard, looking for snacks. Y'all should talk to the boss before you do anything crazy."

Sienna scanned the woodland but felt nothing. She rested her hand on the hilt of her weapon, one of Rocky's homemade machetes.

"We'll need better weapons," she muttered.

Witek finished a mouthful and looked up. "We must stay wary of the sky too. Kilo said he learned nothing examining the Lite Shot."

"Wait, Kilo handled the drone?" said Sienna. "He's not worried you might have breathed pathogens all over it?"

"I think he knows I am not infected. Just as he knows which bodies I found – and I suspect he knows how they died. We did not speak about any of that though."

Sienna lifted her arm again to study Witek's photos.

"So, that's probably death by shotgun on that guy – and we know who owns a powerful shotgun. Why would he kill them? Think they were infected and he just put them out of their misery?"

"I have had a lot of time alone to think but we can only speculate about what killed those men," said Witek. "Plague? Kilo? Monster? Drone? Where did they die? How did the bodies get there?"

Chad shook his head. "Dunno, man. Should we be worried about what the boss man's got in store for us?"

"Best to play along for now," said Sienna.

Witek frowned. "I worried my cousin Marcelina had a similar fate. Remember those rumours about disappearing workers? She is among them. That Lite Shot drone was hunting her and I want to know why."

Sienna flipped to the next image. "What about these footprints, the small ones?"

"I thought I heard voices in the woods last night, right before that thing turned up, no doubt just echoes from you guys at Kirilia. I only believe in what I see. The beast is real, yes, but not necessarily connected with the other footprints. There will be a plausible explanation for those. It looked like children had been near the bodies but they were probably playing in there long before there was anything to find. That place was very sheltered, which is why their prints remain."

"You sure about that, bud? Maybe we're being hunted by a tribe of cannibal kids as well."

"Be careful, Chad. There are always plenty of feral Australians around," said Sienna.

"Oh," said Witek. "You mean those, what do you call them? Boogerns?"

Sienna laughed out loud and had to take a breath to calm herself and explain.

"Bogans. They're an Australian sub-culture. 'Boogerns' sounds pretty funny though. Very fitting."

"Like rednecks or trailer trash, aren't they?" said Chad.

"Kind of. I mean sure, crims, shoplifting mall-rats and welfare cheats might be bogans, but there are also the cashed-up bogans and others who may act rough but always help out their mates. What they've all got is that really broad Australian accent, the bogan cackle laugh, drink and swear more than others."

"Oh, you mean like Jazlyn and Chaylarna," said Chad. "I once thought all Australians were like that."

"Come on, dude, we're not. We're more mixed than ever these days. But oh, those two are bogan as... I probably sound totally elitist."

"I think it's funny," said Chad.

"I am so confused," said Witek.

"Look, I grew up surfing with plenty of bogans and they were awesome. I felt like the impostor. My parents were professional people and we spoke differently, but they always said not to dumb down our speech or use too much foul language just to try to fit in."

Sienna heard loud fluttering in a tree and remembered where they were. This was one of the first times in a while she had enjoyed a good conversation with others. It felt good to open up and laugh a little, like things were normal again.

She turned away and wandered into the woodland. She hoped to see the owl or whatever bird of prey Witek had observed.

"Hey you, be careful," Chad called out. "Where you going?"

"Just looking around."

"Come on, don't play the rash heroine. Charging off alone into the woods without a gun ain't such a good idea."

Sienna huffed. However, she stopped, put her hand on her machete again and scanned the area. The woodland here, south of the hills, was open and criss-crossed with trails. The kind of terrain trail bike riders enjoyed.

Something caught her eye, an odd carving in the smooth bark of a tree.

"Witek, have you been scratching trees?"

"No, why?"

"There's something here. A kind of symbol, like a glyph or rune."

"Indigenous Australian art? One of those scar trees? Hope we're not disturbing some kind of sacred site," said Chad.

"No. It's not like anything traditional I've seen. But it looks kind of fresh."

Sienna traced the marks with her finger, trying to feel some kind of connection. She did not gain any clarity so rubbed her head with her free hand, tilted her wrist to take a photo then rushed back over to Chad, who shook his head after taking a glance.

"I got no idea. I mean it kinda looks like a question mark with arrows shot through it, although that part is like a waving hand. Weird. Nu-tooth me."

Sienna nodded and transferred the image.

"Cool, got it. Screw this. You're not sick, man," said Chad, walking over to Witek. "Check this out."

"Wait, Chad," said Sienna. "You called me rash, now you're breaking Kilo's quarantine."

"Everyone's saying the Big V has a short incubation time and kills you in a couple of days. Wouldn't be doing this if I thought there was any chance this man has some freaky disease."

She sighed. It seemed the Texan considered that rules carried a certain amount of flexibility. However, she too doubted Kilo was serious about this quarantine. He had been happy enough for people to wander over unsupervised to deliver food and water, then return without saying how close to Witek they had been. She knew Vlad and Karmen had visited him almost daily.

"Buddy, I expected you would be reeking by now," said Chad. "When did you last take a shower anyway?"

"A shower? In Canberra. I explored this area thoroughly. I soon found water to wash in. Farm water. Plenty of channels down that way."

Witek waved vaguely to the south and continued. "Made my head itch. I am glad I do not smell offensive. Anyway, I agree you should not have come over – but I think you are quite safe. Let me see."

Witek studied Chad's phone for a few moments. "I have no idea. Probably just state forestry symbols or something. I saw nobody over there."

"There is something else out here," said Sienna. "I can feel it. Something not quite normal. A feeling that's… uncanny."

Witek looked over at her sideways. "Uncanny? Come on, there will be a perfectly rational explanation. Dog. Cat. Whatever the feral animal is, when it is dead, all that will remain is ordinary Australian countryside. If this beast is not responsible for missing workers, then it is people. People with drones. We must focus on dangers that are real. Forget the campfire stories."

Sienna folded her arms.

Witek sighed. "If it makes you feel better, I will examine my own photos again once I get back and recharge my Marektek."

"Agreed," Sienna replied. "Let's meet up. We can share everything we know, decide what we should be worried about and make a plan."

"Very well. No secrets between us, my friends."

Witek grabbed the knotted rope and skilfully climbed up to his platform. Vlad had mentioned his friend had had military training — Sienna could now see he would have left others for dead were this boot camp.

Chad grinned. "Oh. Karmen said she'll come visit you again later. I think she likes you, buddy."

"Likes to argue with me, I think you mean. She has… different views on some things. Thank Putu for the meal. I will sleep awhile now."

Sienna waved and began walking back, scanning the woods. She felt a stray trickle of sweat run down her cheek and slowed her pace to let Chad catch up.

"What are you thinking, Sindy?"

"Ordinary Australian countryside — I'm not convinced. Maybe we should stand guard so he can sleep awhile."

"Kilo might as well bring him back now," said Chad.

"Yeah, but Witek seems so relaxed. Totally at home doing the whole survivalist thing, even with some creature lurking about."

"Heard he did some kind of border patrol back in Poland. I'd say he's used to camping out with all manner of nocturnal critters."

"Well, Chad, I don't think I'd sleep well, day or night. Something freaky is out here and I'm not convinced this beast will be the end of it. Bet if I took a nap, I'd probably wake up to a bunch of cannibal kids, murderous drones and strange dudes scratching at trees, all looking at me like they haven't had a good lunch in years."

"I agree. Especially wouldn't want to be eaten by a drone. Man, that'd be a weird way to go. Ah, here we are laughing about this messed up shit in the 'Awesome Aussie After' and we don't even know what the hell's really in store for us."

Sienna tilted her head. "Those bodies... I wish it was clearer what happened. All we know is they're dead, wearing Dragons uniforms and may have had a whole heap of visitors."

"Could be we've got it all wrong," said Chad. "Those corpses might have nothing to do with Kirilia. We've been assuming the real boss man is among those dead-uns. Sometime soon he'll probably roll in, alive and well and all patched up. Take up the reins again. Relieve Kilo of his duties."

"No, Chad, he will not," said Kilo stepping out from behind a shrub, pump action shotgun in hand.

Sienna took a step back in fright even though the intimidating weapon was pointed down at the dusty earth. She had failed to sense he was hiding there.

Kilo looked down at the gun then straight at them, his face blank, calm, cold, unreadable.

"I made sure of that."

11

Harrison

A nudge forced Harrison to open his eyes. His hope these visitors were merely a mirage was fruitless.

"What kind of motorbikes are they riding?" said Junior.

Harrison shook his head, unable to speak.

"I did not even hear them coming," said Amahle. "Only the dogs."

"They are barking more than usual," said Jacko. "Not enough to drown out engines."

Finding his voice, Harrison said, "Depends on the type of engine. Most conventional fuels ran out pretty soon after the ports shut down."

"Then what are the Blues using to fill their tanks?" asked Aditya.

"Unless they're electric vehicles, most run on liquefied natural gas," Harrison explained. "Australia's old oil refineries shut down years ago. When all that strife flared up overseas, the government got worried about fuel security so they lifted environmental bans on coal seam gas exploration so we'd be less reliant on imported fuels."

"I know," said Jacko. "My aunty was one of the protesters arrested when the farmers and greenies got together for once to blockade the gas wells. It all got way out of hand."

"Correct," Harrison continued, straining for a better look at the gates. "Apparently one of the big companies started fracking to extract gas out this way — could even still be operational if it's within the zone. The government will be demanding as much fuel as they can get."

The visitors were definitely Blues, their mounts almost silent in comparison to regular motorcycles. Electric.

Jon-Jon, aware of their presence now, emerged from his house. Harrison could hear him cursing about "unexpected friends from Budgieweir" as he marched over to secure his dogs before letting the men ride through the gates.

Harrison did not recognise the pair, who parked by Jon-Jon's house and remained helmeted. The overseer jogged over to where they waited, offered them a meal and they went inside.

Harrison exhaled, realising he had been holding his breath, but kept his ears open. All he could hear inside the house was unintelligible words and the occasional muffled outburst of laughter.

When the workers had finished their own dinner and were cleaning up the cooking area, Jon-Jon and his guests re-emerged. The two riders, helmets now off, were unfamiliar, both sporting neat nondescript haircuts. Harrison did not recall seeing either man with Sergeant Selvin.

He tensed again as Jon-Jon pointed at the workers. No... at him.

Harrison felt his face flush and his legs become jelly as the overseer approached. He knew he was screwed but his mind raced, trying to think up some kind of bullshit excuse.

Jon-Jon stopped some metres away, curling his finger. Harrison shambled over, his glasses fogging a little. He felt beads of sweat forming.

"These gentlemen apparently know something about your technical prowess. Want to pick your brains, if you can spare a moment."

Harrison said nothing and nodded with forced enthusiasm. It still sounded ominous. The overseer was unreadable and he could only cling to the hope these men genuinely wanted to enlist his expertise.

"I'll leave you to it then," was all Jon-Jon said before striding right past him, shouting, "How's the dinner clean-up coming along then?"

Harrison swallowed and approached the Blues. He could tell by their insignia one outranked the other, despite their similar age, both perhaps just a few years older than himself.

The officer sported a shiny metal seven-pointed star on each upper sleeve and on both sides of his large popped collar. The other bore a single white chevron sewn onto equivalent places on his uniform — a mere trooper.

"I am Lieutenant Michael. You are Harrison Fletcher, I presume?"

He wondered if Michael was his given name or surname and also why a lieutenant was not travelling with a larger escort.

"Yes sir, that's me," was all he could manage.

"This is Trooper Garcia," the lieutenant went on, then turned to his companion. "Please check over the bikes, would you? This won't take long."

The trooper nodded to both of them and hurried away.

Lieutenant Michael walked Harrison around Jon-Jon's house,

ambling towards the veggie garden. As they passed a window, Harrison heard giggling coming from Jon-Jon's girls. He wondered what extent of hospitality the overseer had offered the young men though the officer glanced at the house and pouted. Perhaps he had partaken in nothing more than dinner.

"I report to Captain McDonald in the capital," said the lieutenant. "He has appointed me as his representative in this zone. I understand you were also approached to discreetly serve as an extra pair of eyes."

Harrison had to stifle a sigh of relief. This was about his mission. His ticket back to comfort. The pair stopped by a section of veggie garden yet to be planted, Lieutenant Michael kicking at the tilled soil with the tip of his boot.

"Ah, why yes, absolutely," Harrison replied. "Not by the captain himself but one of his men, yes. Anything you want to know or need me to find out, just ask."

"Right now, there is just one thing. We are looking for a young lady – Sienna Jones. Name mean anything to you?"

Harrison had never heard of such a person and cursed the fact, knowing comfort in the capital would have to wait.

"Ah, no. Can't say I know her. There are quite a few girls in our group but there's definitely no Sienna. I will keep my eyes and ears open for sure. Any idea where I should start looking? Maybe another farm?"

He hoped for any excuse to escape his confinement within Farm 1469's dog run.

"We think she may be using another name. There is reason to believe her family all are involved in subversive activities, acting against the government. The others were intercepted but Sienna slipped through our net."

Harrison digested the information before speaking. "We were all face scanned by drones at your outpost the day we arrived. Wouldn't the facial recognition software match someone in a government database?"

"This is the problem," explained the lieutenant. "They are trying to rebuild a small local database, but our records back in the capital are... gone. The whole lot. The techno geeks said some sort of computer virus got past firewalls and into everything, just before the internet itself went down. Crazy amounts of data were lost and most computers crashed."

Harrison remembered technical problems at work at the same time cases of a mystery illness were first reported.

"One virus brought down humanity while another took out our best tools, memories, records and comms. Not completely though."

The lieutenant patted a handheld radio at his belt. Many small devices like Harrison's own phone had been spared, maintaining full functionality and local interface with other devices via nu-tooth technology.

"Do we know what this Sienna Jones looks like?"

"Not exactly," the lieutenant replied. "She's Aussie. The captain said look for a blonde, but her hair might be green and purple by now. Here's a rough face sketch."

Harrison took the piece of paper offered and studied the likeness of a girl with twin braids in her hair, which met in a kind of V-shape at the top of her forehead. She had freckles splashed across her nose and large dark eyes but nothing else distinctive.

He wondered if this was what it felt like to be a detective or sheriff back in the old days, before data communications.

"Anyway, keep sniffing around," the lieutenant continued. "I will be your local contact. Next time I swing by, let me know if you've heard anything about her — or anything else we may be interested in. Better head off. I have another farm to visit then a convoy to escort."

He wondered what other duties the lieutenant had. Sergeants had brought them to the zone but perhaps larger convoys bringing valuable produce to the capital had bigger escorts led by more highly ranked officers. Maybe this guy was lucky enough to return to Canberra often, to meet with his captain. Harrison was glad to have a useful contact and looked forward to the day he would be riding in an east-bound convoy.

He indicated the electric motorcycles. "Very cool. Though won't you be a bit exposed out on the open road? Your mates who brought us here rode in armoured vehicles."

The officer raised his eyebrows and appeared less formal and more human for a moment. "These bikes run in a way it's like… you're almost gliding over the highway. Gives you a real sense of freedom. Something I get to enjoy inside the ag zone only. Once outside, I'm encased in metal all the way."

"No trips by rail?" Harrison asked.

"A bridge is damaged. We have neither the resources nor manpower for ongoing track maintenance, especially in dangerous areas. No amount of armour will help if a train is derailed and crashes if someone sabotages the line.

"That's irrelevant because the Budgieweir line doesn't go straight to Canberra — we'd have to travel through even more dangerous territory closer to Sydney, then backtrack via the branch line to the capital. It's simpler and safer to take the shorter, most direct route, which is by road. Speaking of which…"

He nodded to Harrison, turned on his heel and marched back to his electric motorcycle, where Jon-Jon was having a quiet laugh with Trooper Garcia. The lieutenant shook hands with the overseer and both Blues donned their helmets. Their shadows were long and Harrison wondered if they would travel all the way to the capital by night.

Harrison found himself wondering what range the electric bikes had and how many charging stations still worked. He was glad the power was on enough to keep both phone and drone charged.

For him and the others, personal electronic devices were more precious than ever, even offline providing a connection to their old lives. While many networked with each another via nu-tooth, Harrison kept his own phone isolated. He suspected the Brit would cyber-bully others, assuming he had the mental capacity to wield his apps in such a way, though he knew the brute did not need to hide behind a screen if he wanted to heckle somebody.

As the overseer escorted his guests through the gates, Harrison spotted the thug leering in his direction, the blonde Sydney girl hanging off him like some kind of parasite.

"Blues have given Doughboy a good bollocking."

Idiotic giggling erupted from the blonde though Harrison was happy to let them think that.

"A more polite term for someone from Norfolk is 'dumpling' but I should have expected such ignorance from a witless chavvy type from up north," Harrison muttered.

Then he turned away to hurry back to Junior and the others and help finish cleaning up dinner. The overseer was already returning to check on them again.

"So, what did they want?" asked Aditya.

Harrison had his answer ready. "Just asking if I had the skill to help out with a rice skipper. I may get to do some drone mapping too if they're short on experts. Said I'd be happy to give it a go should they ever need me."

That seemed to satisfy everyone for now so he set about cleaning, saying nothing more.

An idea came to him. Harrison held back a curse for not thinking of it while Lieutenant Michael was still here. It was plausible a blonde Australian called Sienna faking her identity might be using another "S" name... why not "Samantha"? Whether the Sydney girl was in fact the one they sought was irrelevant, though he doubted the bimbo was capable of doing anything the authorities might give two shits about, unless she was an exceptional actress.

In any case, if he suggested she was Sienna in disguise, they just might whisk away the annoying bitch and with luck, he would never see her again, while earning himself a ride back to more luxurious lodgings.

Harrison had missed this chance to join the lieutenant's convoy but resolved to develop the idea for next time, perhaps fake some evidence implicating "Samantha" in a plot to sabotage what the authorities sought to achieve in the zone. Any bullshit would do, as long as it was convincing.

Looking beyond the gates, he watched the Blues peel away from the driveway out onto the road, wondering if they had eyes in every camp and how dangerous the real Sienna might be.

It seemed the bikes were not accelerating. To Harrison's surprise, they turned around, stopping back outside the gate. The pair were looking along the road northward, in the direction of the main highway.

The dogs started going berserk, but were no longer barking at the Blues near the gate. They bolted along their run in the same direction as the riders' gaze. Harrison saw nothing but strained to listen, thinking he heard a motor between barks.

"What is this?" asked Junior.

Harrison shook his head as the others gathered around and squinted at the road. He considered risking a drone flight to get a better view but knew there was no time. The engine roared ever louder.

One of the of riders waved both arms about. The other drew his firearm, taking a defensive position in the driveway.

Then Harrison caught sight of some sort of old car speeding down the road. The vehicle was quite colourful, its panels apparently sprayed with graffiti, though it was still too far off to make out much more.

The vehicle complied with the command as it neared the farm entrance, and Harrison heard the sound of its motor fade. Then it roared again, the driver charging as the trooper swung his bike around to get out of the way.

A long pole appeared at the side of the car as primal howls came from the vehicle's occupants. Harrison could see the passenger wield the pole like a jousting knight. The driver veered off the road a little, helping the lancer correct his aim. The rider had chosen the wrong side of the road to evade the attack and Harrison gasped as the young man was skewered.

"What the hell?" shouted Jon-Jon, from somewhere.

As the rider toppled from the seat of his bike, flopping onto the road like a limp discarded toy, his companion opened fire. Harrison could not tell if he hit anyone as the car sped by.

The driver hit the brakes, causing a loud screech, then sped backwards, swerving about, two fat tail pipes roaring. Before the second rider could be struck by this reverse charging manoeuvre, he took his bike off-road onto the weed-strewn verge. He took aim and fired twice more.

There was a brief stand-off, the driver revving the engine but keeping his foot on the brakes, spinning the wheels. The rider was aiming with care. Sunlight glinted off something on his shoulder – a metal star. It was Lieutenant Michael. Harrison wondered how much ammunition the officer carried.

The attacker's burnout was generating a lot of smoke and with the sun in his eyes it became hard to see.

"What's that other noise?" said Amahle.

Harrison squinted, thinking he saw something airborne, diving out of the sun. He extended his arm and held out his thumb, trying to block the solar glare.

The motor growled. There came another gunshot, followed by a bright flash, then Harrison saw nothing. He instinctively crouched, covered his ears and squeezed his eyes shut. Some kind of shockwave made him roll over and there was a terrible noise. Then silence.

He blinked, trying to regain his vision. For some reason, he kept feeling his face, making sure it was there. It was. He was fine. As he and the others slowly stood, they saw the road, the verge, everything outside the gate, all aflame. A plume of smoke billowed skyward. Through it, he spied an aircraft, turning slowly then flying low and fast back into the sunset.

They waited silently, speechless. No rider or driver emerged from the flaming carnage.

Harrison panted in hopeless despair. His only useful contact, his singular connection to the world outside this farm, the one man who was his ticket out of this place, had been incinerated.

12

Witek

"Where have you been, Vlad?" asked Witek. "Making music some-where?"

"Not the music you are thinking of. Hashtag Bali bum gun."

Witek cocked his head, trying to understand the jest.

Sameera spoke up. "You used the Eastern-style toilet?"

Vlad squatted then sprang back to his feet.

"The regular ones were taken. In my family, we have always been adaptable."

"I hope all our families are resilient enough to endure this crisis," said Witek.

"We will see them again, my friend. So, you have won the favour of a killer," said Vlad, clapping him on the back. "Congratulations on your promotion."

"Tough audition," said Riku. "Hey, did bugs crawl all over you in your sleep while you were out there?"

Witek wondered if Riku, clad in puffy bright orange pants and a metallic green jacket with matching moon boots, was trying to emulate an insect himself.

"The tree was fine. Watch for ants' nests if you ever camp on the ground."

Kilo had said he respected the way Witek conducted himself in the woods and cleared him to return just hours after his visit from Chad and Sindy. Commending his resourcefulness, Kilo had requested he command a small team and sought his opinion on how trustworthy and competent potential candidates appeared.

The overseer was also now aware of all they had seen and discussed, politely asking Witek to keep it quiet, promising to explain his full story.

"So, we're the boss's inner circle," said Sameera.

"His 'Magnificent Seven' right?" said Chad, doing little to hide his sarcastic tone. "Should we be honoured?"

"This man has killed people," said Karmen, her normally fair face twisted with scepticism. Her intonations were rather theatrical. "Surely this is a classic case of keeping your friends close, your enemies…"

"Maybe this is true," said Vlad, fingering the hilt of the crude knife on his belt. "He might just be playing nice, probably has to, with so many guests here, but is plotting to murder all seven of us at the first opportunity."

Witek looked at his friend thoughtfully then cocked his head at his rifle.

"Keep your weapons close. Though remember, he could have taken me out while alone in the woods. Instead, I was given a weapon, food and materials to build a defensive shelter. Also, Kilo was the one who insisted we all keep ourselves armed. We should hear what the man has to say."

"He's using us," Karmen said. "So, Kilo sent you supplies. In return, you did all the hard work building a watch tower."

Witek was glad the crude structure had been established, should there ever be a need to watch the southern approach to Kirilia but acknowledged her point with a nod.

"Perhaps my toil has made me less expendable, Karmen."

She sighed. "Maybe he views each of us as merely tools to help him achieve some larger goal."

"What goal then?" mused Sameera. "What's his master plan?"

"Shh. Heads up. Rocky," warned Riku.

The group hushed and watched the older man unhurriedly swagger down the hill towards them.

During Witek's exile, this group had bonded, drawn together during the drone attack. Vlad, who could draw a crowd with koncovka music alone, had befriended them. Seventh in the group was Sindy. The Australian was quiet but perceptive and had some interesting stories and unique insights about her own country. Someone good to have at their backs, Witek hoped.

He was mentally stronger alone in the woods. The others had no idea how he felt about leading. Responsibility for their welfare was the last thing he wanted. Witek had striven so hard to forget his time in national service, his weakness, his failure, the pain and shame of how it all had ended.

"Focus on the present, look only to the future." Marcelina had been the one to offer those words, to help him cope. She was the only one he was supposed to be looking out for in Australia.

Rocky now reached their group, puffing on the last of his cigarette before spitting out the butt and squashing it into the ground beneath his boot. Though he looked like a shifty old criminal, Witek liked the man. Rocky had only two facial expressions – poker face or gold-toothed grin. He gave away little of his past. Witek had gleaned he was originally from the north of the island of Bali and had worked at Kirilia for many years.

Putu hurried over, giving Rocky a fresh packet of cigarettes and offered him some matches. They exchanged a few words in a language Witek did not understand then Putu nodded and rushed off again.

As far as Witek could tell, Rocky acted as a kind of quartermaster and knew where to find anything on the property. He was open to bartering too, which well suited Witek's own style of trading goods or information. He and his comrades in national service had done so time and again to acquire "unofficial extra amenities". He suspected a barter economy might be the main form of trade in the near future.

"Follow Rocky. Time to see boss," the man croaked before turning on his heel and walking casually back up the hill, into the gardens.

Perhaps Rocky was reading Witek's thoughts as he spoke over his shoulder, "Now you see the boss's house, first time?"

None of them had been inside the stately main house. The double-storey building was comprised of chunky light red-brown bricks of variable size and looked decades old. Witek noted the intricate architectural details adorning its eaves, elevated veranda, railings and the two white pillars rising from the front porch, with its impressive solid-looking timber double doors apparently serving as the main entrance. The pillars rose on up to serve as corner posts of a small balcony directly above the doors, then terminated at the roofline.

"Hey, maybe we'll get some answers about that smoke and noise," said Riku.

"Swear I heard distant gunfire just before that boom. Let's ask the boss," replied Sameera, nodding to Riku.

"Those guys do not look bothered about it," Riku continued, waving at some workers. "But whatever happened out there, I have bad feeling it was not good."

Witek watched the people toiling in the garden. Duc, the slim guy from Sydney whose face wore an expression of constant stress, was hoisting a metal frame to serve as a trellis.

Further up the hill, Jazlyn and Chaylarna were assisting Kyle, an extremely muscular young man who was breaking up the hard soil with a pick. Sweat glistened on his prematurely balding head. The two girls were leaning on their tools.

"Hey hey, there are the boog... ah, bogans," Witek whispered over his shoulder to Chad and Sindy.

"Those girls have been asking about you, bud," Chad murmured, with a subtle smirk. "I think they missed you. You're the real reason they decided to stay on here that first night."

Vlad nudged his friend, stifled a snigger and continued the teasing. "Yes Witek, I think they will both pay you a little visit tonight. They said they really like guys with strong accents."

Karmen spoke up. "Kyle's Canadian accent is all they want to hear tonight. Last week it was Iosefa, until he realised how shallow they are."

She strode past Witek, her narrowed eyes fixed on the two Australians, then tossed her hair.

"I'm sure Witek has far better taste in women," Karmen

announced, chin raised.

Chad swung in beside Witek and pointed at Karmen's back with both hands, struggling to contain his mirth. He was barely audible as he whispered, "Told you, buddy. We know who Miss Argentina wants to be her bae."

Witek felt himself flush as he glanced at the cascade of hair covering Karmen's back and felt something stir inside him. He had to admit she was an extremely attractive young woman, irrespective of her headstrong opinions, which did not always align with his own, sometimes flowing a little too freely from her wonderfully full lips.

No. This was no time look at women. He could never allow himself to become close to someone. Especially not now, with a leadership role. He tore his eyes away from Karmen's shapely form.

Rocky led them to the back of the house. A detachable ramp resembling a ship's gangplank led up to the veranda. Witek had noted a curious custom in rural Australia where guests would enter homes via the back, rather than utilising the more impressive-looking front doors that adorned many residences, such as this.

The group filed up the ramp, and Rocky led them along the veranda encircling much of the upper floor, ageing furniture haphazardly scattered about its length. It overlooked the garden and bushland beyond.

Rocky knocked on the wooden frame of a flyscreen door then wandered away.

Agus opened the door, waving them inside with a wide grin.

It took a moment for Witek's eyes to adjust to the dim room within. There was a large square table surrounded by wooden chairs in the centre of the room, books and paper documents piled neatly in one corner, a tea-service tray in another, steam rising from two small teapots with intricate Oriental decorations, encircled by eight matching small cups.

Framed upon a wall was an old enlarged aerial photograph of Kirilia. Its surrounding fields and forest were also visible. Before Witek could study the landscape and look for his tree, Agus ushered them into a hallway.

"He's waiting at the far end. Please, go on," Agus instructed.

The group's boots made a collective commotion on the floorboards. Despite the house's apparent age, modern light fittings hung from the ceiling. Closed doors flanked the central passageway.

The tall silhouette of the overseer, framed by light from a large window, was the first thing Witek saw as they entered a large room. Kilo was whistling to himself. The tune was unfamiliar, not a pop song or any well-known piece of music. It was a haunting melody, both sombre and epic.

The man, clad in his heavy great coat, turned to face them, hands clasped behind his back. Witek realised the window was a doorway leading onto the small balcony above the main entrance. Only a fly-screen door was closed, allowing a pleasant breeze to enter.

"Please, take a seat, if you wish," said Kilo, indicating a grey leather lounge, "and help yourselves to some green tea."

Agus set down the tray from the other room on a low coffee table.

"Thank you," said Kilo, pouring a cup for himself and nodding to Agus, who left the room, closing the door behind him.

Only Witek and Sindy chose to remain standing. The room was

large, well-lit and offered an excellent view westward over the fields of Kirilia and other farms in the wide valley beyond.

The furnishings were an odd blend – the lounge not especially outrageous compared to the bright-green modernist stools that lined a bar along one wall. The main light hanging from the ceiling was set in a small chandelier. A simple wooden desk with a swivel chair was set to one side, a laptop computer folded shut upon its surface beside a portable document file. Plants with sharp spiny leaves grew in large pots set to each side of the balcony door and softer leafier plants were elsewhere.

Of most interest to Witek was the collection of old weapons mounted on one wall. Unlike Rocky's improvised blades, these were genuine antiques: swords, axes, pistols, a Gurkha's kukri, an old cavalry sabre. He recognised a few mass-produced replicas, but others were authentic, and Witek suspected their former owners were people with fascinating tales.

"My aunt and uncle's collection," said Kilo, addressing Witek's curiosity. "They never had children and they kept themselves busy with hobbies. Collecting, hiking in these hills. With farm commitments, they rarely took holidays, so I do not know when they had the opportunity to visit antique stores and gather these. Online perhaps. Anyway, as to why you are here…"

Witek wondered where the man would start.

"Well, I came to Kirilia seeking the two family members who may still be alive, hoping this relative isolation allowed them to hunker down and avoid the pandemic. They never even liked going into Budgieweir unless they absolutely had to. So, I figured if anyone had a chance…"

Kilo gazed outside; eyes distant, unfocused. Then he whirled, facing them.

"When I arrived, something felt wrong and I approached with caution. Any place now might harbour the infected, the desperate, thugs, traps… I hid in the bush and watched, waiting for darkness, then crept in to check each building.

"I found Rocky, chained in a shed like an animal. They'd left bolt cutters just out of reach, to torment him. A mistake."

"Who…" Chad ventured, but Kilo held up a finger.

"Before Rocky could explain anything, his tormentors revealed themselves. Three smug company men had made themselves quite at home here. Not even locals – they were cocky bloody Dragons from overseas. On my family's land.

"I later learned they began their stay by killing and eating all the chickens, followed by my uncle's kelpies. By the time I arrived they had moved on to amusing themselves by treating my family's loyal workers like animals."

Witek did not miss the glint of fury in Kilo's eye nor his voice steadily rising in volume. Kilo paused, took a breath then sipped some tea before proceeding in a more even tone.

"Bastards must have found my aunt's wine collection as they were staggering down the hill, ordering Putu and Agus about like slaves. They were armed with pistols. Did you know that Lucky Dragons security personnel working in Australia are permitted to carry firearms on any of their land acquisitions, even before the pandemic?"

Sindy, who had been quiet all day, spoke up, fire in her voice. "Government buddy deals with multinationals and property developers. My parents despised the way those types could be a law unto themselves, while the rest of us have to conform and obey the rules like sheep."

She stopped, looking flushed, then lowered her voice. "Sorry. Please go on."

Kilo raised an eyebrow. "Yes. There is truth in this."

The overseer swirled his teacup and stared into it before continuing.

"One of the men had a slingshot… any of us would be fined for carrying one. Apparently, they liked to shoot small pebbles at Rocky for entertainment. Not anymore."

He laughed, without cracking a smile.

"When they blundered into the shed looking for Rocky, they found me. The one who seemed to be in charge had a hole in him before he could utter a word. Instead of drawing weapons, the others fled. Rocky was waiting in the shadows and made short work of one man, while Putu and Agus ran down the other and tackled him. It crossed my mind to keep that one alive for questioning but it was not my place to deny the men their vengeance.

"Under the cover of darkness, we took their bodies to a place we expected nobody would find them anytime soon."

Kilo looked at Witek for a few seconds. He had not been asked a question and chose to remain silent.

Sindy drew the man's attention with a question of her own.

"What about your family? Did those three take Kirilia by force?"

"My aunt and uncle disappeared before the Lucky Dragons arrived. Rocky said they went for their regular bushwalk but failed to return. He searched for them and kept the farm running as best as possible.

Then the pandemic hit and the Blues showed up, saying the Dragons now had administration of Kirilia. Evidently, conducting background checks was not part of the overseer appointment process."

"Those freaks would be using us all for slingshot practice right now," said Chad. "You did us a favour, man."

"Depends on how prepared you were to fall into line, I guess," Kilo explained. "Apparently, when they came here Rocky refused to cooperate, told them they were trespassing. Before departing, the Blues insisted that the workers obey their new managers but the men sabotaged all that they could. The Dragons' patience ran out, but instead of calling on the Blues to arrest and remove the men, the overseer chose his own sick form of discipline."

"Wait a minute," said Sameera. "Surely the Dragons did not think they could motivate all of us new arrivals when they're inflicting violence on their existing workers."

"I suspect after their bit of fun, the Dragons planned to eliminate them before you were sent here," said Kilo. "Three different bodies would now be rotting somewhere out in the bush."

"So, what happened to his head?" asked Vlad, scratching his forehead.

Kilo's brow furrowed. "Whose head?"

"The Lucky Dragons overseer," said Witek. "Things were messy but he was definitely headless."

"In my trophy case, of course."

Kilo scanned each of their faces. The room was silent for several seconds. Then he burst into laughter.

"Honestly, I have no idea. We had neither the time nor reason to dismember those vermin. Some scavenger must have taken it.

Maybe that beast in the woods."

"What are we going to do about that?" asked Riku, jiggling his knee.

"Everyone in Kirilia must remain armed and stay together until we know what we are dealing with. Do not wander off alone."

Riku nodded. "Fine, but there is another danger. What will happen when the Blues return? Sergeant Booth will ask why the appointed guy is still not here and why you remain as acting overseer."

Kilo finished his tea, looking thoughtful. "Agus said our friend Booth probably never met the man – a different squad of Blues escorted the Dragons to Kirilia. Our story could be that we had to isolate the Dragons as they appeared infected. We'll say they died horribly, forcing us to burn down their quarters to stop the spread."

Witek glanced at Chad, the Texan's eyebrows dancing, then over to Sindy, whose face remained impassive, aside from her lips, on which played the smallest hint of a smile.

"We may say they were quarantined in a small building where we now have a fire pit. I doubt the Blues have a surplus of bored forensics teams on hand to verify such claims. I hope they do not care who is in charge, as long as we are producing a harvest. I know you had face scans and so forth but with their computer networks in such apparent disarray, their database records are likely far from perfect.

"I fear the Dragons themselves may come sniffing around for their missing staff. They are more pedantic about such things. Before all this they had a reputation for chasing every cent owed and would be more inclined to seek out lost assets, be it money, equipment or personnel. Even now.

"We should still remain guarded when dealing with the Blues though, Riku. They have sophisticated surveillance and weaponry. We must ensure there is no reason for them to use their resources against us."

"Forgive me for asking," said Riku. "Regarding their surveillance – when you took over, did you consider they might have seen the whole incident? They may even be watching us right now. The overwatch drones – they surely detect heat signatures, otherwise they would be useless at night."

"Depends on who is monitoring their signals and what is considered suspicious. Overwatch drones are for detecting larger threats, such as unauthorised vehicles approaching. Their signals are monitored in Budgieweir and most are set to patrol the restricted areas just beyond this zone's border."

Sameera cracked her neck. The movement looked painful to Witek and he fought the urge to cringe.

"How do you know this?" she asked.

Kilo strode to the desk and retrieved the portable document file.

"I found the official Overseers' Handbook."

He set down the file on the coffee table, opened it and removed a bound paper document from the its back-most partition.

"Old school," he said, opening a page at random and setting it down before them. "You are welcome to peruse this. With the internet gone, official communications are being distributed in paper form, just like in the old days."

Witek knew this was an alien concept to much of his generation, whose personal electronic devices were all they ever needed to access information.

"The handbook is not comprehensive," Kilo went on. "I anticipated your arrival after reading the part about making room for new workers. There is very little about staff management. No indication of worker numbers. I expected six or seven, not a bus full. Our automated gear requires one or two operators. I have already assembled a core farming team based on training, experience and familiarity with the machinery."

"Karin's group," stated Karmen, arms folded.

Witek had been briefly introduced to these farmers during a meal. Karin was Canadian, he recalled. The others hailed from all corners of the world.

"Isn't Ahmed in that group too?" asked Chad.

"Yes," said Kilo.

"Who is Ahmed?" asked Vlad.

"Guy with the gold tooth," Chad explained. "It's kinda funny, when you think about it – who'd have thought a guy from the Maldives, out there in the ocean, would end up in this dustbowl and make the agri-techie team."

"Jealous you did not make the cut?" Sameera teased.

"Not at all," said the Texan. "I think it's really cool. Shows where a bit of dedication can get you no matter where you're from."

Kilo intervened. "Ahmed was a few years into his agricultural science degree at a university not so far from here. He knows this terrain and is well-versed in the latest farming techniques. Karin grew up on a farm in Saskatchewan, was set to make a career of it herself and says farming is all she knows. She has watched the machinery and methods evolve.

"This knowledge makes them indispensable. They must remain

safe. We are relying on them to satisfy the Blues' demands. There-fore, it falls to you to protect the farming team and support them in doing what they do best.

"Also, I am forming a third team led by Nestor."

"Which one is Nestor?" asked Witek.

"Big, broad shoulders, Russian, you cannot miss him," Vlad replied.

"Correct," said Kilo. "He has excellent ideas about farm defence and we will work on making our perimeter more secure."

"I see," said Witek, folding his arms. "Is Nestor aware of any threats right now? We observed smoke not far to the south and heard an explosive sound, right after a possible gun battle."

"Yes. Something happened but I cannot confirm what it was. There is nothing strange about fires on farms, but I would be a fool not to take those sounds into account. You know what kind of people are out there. The threat of raids is real."

"Very well," said Witek. "So, this is why you want some of us to perform specialised roles."

"Correct. Everyone will continue helping with cooking, cleaning, the veggie garden and so forth, but things will be more structured now.

"So, we have three teams of seven, with three workers in reserve. Seven per team can watch each other's backs if there is trouble, without being so numerous as to get in each other's way."

"Interesting," said Sindy. "Seven individuals will also give a diverse range of opinions on how to proceed with a task. More than that and we risk too many opinions and debates that go on forever and no work gets done. I mean, just look at our politicians."

"Hey, hey, President Sindy has entered the room," said Chad.

"I'm serious, Chad. Imagine say, seven teams of seven, where each team counted as a vote on larger issues. An odd number of votes means there's always a majority and a decisive course of action."

Witek found himself nodding. "Logical. This makes good sense."

"Oh yes? Then what do you propose these extra teams would specialise in, Sindy?" asked Karmen, who remained looking at him, not the Australian.

"I don't know. Exploring, scavenging, trading with our neighbours…"

"We are talking about many more mouths to feed," said Kilo, rubbing his chin. "Even so… seven by seven… I like the concept."

"What is that thing?" said Sameera, staring outside.

Witek strode to the balcony door. Several vehicles were approaching a farm in the valley below, a few kilometres away. They were accompanied by a large aircraft, swinging about the property in wide circles.

"What are we looking at?" Witek asked.

"Higginson Farm," Kilo replied, "and I believe that is the biggest drone I have ever seen."

13

Phuong

A dog was barking somewhere. No, perhaps she had imagined this. A dream. Phuong realised she had fallen asleep at the small table by the window overlooking the fields. It was dark now, her only illumination coming from the rice skipper's control tablet, which had auto-dimmed.

She had worked herself to exhaustion, flying the drone, mapping the farm, analysing data, remaining indispensable. If she stopped proving her worth, Horace would no doubt think of… other uses for her.

A door squeaked then clattered shut. Horace's house. Footsteps. Two people. One much more heavy set than the other.

Phuong peered down from her small loft as the front door of the outbuilding in which she worked and slept swung open.

Horace was of late middle age and not the finest specimen among his peers. Clad in old jeans and a stained, moth-eaten polo shirt, his overweight form ambled inside, shoulders slouching over his gut. This physique was crowned by a less-appealing head: a greasy bald noggin, bulging eyes and an overlarge protruding bottom lip, which glimmered with spittle. To Phuong the man was a terrestrial incarnation of a dopey bloated fish.

Despite his appearance, Horace was well-connected, a man of status in the area. He was an old friend of Jon-Jon, enjoyed good relations with the Blues, had lived on this farm all his life, and had boasted a bank balance more well-nourished than his ample stomach, right up until when the fiscal world collapsed.

Horace's farm had no name. On arrival, Phuong had noted the main access route was unremarkable aside from a narrow bridge allowing vehicles to cross the channel forming the roadside boundary. There was no gate or signage, just a gravel driveway leading to Horace's ageing fibreboard house. Therefore, Phuong did not know precisely where she was, though at night the lights of Budgieweir were visible a short distance away.

She wondered if her friends were still billeted with Jon-Jon or had also been sent away. Since leaving Farm 1469, Phuong had eaten very little, her stomach perpetually cramping with knots of anxiety. She did not trust Horace one iota given his dubious network of acquaintances and took great pains to remain in the sanctuary of the loft where she worked, ate and slept.

Her refuge was only accessible by means of an old wooden ladder. Horace did not possess the agility to climb and she doubted the ladder would take his weight. Phuong usually only climbed down to use the old workers' bathroom on the lower floor or to tinker with the rice skipper, which had been trucked over from Farm 1469, charging cradle and all, by some rough-spoken Blues.

Although the bathroom was the coldest part of the outbuilding, she was grateful it was there. It meant she did not need to enter the confines of Horace's house, where she would be far more vulnerable to unwanted advances.

As feared, Horace was as grotesque and sleazy as his mates. Phuong wondered whether it had always been so among these old beasts, who from the seclusion of their farms could regard women as little more than useful working playthings, with nobody around to call them out or expose their misdeeds. It was clear the present crisis, so lacking in genuine law and order, had delivered these men a smorgasbord of fresh new vulnerable and isolated women.

Phuong had tried to befriend a pair of girls who had been there a while. Both had vacant eyes and did not speak so much. She wondered to what extent they belonged to Horace and how loyal they were to him.

Najwa, the more taciturn of the two, was from Malaysia. Phuong had only learned this from the relatively chatty Rea, who had been in Australia longer and had escaped the Philippines just before its partial annexation. Before the pandemic she had lost contact with her family on their home island, now occupied by resource-hungry invaders. Despite the probability they had ended up in a re-education camp, likely making cheap goods for some mega-corporation, Rea prayed daily for their survival. Phuong feared the plague had been unkind to those living anyplace cramped and confined.

The person who had accompanied Horace over to the outbuilding turned out to be Najwa. Horace waved for her to join him inside and she hurried to comply, standing behind him, head bowed, holding a bundle in one hand, a dinner tray in the other.

Horace looked around the building then up at Phuong in the loft.

"Come now, workaholic," he said in his jolly, goofy voice. "I admire your dedication and progress but now it's time for a bit of R&R. I need all hands on deck for the party. A mutual friend of ours has won himself a promotion and is keen to celebrate."

Being so absorbed in work, Phuong was oblivious to the reason for the day's activity in the alfresco area, which boasted large canvas shade sails, barbeque, bar fridges, a fire pit for cold winter evenings and sun lounges. The centrepiece was a hot tub, large enough to accommodate eight. She tried not to contemplate the identity of Horace's special visitor.

"I found something just about your size that a former guest left behind. Come on, girl, set down Foo's dinner and show her."

Najwa stepped forward and put down the dinner tray, which was laden with two steaming bowls smelling of fried rice, then unfurled the bundle.

It was a dress, its light metallic blue sheen suggesting satin. Phuong had never worn such a tacky-looking garment.

"Try it on. Najwa will help you after dinner. I'm sure you'll look just the part," said Horace.

Caddy-girl at a tropical overseas golf resort catering for fat ageing Western businessmen was no doubt the part he envisaged.

"Make it an early night tonight," Horace went on. "We'll finish cleaning my party area straight after breakfast."

Phuong faked a grin. "Sure thing… and thank you. I am sure it will be a lovely fit. Just need to run one more night test with the skipper before bed."

In truth there was nothing more to do. Everything was optimised, running fine, fields mapped, all long before the actual rice sowing was due to start. She had considered suggesting some small test sowing runs, to keep Horace from reassigning her to new duties, but now she was out of time.

Phuong looked at the rice bowl. Perhaps she could become ill from a fake stomach bug and avoid the party that way. She already had genuine cramps.

"OK, girl, OK. Don't stay up too late. I'll leave you both to it. I have a glass of wine waiting. Eat up while that's nice and hot."

Horace turned and waddled away. Phuong heard the door to his house squeak once more then climbed down from the loft.

Najwa politely waited for her to descend, passed her a bowl and they ate in silence, seated on old but sturdy wooden chairs. Phuong had not realised how hungry she was. The rice was adequate, if overladen with soya sauce.

She was still unsure if she could trust the silent girl. Phuong looked over at the dreadful dress, draped over a bench, and emotion got the better of her.

"How can I wear that?" she blurted. "I'll look like a total whore. I know they want me to look all exotic. I am third-generation Australian. I've never even left the state except for a stay in Canberra but…"

Phuong shook her head.

Najwa said nothing but her eyes widened. Then the girl stood and hurried to the exit with quick small steps.

Phuong felt sick and closed her eyes. The girl was running straight to Horace.

There was a noise. Phuong looked up and saw Najwa at the doorway, peering out into the gloom. Then she turned, finger at her lips, and rushed back, feet pattering softly on the concrete floor.

Najwa resumed her seat, leaned in close and looked Phuong straight in the eye.

"If you want to get out of here, now is your only chance."

Phuong gasped, unable to find words.

"Trust me, you don't want to be at the party. It's for that Selvin — he's just been promoted to lieutenant."

Phuong cringed at the mention of his name as Najwa confirmed her suspicion.

"He's worse than these old guys. I came here with three friends."

Najwa paused and stared at the satin dress for a few seconds.

"When we learned what Horace was like, two of them tried to run to Budgieweir and report him to the Blues. I was scared and Rea said to stay and wait.

"The next evening Selvin was talking to Horace. I heard that my friends only reached the solar farm down the road and ran into Selvin's squad there. The sergeant said he had taken them some-place they will never stir up any trouble again.

"Horace told us it is pointless to run off as there is nowhere better or safer than here. After that, we heard nothing more of our friends."

Najwa gave the doorway a furtive glance.

Phuong had never heard the girl speak so much in all her time here and it was unfortunate every word was bad news.

"How did such a horrible man get promoted?" Phuong whispered. "The Blues are supposed to be protecting us."

"Rea says the boss in charge of all Blues in the area is some lazy old guy. Selvin acts like a charming prince and the boss guy can see him do no wrong, especially now he's collecting gifts."

"What kind of gifts?"

"Things like extra food, even alcohol. Rea heard they all love him in Budgieweir for that. So, when one of their lieutenants was killed by bandits, Selvin was the preferred candidate for promotion."

Phuong sighed. "Are there any good, honest Blues we can turn to?"

"Foo. You need to understand. Most of the Blues here were never real policemen. Selvin was a nightclub bouncer and worked street security at the Budgieweir taxi stop. The lieutenant who died was a good guy, so maybe he was a policeman. Selvin suspected the lieutenant and his men were investigating his bad behaviour. But they all died during raids on the zone before they could report any-thing."

"Bandits. How convenient," said Phuong. "Sounds like he's capable of doing anything for power and position."

Najwa nodded. "And this is why you must go – far from here."

Phuong contemplated this, frowning. "Najwa, how exactly do you know all this?"

"Horace is so loud, especially when he's drunk. He's always joking and gossiping with his friend Jon-Jon on the radio. He thinks girls like Rea and I are stupid, scared little foreigners who don't understand. We may be quiet and obedient and play along but we are always watching, always listening."

Even now Phuong could hear Horace's idiotic drunken guffaws.

The thought of fleeing into darkness terrified her. She might stumble headlong into a patrol too. However, quiet compliance with Horace's wishes carried its own risk. This time tomorrow she might be the plaything of a drunken Selvin.

There would be no more windows of opportunity. Indecision would be costly. Najwa was right. She had to act now.

"If I go, will you, Rea or any of the others join me?"

"No," Najwa said in a soft voice. "Not knowing what they will do if we are caught scares me more than the party. I was so scared to even speak to you at all. Rea said you are our best chance. If you could get away, find good people, bring back help."

Phuong nodded as she listened.

"Some of the older girls are loyal to Horace – if several of us are missing, they will quickly notice and tell him. You always sleep out here though. You could be far away when they find out in the morning that you're gone."

"What if Horace wanders back now to see me wearing my lovely new dress?"

"When he sits down to drink wine, he usually does not get back up. There is plenty of alcohol in the house, ready for the party. I could put some spirits into his next glass, make him sleep faster."

"Spiking drinks? I thought you were a good girl, Najwa."

The girl gave a hint of a smile, the first Phuong had ever seen. There was something else in her eyes. Hope. She could not let these poor girls down.

"I am so sorry your experience of my country has been this horrible, Najwa. If you spike his drink, use just a little. We don't want him to suspect anything."

Phuong would have never contemplated escaping Jon-Jon's farm.

However, Horace had no dogs, no guards, no perimeter patrol and hopefully no cameras.

"If you were the last person to see me, they will ask questions," said Phuong.

"I will suggest you ran off west to Budgieweir seeking help, like the others."

"What about the Blues' overwatch drones?" asked Phuong.

"People say they mainly watch for bandits. I do not know if this is always true. Remember there are people working on some other farms, sometimes even at night. From up there you will look like just another worker."

This made sense. If she stayed off the roads and stuck to fields there was a chance. Phuong was more concerned about drones capable of facial recognition, like the one that scanned them at the Blues' outpost. Even with computer networks offline, an individual drone could fly back to its master and report her position.

"What about the farms next door? Is Horace friendly with his neighbours? I haven't spotted anyone nearby during my drone work here but..."

"His neighbours died before I got here," Najwa explained. "The virus got them. I know this because he wants to use their fields for summer crops."

Horace chortled loudly again.

"I should go back to keep him distracted," said Najwa, turning to the door. "Take a blanket with you — it is very cold here at night."

The drab grey woollen blanket she had used when sleeping on the foam camping mattress up in the draughty loft would be perfect, its colour inconspicuous.

"Thank you so much. I promise to find help, if I can."

Najwa nodded and hurried away. Phuong climbed to retrieve her blanket. She also grabbed a water bottle and some homemade dry biscuits baked by one of the girls, placing them in a clear plastic ziplock bag, which had held screws and other small spare parts for the rice skipper.

Then she grabbed the tablet that controlled both the survey drone and skipper. This mapping drone was very small and portable, more compact than the one at Farm 1469. She knew it could prove invaluable for scouting.

Phuong took a deep breath and made for the door.

Her path was blocked by Rose, the eldest of Horace's guests, beady-eyed and pouty. Phuong held the small drone out of sight, obscuring it within the blanket.

"Where you going?" Rose demanded. "You try dress on already? You sleep now, working hard in morning."

If Rose had been here as long as Phuong suspected, Horace had never cared enough to help hone her mastery of English.

Rose peered at her with folded arms, eyes flicking to the dress draped on the bench. Then Phuong remembered what she had told Horace.

"I am taking the rice skipper for one more night test. I will go straight to sleep as soon as it's finished."

"Hmph. Well. You see party lights here? Horace said in box."

"The only boxes are on the corner shelves, over there."

Rose followed her gaze and tottered over, looking about. Phuong pretended to examine the skipper while Rose retrieved a carton and withdrew a length of dusty coloured glass light globes fixed to a cord. Phuong wondered how many still worked and hoped she would not be around to find out.

Satisfied, Rose began to depart. Then she turned back and stared at Phuong.

"Hey. You do night test? You keep warm with high-vis, not blanket. Blanket for sleeping, not get dirty outside."

Rose cocked her head at the high-visibility jackets hanging from hooks by the door, all faded yellow and stained with red dust.

Phuong nodded. "Thank you. I will."

Rose spun on her heel and returned to the house.

The high-visibility jackets looked overlarge and were designed to be conspicuous. However, labourers wore them universally and Phuong realised she would not look out of place. She put one on. It was huge, the sleeves covering her hands. It had several pockets, deep enough to contain biscuits, water bottle, even the drone.

She unbolted the second metal door and swung out both of the double doors to accommodate the girth of the rice skipper then began her feigned test.

The rice skipper lifted from its dock and hovered around half a metre off the ground. Phuong guided it outdoors using manual control settings on the tablet and walked out in its wake into cool twilight air. She lifted the wide hood of the hi-vis jacket over her head.

Rose was nowhere to be seen and all she could hear over the noise of the skipper was Horace guffawing within his house.

As she steered the skipper out into the nearest field, an idea came to her. After setting a simple navigational routine, Phuong extended the skipper's seeding arm. Then she used the arm to climb aboard the vehicle, doing her best to tuck her feet into the rungs leading to a service panel atop the machine. The skipper wobbled but remained airborne.

Gripping the metal frame of the skipper's arm with her left hand, she clutched the tablet with her right. With some difficulty she stretched her thumb onto the touch screen to execute the nav program. The skipper lurched forward, and Phuong nearly dropped the tablet as the vehicle accelerated.

The air felt icy upon her face as she rode the skipper across the empty field. It gathered pace and the hood of her jacket blew back. Despite the wind chill and her awkward, precarious grip, the experience was exhilarating.

Horace's property extended some kilometres from the house and this was proving an effective method of spiriting Phuong a healthy distance away in a very short time.

Phuong saw little of her surroundings. The skipper was equipped with safety lighting – its bluish-white headlamps at the front lit up some of the ground but only a short way, as it was not designed to be manned. There were also a couple of dim red lights to the aft, an orange strobe light on the underbelly and an identical one at the far end of the seeding arm. These could not be disabled, as the vehicle had to be compliant with safety regulations. Phuong knew she would need to abandon her transport or risk being located once it became known that she and the valuable rice skipper were both missing.

Her programming was precise. The skipper slowed upon reaching the far corner of the field, swayed as it adjusted course, then moved through an open gate into the next paddock. The vehicle was a precision instrument, designed to carry its payload within the main body, not clinging to one side, and she was glad her forty-something kilogram frame had thus far been supported. Were someone like Horace aboard, she suspected it would roll over and crash.

Phuong approached the pre-set destination. It would be easy to set the skipper down there and she could continue her escape on foot.

She crossed the second field faster than anticipated. There was no more time to weigh her choices. The skipper stopped, hovering in place above the tilled earth, in the exact location where she had sent it. It appeared local GPS base stations were sufficiently scattered to allow precision farming anywhere in the zone.

Phuong craned her head around, looking back. Dust filled her eyes, agitated by the vehicle's forceful downdraft. The lights of Horace's house and outbuildings were dim and distant. There was no indication of movement or pursuit.

Phuong paused and took several deep breaths. Though petrified and alone in a strange dark land, at this moment she was free.

14

Witek

"Higginson Farm, are you on channel?" Kilo spoke into the two-way radio.

Witek feared it was too late. Something had happened. There was only silence. After two more attempts at contact, Kilo gave up and stood.

"Who the hell is this and what do you want?" The voice was female, with a harsh tone.

Kilo sat back down at the desk, grabbing the radio. The speaker continued before he could respond.

"Hang on. I never forget a voice. You're that Mexican kid who used to come up and stay with George and Iris. The nephew."

"If there's one thing this Texan knows for sure about that man — he is *not* Mexican," Chad murmured.

"Why would she say this?" asked Witek.

Sindy chuckled. "I think she means he's from south of the border — the state border. He's Victorian. She did well to pick his voice though."

Witek wondered whether Kilo's family were liked by their neighbours.

"Hello, Mrs Higginson. How are you going?"

"Just great. I've got a sick husband and a farm to look after, this lot to babysit and now those blue bastards come along and take everything. Filthy pigs."

"I thought we were supposed to deliver bulk crops to a depot and nothing more."

"Hmph. This visit was no official collection. What can you do when they point a gun to your head?"

"What was that aircraft?"

"Rocket drone. Should be protecting us from raids. Instead, those scum are using it to do a bit of unofficial pillaging 'emselves."

"Would they blow up workers who resisted? Know anything about what happened off to the south?"

"Not many people on channel these days and the Blues won't let us go to town. So, we know about as much as you, which is bugger all."

"Where is the drone now, Mrs Higginson. We have lost sight of it."

"Moved up the valley, probably to hassle another farm, I reckon. Anyhow, what's the deal with you? I heard those Dragons were gonna take over up there after George and Iris disappeared. You workin' for 'em?"

"The Dragons? Not at all. I am in charge here and we have no Dragon guests on the farm. I am here with my own crew. You were sent workers too, I presume?"

"Yeah. Good bunch of kids. Been keeping 'em busy, don't you worry 'bout that. But how can they live on just rice? Blues nicked our fruit and veg. Most of our grog too."

"I might be able to help. Most of our vegetables are only just getting established but I am sure we can spare something. In fact, we were just speaking of establishing trade with our neighbours."

"Appreciate it. Swing by here later on. Probably should stay off-air. Bastards are probably listening in. See ya later then?"

"Will do. Out."

Kilo stood and looked directly at Witek.

"We need to support each other in the valley. Expanding our vegetable garden to diversify our food was a task that will soon serve us well. Thank the Gods we are blessed with spring water at Kirilia because it practically never rains."

Thank the Gods. Witek wondered if the overseer was a heathen — a follower of a polytheistic religion, unless it was just part of the way he spoke.

"The spring is one reason I chose to remain here after rescuing Rocky and the others. It made sense to wait out the crisis in familiar territory. Of course, staying in Kirilia meant I had to become the overseer."

A bird chittered out in the garden somewhere. Witek noticed an expression of annoyance on Kilo's face as he turned his head to look.

"So, our team of seven — what exactly do you want us to do? Security patrols around the fields? Watch the approaches to Kirilia from suitable vantage points?"

"Well yes, these are important necessary actions," said Kilo, brow furrowed, eyes fixed upon the valley. He began poking about among the plants by the balcony door.

Riku's knee jigged up and down as he continued flicking back and forth through his image gallery then looked up at Kilo to speak.

"Do not forget the threat of raids from beyond the zone. How are the seven of us going to take down anything? I am honoured to be chosen along with my friends here but I am not a soldier or a policeman… hey, I have never even fired a gun. I apologise if I sound insolent for asking but… why us?"

The tall man looked thoughtful as he picked up a bit of dirt from a pot plant, twirling it between his fingers before addressing Riku.

"Intel," he said. "We need to learn more about the situation outside Kirilia. Watch from the shadows, scout the area but do not engage any threats unless there is no other choice.

"Why you? Well, Riku, the fact that you are thinking things over and worrying is something I see as an asset. Other workers keep their heads down, which is fine. They are happy to let themselves drift along with the wind and obey orders.

"However, everyone present in this room has been a little more vocal in questioning our circumstances. This is good. We cannot afford complacency. Keep well-informed while still remaining anxious. It is about balance. You seem to grasp this fact and therefore are the best choice for a reconnaissance team."

"Blissful ignorance can kill just as easily as heroic idiocy, no?" said Witek.

"Correct," said Kilo.

"Other workers may be quieter but do not think they care any less about the situation," said Karmen, scooping her hair across one shoulder.

"Perhaps," said Kilo.

"Our generation was already jaded before this 'Big V' – I bet some here were climate activists," Karmen continued. "We grew up being told to accept things like famine and extreme weather events were the new normal. Why accept when we could act? We urged politicians to clean up their messes yet they continued to do nothing unless it was profitable. Forgive us for having little faith in people in power."

There were several nods and quiet, sad murmurs of assent.

"Excuse my language, ladies and gentlemen, but the planet's well beyond fucked up now," said Chad. "I wonder how many politicians are even left to try to clean up anything."

Witek had never seen him look so serious. There was no hint of humour on the Texan's features.

Kilo gazed at nothing in particular, eyes remaining unfocused as he slowly spoke.

"This is true. I acknowledge everyone is equally concerned about the future, even those less vocal. Some perhaps cope better by burying themselves in work. Which is why I must find useful tasks to keep everybody occupied."

Kilo rubbed his cheek and sighed.

"I fear the time is coming when the worst of humankind will arrive on our doorstep. Conflict is inevitable. Being an effective worker will not be enough. Everyone may have to stand and fight. If only we had better armaments."

Kilo took a firearm from the wall and cocked it.

"Is that a BB gun?" asked Chad.

Witek then saw Kilo was inspecting a very small pebble held between his fingers, with which he loaded the air rifle. More chittering came from outside and Kilo stepped out onto the balcony to take aim at something in the garden, then fired.

Witek walked to a window in time to see a dark bird take wing with a commotion then crash back to earth, dead.

Kilo returned, looking satisfied as he returned the old weapon to its place. "Bloody blackbirds. Harassing native birds, digging up our new garden… Damned feral creatures, they don't belong in this land. I consider it very apt that their genus name is *Turdus*."

Witek's companions looked at each other with blank faces, except for Sindy, who giggled to herself until she realised heads were turning her way. She went silent, looking flushed. While the girl was clearly astute, Witek suspected an odd sense of humour. Perhaps she was a little crazy. He figured the crisis was probably affecting people's mental health in all sorts of ways.

Kilo turned back to the group. "It will take more than BB guns to defend ourselves. Information will help just as much as weapons – it is another commodity we can use to forge stronger bonds with neighbours."

Chad nodded. "Yeah man, good to get a heads-up if them old Blues are snooping around the 'hood, right?"

"Er, about that… ah Chad… too late, th… they're…" said Riku, trailing off. The look on his face made Witek's stomach knot. Riku raised a shaky hand to point outside.

Kilo whirled and strode back out onto the balcony. Witek was at his heels.

Putu was running up the garden path, pointing back over his head. "Blues… they just broke through the west gate."

From this vantage point, Witek could see vehicles speeding up the driveway.

"Where's Rocky?" said Kilo, storming back into the room. "He was going to clean my shotgun."

Agus called out from somewhere inside the house. "He did. I have it here. Coming."

Witek's mind raced. He visualised Kilo unleashing his rage upon that man who was now rotting beneath a cliff. Violent action against the authorities was another matter. If Kilo did not keep his cool, a bloodbath would ensue and Witek knew he had to intervene for the sake of everyone at Kirilia. He stepped in front of Kilo.

"Let me face them on your behalf. It can be our team's first task. You stay hidden while we learn if they are here with questions about who is overseer or just intend to take supplies."

"Just…?"

Sindy came to Witek's side. "Information is everything, like you were just saying, right? We're your recon team – let us gather info."

"Then we will use it to plan our next move," Witek added.

Kilo exhaled. "Very well. Your plan is sound and logical. Hurry down then."

"One more thing," said Witek. "Where is the drone that hunted me?"

———

Putu met them in the garden, gasping. "They're taking food."

The team rushed down to the shed that served as both pantry and kitchen.

Witek slowed, stiffened and marched, recalling military drills, trying to project confident authority.

"What is this?" he demanded, lifting his chin. "There is nothing in the handbook about unscheduled direct collections. We have no harvest – this farm is just starting out."

Witek saw four Blues had arrived in two utes. None had been aboard the bus from Canberra. He did not like the smug looks they wore.

"Care factor…" said a young trooper, doing nothing to hide the mockery in his tone.

The rear tray of one vehicle was laden with farm produce – not grain crops but fruit and vegetables. Witek noticed a small crate with several bottles of alcohol packed in there too. He wondered how many farm larders had been emptied so far.

One man had two chevrons displayed on both sleeves and the collar of his uniform, signifying the rank of corporal. Witek turned to him.

"If you are seeking lost property, we found this battered drone by the roadside when we were brought here. Is it yours? Could it have fallen from one of your convoy vehicles?"

"Sure, we use them drones," said the corporal, glancing at the UAV with disinterest. "Not one of ours but. Wrong paint job. Keep your trash."

A trooper emerged from the kitchen. "Which spices?"

"All the spices. Take the lot," instructed the corporal.

"Dude, are you serious?" said Sindy.

"Orders from above. Don't like it? Take it up with headquarters in Budgie."

Another trooper was kicking around some traditional Balinese Hindu offerings left outside the door by one of the workers.

Putu stared in dismay then stepped forward. "Oh, come on –"

The trooper grabbed Putu by the collar with both hands, swung him about then pinned him against the shed.

"Yous farmers want our protection?" said the corporal. "Well, your bodyguards gotta eat well too. Don't worry, we won't let you starve. Here."

The corporal retrieved a swollen sack from the back of the ute and dumped it on a bench.

"Great, more goddamned rice," Chad muttered. "Probably just needed more room in the vehicle to stash all our good stuff."

A trooper handed a rifle to his superior. It was the .22 Witek had been given during his quarantine, which he had left with Rocky at the workshop.

"What do yous need this for?" demanded the corporal, putting the rifle inside his vehicle.

"This is a farm," Witek began, "and there are feral –"

"In fact, what're they for?" the corporal cut him off. "Hand over them choppers yous are carrying."

"This is bullshit," said Vlad. "It is dangerous out here and we need to protect –"

Without warning, two troopers shoved him to the ground, disarming him and passing his blade to the corporal.

"All o' them blades."

Witek handed over his blade and nodded to his team, who followed suit while he helped Vlad to his feet. Then he stepped in front of his companions, feeling stress rising and an odd sensation of breathlessness.

"Who is your superior?" Witek demanded, forcing the words. "Sergeant Booth?"

"Booth?" mused the corporal.

One of the troopers sniggered. "Oh, that'd be 'By-the-book

Booth' – they stuck him out at the Eastern Outpost. You know?"

"Oh, the old cop," said the corporal. "Yous won't see him again. Trouble on the highway keeping that lot busy. No. It's the Budgieweir squads you'll be seein' from now on. We answer to Sergeant Selvin. He's gonna get a promotion so yous ought to stay in his good books."

Yous. Witek had heard the likes of Chaylarna speak in this manner. The corporal was evidently just a bogan in a uniform. At least in his uncouth ignorance he appeared unconcerned about who was in charge at Kirilia.

There was nothing more Witek could do but root himself to the ground, not wanting to appear submissive by backing away. He reflexively clenched his fists. The corporal spied the motion and rested his own hand on the hilt of his pistol, raising his eyebrows, tilting his head.

Sindy stepped between them. "You can tell your Selvin to go –"

There was a roar overhead and Sindy ducked. The drone they had seen above the Higginson farm was intimidating up close. It swung about in an overt display of force then stopped suddenly, hovering in place.

Witek had seen a similar prototype in an online video. Military hardware had continued to interest him, even after he left Poland. This type of UAV made a distinctive sound when airborne, like an oversized vacuum cleaner.

Bristling with rockets, the airborne behemoth glared at them from the well-encased fore camera in its nose cone, giving it a cyclopean appearance.

The corporal grinned. "What's that, mate? What ya gotta say to the Sarge?"

15

Sienna

The recon team's first expedition outside Kirilia came sooner than expected. Sienna was excited, even if they would not venture far.

Kilo stomped about, incensed by the Blues' plundering, unable to hide his hunger for immediate retaliation. He proposed a counter-raid, acknowledging the need to be clandestine about it given the potential consequences of any overt moves made against the Blues. Sienna, angry at seeing her companions shoved around, was vocal in her support for this. She did not like the way that corporal had ogled her either.

Then there was the matter of being disarmed just as everyone learned a beast was lurking in the bush. Sienna missed the familiar security of the machete she had worn at her side and suspected other workers felt that way too.

On top of that, word spread that a farm had been raided overnight by bandits somewhere down south, near the river. Workers from an adjacent farm were first on the scene, arriving long before the Blues troubled themselves to investigate. Nobody survived the attack.

With the rocket drone being used to bully the zone rather than protect it, Sienna understood the necessity of self-protection. Rocky was already creating new hand weapons for everyone but Kilo wanted more and he gathered the recon team to discuss his plan.

"The neighbouring property north of here has an empty house. Go on foot. The old stock route track is so rough and rutted in that direction you will struggle to get a vehicle through. We can try later should you find anything worth bringing back that is too heavy to carry.

"Scout the old farmhouse. You cannot miss it on your left, over the next field after you pass our cattle. Stay there the night if you please. Pick it over. Be thorough. Bring back whatever you can carry – food, firearms, anything worthwhile."

"Could sure use a doomsday prepper's shopping list right now," said Chad.

Sienna recalled watching shows about such people and tried to recall the things they hoarded.

"In particular, I want you to bring back any keys you find," Kilo continued. "Our radio will remain on. Report danger or any significant discoveries."

"What if we find the beast waiting there?" asked Witek.

"Use this," said Kilo, handing over his shotgun. "Do not lose it. Hide at the first sign of any Blues."

With that, the seven set out along the rough track, its ruts up to half a metre deep. The old road had become a watercourse at some stage, eroded to the point it would be easier to drive off-road unless one was in a monster truck.

They passed a small herd of silvery-dun cattle in Kirilia's poorly vegetated northern paddock. Sienna was unfamiliar with the breed, a fact that amused Karmen, who had gone on to enlighten everyone that they were an Australian breed known as the Murray grey.

"I grew up a beach girl, not a farmer's daughter," Sienna protested.

Karmen sighed. "I only know this as I once read something about Australian cattle being brought over to Argentina and Paraguay for experimental crossbreeding, to improve the characteristics of our local stock. Their condition is poor. Some of the workers are saying they should be set free."

"Kilo is considering trading them away before they deteriorate further," Sienna explained. "Cattle farming can be far too resource intensive."

Witek pointed across a barren field to their left then proceeded to march across it. Sienna watched eddies of dust rise as they traversed the parched open ground, before turning her gaze to the Cooper Hills. A tingle caressed her spine and she felt a strong desire to explore further along the stock route. Another day.

The neighbouring farm was empty and overgrown, untended lawns surrounding the farmhouse suggesting no occupation for some time. The house itself was an old musty wooden structure, its roof covered with streaks of rust. Indoors it appeared habitable, if overdue for recarpeting and a fresh paint job. Access proved easy, the locks having already been broken open. The place was furnished, though untidy, and Sienna wondered if the mess was made by looters or former inhabitants.

She did not like the atmosphere indoors. In the lounge room, an old yellowish painting of a pair of forlorn-looking children staring out at her with dark eyes gave her the creeps.

There was a lot of sporting memorabilia, which piqued the

interest of Sameera and Chad. Sienna was less interested in these dusty items and wandered into the kitchen.

She opened the refrigerator door then slammed it back shut, screwing up her nose at the stench issuing forth from the rotting food she glimpsed within. Then her eye was drawn to a bobblehead of a sporting mascot atop the refrigerator, some kind of white bird. On closer inspection, its hollow base revealed a hiding place for a small key ring, its little tag bearing the characters "8YT".

"Bingo," she exclaimed then held up her find to show the others.

"Excellent," said Witek. "Keep searching for anything useful."

The team took their time but found nothing of exceptional value. They gathered some nearly expired medications, jars of spices and seasonings, baked beans and other tinned food, matches, candles, an array of knives from the kitchen drawers and several rolls of toilet paper.

Vlad found a hockey stick, wooden and ancient but solid, unaffected by the decay of time and quite capable of taking down a drone that flew within reach — or at least he expressed the desire to attempt such a feat.

As evening fell, the question of whether to stay arose. Chad favoured the idea. Vlad was also enthusiastic, making himself comfortable, playing folk tunes on his wooden koncovka. Witek said it made practical sense to stay, as it fitted with the goals of their expedition and Karmen promptly agreed.

Riku, Sameera and herself had not been so keen but were outvoted. Sienna did not wish to stay a moment longer.

"We could be back in our own comfortable beds in less than half an hour," she said, and held up the keys, shaking them. "We have what we came for and more. What will we gain by staying on?"

Vlad played a brief melody that sounded suspenseful to Sienna, then spoke. "Another chance for Witek to hunt the hunter?"

Witek said nothing but raised his eyebrows, nodded and scanned the land outside.

"We are a team now," said Sameera. "Guess we should see this audition right through to the end together."

Night fell. There were enough mattresses and lounge cushions to provide a bed for everyone.

Sienna squirmed as she sat in a lounge chair, unable to relax, and volunteered to take first watch with Chad. They seated themselves on outdoor furniture in an annexed area, listening to the sounds of twilight coming through the fly screens. Chad proved tired and less talkative than usual, more yawns than words emerging from his mouth.

Sienna's attention was drawn to the hills, their outline dark against the starry sky, and felt their pull. No predator came forth to meet them and she spent most of her watch fidgeting with her medallion, thinking of her family.

Eventually she was relieved by Witek and retired to the lounge room. Chad promptly fell asleep in an armchair, but Sienna was unable to stop her mind racing. It took time to get comfortable atop lumpy cushions, under the gaze of those miserable kids in the painting, before she nodded off.

Her dreams were troubled. She wandered along a path with her family, surrounded by gnarly trees and coastal scrub. It led to a lookout near her home on the Gold Coast. Then the familiar scene darkened. They found themselves hunted and chased down suburban streets by uniformed men. Sienna became separated from Craig and her parents, hearing their voices but unable to find them. She hid in darkness from their pursuers. Then things became worse.

The thing that had stalked her dreams was back. She sensed it in the shadows. Visible yet shapeless, it emerged from the gloom and billowed towards her like some horrific unnatural cloud of incense smoke. Its awful deep rushing sound, reminiscent of the surf or a cold bitter wind, filled her ears as the thing engulfed her. She was paralysed, unable to scream for help, as the ethereal entity reached inside her neck and chest and feasted upon the very essence of her being.

Then the white-haired man was there. His unblinking ice-blue eyes were watching.

As always, Sienna fought to break free, struggling to end the horror, to escape back to full consciousness.

Then she was awake, finding herself in that awful house with its own musty shadows. Chad snored away, oblivious to her torment. Not wanting to wake him, she sat up, pushing fear aside. She felt very much alone.

This nightmare had sporadically plagued her sleep since she was a child but had not bothered her at all in Kirilia, where she slept in peace and comfort every night.

She gasped when she heard an unexpected whisper. "Sindy. Are you OK, Sindy?"

It was Witek. She wondered why he was skulking about indoors during his watch. It didn't matter; she was grateful for company.

"Nightmare, yes? Come."

He helped her to her feet and led her to the annex. It was cool in the night air and she folded her arms but was comforted by the sounds of nature.

She spied Sameera armed with Kilo's shotgun, sharing a cigarette with Vlad by moonlight out in the yard, their quiet conversation peppered by laughter. Thankfully they were downwind, the smoke inoffensive until the pair returned to the annex and Sienna caught a whiff on their clothing, forcing her to suppress a sneeze.

Sameera handed the shotgun back to Witek, who nodded and remained seated in silence, staring out, scanning the night.

"I hoped to find a trace of Marcelina here," he said after a while. "Kilo says he never came across her but she must have been in this area before our arrival."

"She might be holed up in the next house we visit," Sienna offered.

Something caught her eye out in the hills, further north.

"Look. Lights."

"I see nothing," whispered Witek.

"Sorry, sis, same," Sameera added.

"I'm sure I saw a flicker, like a campfire."

"You are overtired," said Witek. "Try to rest."

Sienna resisted sleep, straining to see something more but to no avail. She permitted herself to relax, feeling more comfortable in the annex among companions, and closed her eyes.

Then the sun was rising over the hilltops. A pied butcherbird was heralding the dawn. The morning was beautiful and Sienna scanned the horizon.

"Good morning," said Witek. "Still nothing out there."

He was wrong. Somehow, Sienna just knew it.

16

Phuong

There was no time to plan. Phuong wanted to sit awhile but rest was not an option.

The rice skipper's headlamps illuminated a closed gate. Straining through dust, she saw it was padlocked. A vehicle track stretched away on the far side. Farm 1469 was somewhere off in that direction. Phuong recalled seeing this laneway while drone mapping. A large empty canal ran along its left flank but she remembered nothing more.

She hooked her left elbow around the seeding arm's frame, freeing her hand, its palm sweating from holding on with such a tight grip. With both hands now free, she could make proper adjustments with the controller tablet. She raised the skipper's idling level higher off the ground, hoping an elevated perspective would improve her view.

A waxing gibbous moon had risen in the eastern sky, obscured by a haze of high cloud, which caused a wide halo to form around it. Phuong felt like a great eye bore down upon her, watching. The moonlight did not illuminate the land as well as she had hoped.

Phuong scanned the rest of the sky. Overwatch drones might be up there somewhere, but she saw nothing aside from some of the brighter stars struggling to force their own light through the clouds.

A flicker to the west caught her eye. It was not the lights of Budgieweir, which winked sleepily further left. Nor was it moonlight reflected from the neighbouring solar farm. She saw it again. There was something moving against the shadowy backdrop of the low western range of hills. Its distance was hard to gauge. A vehicle. It flashed brighter now, its source now facing her direction.

Phuong knew it would be logical to set the skipper on the ground, shut it down and thereby kill its safety lights. However, panic set in, an instinct to move away as rapidly as possible. Realising she had just enough height to clear the gate, Phuong jabbed at the touch screen and manually piloted the skipper straight over the top.

Following the laneway, she sped eastward, eyes fixed upon the screen. This offered a clear forward view, directly relayed from the skipper's sensors – better than her own eyesight at night.

The track stretched on, fortunately along straight and level ground with no sharp corners. Phuong wanted to wipe the grit and dust from her eyes but dared not risk dropping the control tablet. On screen, a small building loomed ahead beside the track and Phuong swiped at the speed control slider, realising too late the long seeding arm, which stretched out to that side, would hit the structure.

She heard the loud clang of contact over the engines and the skipper went into a slow, flat spin. Her feet slipped and she scrabbled for support against the machine's body. Her left arm, wrapped as it was around the frame, was jarred badly. She regained her footing but fought to avoid falling off. She squeezed her eyes shut.

Even when the spinning sensation stopped, the skipper rocked nauseatingly, and something in her pocket crushed against her side, until the stabilisers kicked in. Only then did Phuong open her eyes.

She found herself facing the direction from which she had just travelled. Blinking away tears, which helped dislodge grit, she saw she was alone. No vehicle's headlights were closing in as feared.

Phuong took several deep breaths, trying to calm herself. The cloud haze had cleared, the night air now much cooler. The moon was bright and she felt very exposed. It was time to ditch the skipper and hide it, if possible.

The small building, clad in corrugated iron, was sturdy enough to withstand the impact. A pump shed. Far too small to accommodate the vehicle, even with its arm retracted.

Most sheds large enough would be near dwellings and there were no guarantees other farmers would be more benevolent than Jon-Jon or Horace. Search parties would investigate all nearby farms.

Phuong eyed the deep trench of the empty canal. No. There the skipper would still be seen from the air. She guided it about, deciding to risk proceeding, though with more care.

Further along, the laneway meandered and Phuong had to avoid the occasional tree growing beside the canal. She could always traverse open fields but right now, the track was her only navigation reference.

The canal veered away, its shadow stretching northward. The pain in Phuong's jarred arm intensified and she did not know how long she could continue. She wondered how close she was to the road fronting Farm 1469 and whether this laneway would take her there. She suspected her friends were mere kilometres away.

Then Phuong noticed a structure in a field to the right of the shadowy canal, indiscernible against the gloomy backdrop of a copse of trees. She would have missed it if not for a glint of reflected moonlight. There were no adjoining buildings or lights suggesting nearby human habitation.

By now, they would know Phuong had not returned from her "night test" and Horace would raise the alarm. It was fortunate these neighbouring farms were completely empty – or if there were people living in unseen farmhouses, they had killed their lights and gone to bed.

So, she made for the trees, determined to find somewhere to set her ride down while she still could. She guided the skipper over a fence and across a field, moving slowly, glancing up to check for obstacles.

The building by the trees was an old hay shed, open at the sides, its metal roof supported by the trunks of long-dead cypress pines.

As she slowly circled the building, Phuong detected the stale scent of dry hay bales. The skipper's engines agitated all loose particles in the vicinity. The shed was only filled to a quarter capacity, yet the hay remained stacked high in places, an L-shape formed by the bales offering enough cover to obscure the interior from two sides. The roof appeared intact. She doubted there would be anyplace better to conceal the skipper.

Phuong manoeuvred inside sideways, the long seeding arm trailing. Normally, the arm would be retracted before entering a confined space, but this was not possible with a human elbow hooked around its frame. Straw blew everywhere as she carefully set the vehicle down on flat earth, having moved as close as possible to the inside of the L-shaped wall of hay. She disentangled her throbbing arm and climbed down, collapsing with relief atop a rectangular bale.

Immediately, she retracted the seeding arm, relieved her earlier crash had not caused enough damage to prevent her from doing so. Shifting counterweights clunked as the arm slid back and it was done. Before shutting it down, Phuong noticed the skipper's battery was at 68 per cent capacity but hoped to never ride it again.

Her ears rang as they reacquainted themselves with silence. She felt secure as darkness surrounded her like a blanket, if in truth the only things settling were dust and straw.

Reaching into a deep pocket, she retrieved the water bottle and took a swig to soothe her throat. Her back and shoulders ached, protesting the unnatural position she had maintained. She wished the skipper's designers had included a small passenger seat and control tablet mount.

Checking her other pockets, she learned the small delicate mapping drone had been crushed during her smash with the pump shed. The biscuits, in a different pocket, were still intact.

Pulling the hood over her head and leaning back, Phuong yawned. She could almost sleep atop the bale of straw. Just a short rest. A moment to think about her next move.

Phuong closed her eyes.

———

Her arm ached. She felt so cold. This was a void. The blackness of space. No, there was some sort of blinding light beyond the enshrouding darkness.

Phuong sat up, rubbed her eyes, then scrambled to her feet, gripping the control tablet. Glancing around, she appeared to still be alone. The only sound was the lazy chirping of crickets.

There was no time to linger. She had to distance herself from the skipper. Hidden as it was in this gloom, it would be easier to locate by day.

With the mapping drone crushed, it was pointless to continue carrying the control tablet. She lifted the edge of a hay bale, slid the device into the gap then lowered the bale, satisfied this would impede Horace and the Blues from recovering the skipper even if they found it.

Realising she was standing on a dusty floor, Phuong knew she had left footprints. They would expect her to try to return to Farm 1469. To her friends.

She walked with purpose in a straight line, directly out of the hay shed through its open eastern side. She continued until the sound of her footfalls changed and she felt herself walking on thick grass, making a soft crunching sound with each step.

The moon had moved further along its westward arc but was still high in the sky and Phuong hoped she had not slept for long.

The stars had wheeled overhead too. On a moonless night they would be spectacular. Even now, Phuong doubted she had ever seen so many. Growing up amid city light pollution, she had never paid much attention to stars and many constellations were a mystery. Duc knew them better, having taken an interest when they first left Sydney and he could observe them in clean, country air.

A bright and familiar arrangement was visible. She knew many Australians referred to it as "The Saucepan" but she recalled a night before the pandemic when Duc explained this was just a small part of the larger constellation Orion, the Hunter. He tried to explain the overall shape of Orion, confusing her until an old farmer present said he looked at the arrangement of stars a different way — he called it "The Arrow Pointing North".

She hoped she was no longer leaving a trail and the grass now felt softer and squishier. Satisfied she had done her best to mislead trackers away to the east, she glanced at the sky once more then changed direction — north.

Duc was somewhere north, though Phuong could only speculate about his precise location. She was afraid to follow the north-south road that ran outside Farm 1469, but by following stars and cutting across fields, she hoped to reach that highway with the railway beside it. From there, she could try to find the dusty road Duc's bus had taken.

Phuong had been too stressed to notice landmarks when their convoy had split, but she remembered that intersection was close to the hills north of Jon-Jon's farm. She could see them now, stark and clear against the sky. It was impossible to gauge their distance.

She quickened her pace, hoping to cover as much ground as possible before daybreak and also to fight the chill, which had gotten into her bones while she napped. She took light steps through the copse of trees, trying not to disturb too many fallen gum leaves, which crunched underfoot, then strode into the open field beyond.

Phuong pushed on feverishly, counting steps to keep her weary mind active, until she reached 100 then started over.

Eventually, her path was blocked by a barbed wire fence. Without friends to hold it open so she could slip through, she could only follow it instead.

A dog bayed somewhere ahead and to the right. Feeling a chill of fear run through her, Phuong followed the fence to the left.

The fence line turned a corner when it came to a canal, likely the same channel she had seen prior to ditching the rice skipper. There were a couple of metres between the fence itself and the drop into the canal, more than enough space to continue walking north unimpeded.

The earth felt hard underfoot on the channel bank and Phuong hoped she was not disturbing any more dust.

Bleary-eyed, she lost all sense of time. The dark line of the canal stretched onward, her journey broken only by the occasional silent pump shed, metal bridges spanning smaller side channels and puddles in the deep trench reflecting moonlight. The unpleasant scent of stagnant water helped keep her awake.

To her right, dogs barked again. They were not close but Phuong was glad to have the fence at her side. These dogs sounded agitated and did not quieten. She wondered if they were Jon-Jon's. Then she froze.

There was something else to her right. Lights. There were three, winking in and out of sight as they bobbed behind trees and unseen obstacles. She heard nothing aside from the dogs. The lights shone an eerie blue-white and moved from right to left, meandering somewhat, keeping close to the ground.

The dogs went silent but the lights entered the field beyond the fence, crossing open space. Search drones. It was time to hide.

There were no pump sheds, trees or other forms of hard cover so Phuong swung into the empty canal. The gentle slope into the trench was not muddy in this place so she was able to lie flat on her stomach, peering over the bank.

Ahead, one by one, the lights bobbed over the fence line. Two crossed the canal but the third dipped down into the trench and lingered there.

Phuong did not move a muscle, pressing her head to the soil, holding her breath. Her large hood fell across her face but she could still peer through a gap with one eye. The light in the canal was very close now. It moved in complete silence. In fact, everything was silent, no dogs, no crickets.

All drones she knew of made some kind of sound. None lit up in such a way. If their purpose was searching, they would project a beam of light. These gently glowed like overlarge fireflies.

This was too surreal. She must be dreaming. The ground beneath felt real enough. Phuong was curious but dared not move.

The light suddenly zipped up out of the canal and weaved its way overland to re-join the others. Then the trio of lights sped away to the west.

Phuong took a breath and lifted her head. Within seconds, the lights winked out, one by one. Shuddering all over, she crawled out of the trench and crouched, staring at the point where she last saw them. They did not reappear.

After some minutes, she stood and looked around, yawning. There was no search party. She was completely alone, save for some creature, a frog perhaps, croaking down in the canal. The moon had sunk further west. Even the Arrow Pointing North had passed its zenith and was descending into the west as well. There was no sign of dawn yet Phuong feared it would arrive all too soon.

After some time, she realised she no longer could see the line of hills she hoped to reach. In her delirium she must have changed course. The position of the moon and the stars indicated otherwise, confusing her.

Then Phuong understood. A much closer hill blocked her view of the larger range. As she approached, it became apparent this hill was artificial — an earthen embankment.

A rooster crowed. Other early-birds had begun singing. She hoped the top of the embankment offered a vantage point for locating a place to hole up and rest.

Something was moving, directly ahead. A shadow. A rather large one. Phuong realised a creature blocked her path.

Perhaps she could go around, find another way to the embankment. There was still the fence to her right, its wires barbed, while to her left Phuong saw water in the canal. In the chilly morning air, she did not fancy taking a dip to test its depth or risk becoming stuck in mud. An awkward climb over the fence was her only option.

As she tested the wire's tension to figure out a safe way to cross, Phuong heard a sorrowful whimper.

The shadow did not come closer but it was watching. Normally, she would have been too scared to approach a large beast, domestic or otherwise, but there was something so mournful about the sound it made. Perhaps she was so tired she forgot she was supposed to be frightened. She moved closer.

The creature before her was a huge dog bound to a long chain, much larger than Jon-Jon's beasts. Perhaps a Great Dane. No. Not tall and lanky enough but the fawn coat, dark face and huge jowls suggested something similar. A mastiff. Yes, though a rather thin specimen. Phuong wondered who the owner was and why it was left abandoned and starving.

Phuong did not want to become breakfast for a big hungry dog and stayed back. Then she remembered the biscuits in her pocket. Taking one from the ziplock bag, she held it aloft, taking slow steps, then threw the biscuit forward. The dog snuffled at the ground, found the biscuit and crunched it. Sniffing the ground awhile, seeking crumbs, the mastiff then turned its attention back to Phuong, cocking its head sideways.

The chain stretched back to a pump shed beside the large embankment. Gauging its length, Phuong held another biscuit high. The dog was transfixed, licking its chops. She threw the biscuit as hard as she could across the canal. The dog plunged down into the trench, splashing into the water. Phuong hurried on as the mastiff lurched out of the water on the far side, seeking its snack.

Reaching the pump shed, Phuong saw the chain was fixed to a post with a simple clip. Looking back, she saw the mastiff finish off the biscuit and strain on the chain, having taken an interest in small shadows that appeared to bound about in a field – rabbits, maybe hares. She was nervous but could not leave the poor dog here to die. Unclipping the taut chain was not easy but it slackened just enough to unhook the clip.

Phuong hurried up some metal stairs, which led from the pump shed up the side of the steep embankment. She did not want a great hungry beast tailing her, unsure if it was grateful for its snack and freedom. The mastiff remained in the paddock, hunting, its dark form moving to-and-fro so Phuong stopped to survey what was ahead.

The stairs had taken her to a narrow metal footbridge spanning a large canal, far bigger than the one she had been following. It was full of water and likely served as the main irrigation supply for the ag zone.

On its far side was a levee bank and just beyond that, a small town.

Phuong saw no signs of people but heard a rooster crowing in a yard. The town was otherwise silent.

It was getting lighter and she hurried across the bridge with careful steps, trying not to think about the treacherous water below. Descending the far levee bank, Phuong found herself on a residential street, which ran along the edge of town, the canal to one side, modest but neat homes on the other. She needed to find an empty one before the sun rose.

Phuong did not have time to be picky – the unmistakable sound of a drone broke the silence. She could not see it but it was getting louder, as if homing in on her position.

Dashing across the road she dodged standard roses in the front garden of the nearest house and made straight for the door. She turned the handle. Locked.

She could hear the drone moving along the street. It was close now.

Frantic, Phuong looked for a side gate. Failing that, she found a council wheelie bin against the high fence that blocked access to the backyard. Without hesitation, she clambered onto the bin and jumped the fence, landing on a turf lawn in the rear yard, steadying her landing by pressing her palms into short bristly light-brown grass.

The home's exterior was plain but the building was quite big. Phuong found a back entrance. Both the security screen door and main door were unlocked.

The drone was almost overhead.

Phuong spun inside, closing then locking both doors with their manual latches, then froze, waiting.

The buzzing sound faded.

Tiptoeing about the house, she heard no sign of life, its occupants perhaps having died here during the pandemic. There was no reek of the dead though, just the faint aroma of the dried herbs hanging from a kitchen rack.

It felt odd being alone in such a large homely place. Phuong glanced around at the family portraits adorning the walls — well-dressed people attending parties, weddings, a buxom bride with long shiny dark hair. The furniture appeared expensive, too opulent for her taste, unlike the plain but practical style in her own family home.

It was cool indoors but more comfortable than out in the fields. Phuong found a bedroom, its neat double bed topped by a thick, inviting doona, its cover black with a white floral pattern stitched around the edges.

Dropping her dusty hi-vis jacket on the floor and removing her shoes, she got straight in, pulling the doona up around her neck and half over her head. Exhausted, she was asleep within seconds.

Phuong woke to the sight of masked men with pistols pointed at her head.

17

Sienna

Exhilaration outshone all other sensations. Sienna was on the move. She always felt at home on the open road, travelling somewhere. Anywhere. She welcomed the sense of freedom brought on by wind in her face.

Her rough night in that abandoned house was a hazy, distant memory. Standing in the back of Kilo's uncle's ute, under warm sunlight, Sienna felt like she was back on the Gold Coast, surfing. This was the best local alternative to riding a wave.

She flipped the nu-tooth headphones attached to her sunglasses down into her ears and launched her wrist-phone's music app. She kept her music database in shuffle mode, so skipped the first couple of songs that came up before settling on the third – an epic tune from an old movie score.

Sienna called on the pleasant rush of goose bumps. As the feeling flowed into her limbs, she became energised by the natural high. It was like an equal and opposite sensation to the terror of her sleep paralysis. She felt ready to take on this messed-up world.

Sienna gripped an old dog chain clipped to the grille behind the vehicle's cabin and leaned back.

Chad was shouting. She lowered the volume of her music. He was sitting in the back of the ute with everyone except Witek, who was riding shotgun inside the cabin beside Kilo, who was at the wheel.

"Sindy. You're crazy, girl. If that chain breaks…"

Chad made a motion with his hand signifying a flight through the air and subsequent landing in the trailer behind them, with ensuing trampling by the cow within.

"YOLO. Come, join me. Hold on to the grille."

The others shook their heads but Chad needed no further encouragement. He stood, gripping the grille with one hand while fist pumping the air with the other, whooping.

Inside the cabin, Witek stared over his shoulder, unamused. Kilo, oblivious or just apathetic, paid them no heed at all.

"Nanny state. Nanny state. We will all be arrested for travel without seatbelts," said Vlad.

"You crazy kids are going to fall out – be careful," said Riku.

The group had managed to convince him to wear less-gaudy apparel for this outing. Riku had insisted on maintaining his own individual "look" by wearing a grey beanie, with two large woollen tufts that looked like ears, which he now clutched against his chest lest it be blown from his head.

"Listen to Riku. Be sensible," Karmen demanded.

They had gathered speed and her words were almost inaudible and Sienna ignored her.

Chad leaned closer to Karmen, who gripped the ute's side with both hands.

"Come on, Mom. Have a little fun up here – you might like it."

Karmen rolled her eyes and turned away but Sameera tugged on Chad's shirt before he could swing back upright.

"Your life is your own but be quiet, Chad. We don't want everyone in the valley wearing blue to come after us."

"Yes, Aunt Meera." The Texan fist pumped the air once more, albeit silently this time.

This rush was a much-needed release, but if they attracted the wrong kind of attention, there was no telling how Kilo might respond. The man's rage had not subsided and Sienna noted the way he kept his mouth set in a tight line, eyes and brows fixed with a certain intensity she had not seen before. Only when Sienna presented him with the keys had his expression changed to a brief grin, though a rather hideous one.

She lurched forward as the vehicle slowed. Kilo's long arm snaked out through the window and he slapped the metal roof of the cabin then pointed at something up ahead to the right. Sienna killed her music and squinted, tensing her muscles.

Twenty or so people were congregated behind a farm gate around some sort of small digging machine, which stirred up dust. Some toiled with shovels.

The properties immediately bordering Kirilia were abandoned, their pastures untended. However, their nearest neighbours, the Higginsons, had a working farm.

A short, battle-axe of a woman with multicoloured dyed hair marched through the gate, a long double-barrel shotgun in hand.

The workers flanking the woman were much younger, unarmed save for their picks and shovels. Sienna assumed they had been sent to work in the ag zone too, although she did not recognise any faces.

She felt like all their eyes were on her. It was probably just paranoia but she drew herself back to sit down among her companions.

The woman frowned, checking their vehicle as Kilo eased it to a halt, giving her a wave.

"Glad to get visitors with no uniforms," she spat. "You haven't aged much, Mexican."

"Thank you for the compliment," said Kilo. "Here is something to help you keep going, as promised."

Mrs Higginson looked over the cow in the trailer. "Skinny, but she'll do."

The woman squinted at Sienna and the others in the back. Her workers stared in silence, all wearing hi-vis shirts of fluorescent yellow or orange tone, and Sienna wondered why such workwear was never issued at Kirilia, not that she wanted to wear it.

"I see they paid you a visit too, eh, Mexican? How'd it go?"

"Hmm," Kilo replied. "Yes, well. They took food, weapons and did a whole lot of chest thumping. However, you may rest assured that Kirilia will not roll over so easily."

"Well, those bloody mongrels won't get back in here so easy next time. They might fly their machine around and make noise, but no ute's gonna get near the house and load up again."

Sienna noticed they were digging a deep trench across the main driveway into their property.

"What if you need to get out?" asked Kilo.

"Don't you worry about that. We have ways. Now what're you goin' to do at your place?"

"Not just hole up and wait. I decided a tour of the neighbourhood was long overdue."

"See what you can take back from 'em, eh?"

"I never said that," Kilo replied.

"Well, you probably won't find much. Brewerton's a no-go zone unless you're wearing blue. Everyone was sent off to Budgieweir for 'health checks' and never came back. There's always more traffic headin' into Budgieweir than comin' outta the place. Folks leavin' home to go there, that ain't good for anyone's health. Dunno why they didn't just lock 'em down like with the other pandemics.

"Anyhow, don't bother driving past Brewerton — it's pretty much Dragonland all the way to Budgieweir. Locals were bought out by 'em long before the shit hit the fan. Solar farm's theirs too. Bastards makin' us Aussies buy back our own sunshine. Oh, Dragons own the irrigation too — even water 'round here ain't ours. They should never have separated land and water titles back in the day — it's a disgrace our governments allowed it."

Sienna knew her parents would like this woman. They had often complained about Australian voters being too apathetic to consider supporting the smaller political parties more inclined to put the long-term interests of citizens first.

"Dragons didn't employ local kids," the woman continued. "They brought in their own company workers — a bunch of robots with no personality, happy to work for crappy wages."

Kilo changed the subject. "What of the pandemic? You mentioned your husband is unwell."

"Bruce?" Mrs Higginson interrupted. "Nah, not the Big V, the Big C. We have a cancer cluster here. Got worse when they relaxed bans on certain agrochemicals. Bruce and I tried to keep things clean on our farm and I know your folks were good like that too, but if everyone else is spraying all over the place, what's to stop the drift coming onto your land?"

"I am so sorry to hear this," said Kilo.

"Bruce would appreciate a visit."

"Once we have things sorted, I will."

"Anyway, if it's plague you're worried about, stay away from Budgieweir. Dunno how many are still alive there. Blues have their base in Budgie though. Probably have a vaccine they're not sharing with the rest of us."

Sienna wondered how survivors dealt with all the bodies and shuddered, imagining what it was like for those tasked with removing them. From what she understood, the disease passed over an area like a wave. She wondered if it lingered on corpses or could even be carried on the wind.

"That digger of yours, what kind of fuel is it using?" Kilo asked.

"LNG, from our fuel ration. Blues have direct access to the source. Why do you ask?"

Sienna wondered if the source was nearby and whether the facilities to extract, purify and store the fuel were all on site and if any farmers were unhappy having a fully operational LNG micro-plant nearby. Touted as "cheap, clean and green fuel", she knew LNG was used to fuel trucks and ships fitted with on-board cryogenic storage tanks but had not realised the technology had developed to enable easy re-gasification for use in smaller vehicles – even mini excavators.

"Hang on, we never got such a ration," said Kilo.

"Do you have the right kind of storage tank at Kirilia?"

"Well, no."

She spat then looked at Kilo. "You want my excavator, don't you?"

"You just might have inspired me with what you are doing here. Yes. I could put it to good use, if you are making it available for hire."

"All right. Everything is negotiable. Your folks were generous neighbours."

"I can be a generous neighbour too."

"Thanks for that bit o' meat there. Bring us a few more presents and we'll see what we can do. Few more cows, extra food, seeds, plants, vehicles... old-school fuel."

"Excellent. Let us do business then."

Kilo gave a nod to the team and they led the cow from the trailer and handed it over. It was placid enough to be taken away by rope.

"While the valley is clear, we should press on," Kilo said, giving the woman another wave, almost a kind of salute.

Mrs Higginson nodded then turned to recommence work.

Before they set out, Witek left the vehicle and jogged over to Mrs Higginson to discuss something in private.

"His cousin?" asked Sienna.

"Most likely," Vlad replied.

The woman shook her head. Witek nodded, grinding a clod of dirt under his boot, then hurried back to the ute.

With that, they departed.

Once they were far from the gate, Sienna stood again. For some reason, she was unable to summon the exhilaration she had enjoyed earlier. She could not shake the memory of being stopped and separated from her family while travelling like this. Part of her wanted to sit back down and be inconspicuous but she remained standing, to help scout the way ahead. Spotting threats in time could help keep the team together.

She saw Brewerton's grain silos before any other structure — plain, blank canvases, awaiting an artist who would never come.

"If I wanted to watch for incoming threats, that's where I'd be," she said. "Hope they haven't already seen us."

"Sindy, don't stress," said Sameera. "Why climb all the way up there when you have drones?"

"Good point."

Kilo slowed suddenly, just outside town, then turned into a property.

"What's up now?" asked Riku.

"Hey, it's a winery, man. Guess Kilo's thirsty," said Chad.

There were only a few buildings and Sienna figured it was a boutique winery.

Kilo parked under a gazebo and jumped out.

"Check the area."

"What's up, boss?" said Chad. "I thought we were going to town?"

"Just a feeling. Let us hang back awhile."

The team scattered, jogging around the grounds, checking for signs of life. Witek moved like a professional soldier, his military background evident.

Sienna approached a building, its access ramp and stairs framed by grapevines sporting fresh spring leaf growth. She hurried up to the entrance, where a blackboard had been erected.

The chalk letters read: "Dear valued customers, regrettably our cellar door will be closed until further notice. Orders can still be placed via our website or visit..." The bottom of the sign had been erased and replaced with other words, written in a different hand: "…come back when the pandemic is over. Uninfected pissheads only."

She peered inside, glancing around the small cellar door's pleasant wooden interior. The door was locked.

The building had been constructed high enough to provide a view over the top of vineyards, with Cooper Hill and the adjoining ranges as a backdrop. An idyllic location for wine tasting. She could even see Kirilia at the base of the hill.

"Sindy, get down here," called Chad, who had ducked behind a decorative wine barrel.

Without thinking, Sienna vaulted over the railing, down into the garden, ducking between two rosemary bushes, where she waited.

"What is it, Chad?"

"Rocket drone. Over the town."

She scanned the sky but saw nothing. "Where's Kilo?"

Chad crawled up beside her, nodding at a tall metal structure supporting elevated metal tanks. The overseer crouched on a lower catwalk, watching. Then he dashed down the metal stairs, out of sight.

Sienna heard an approaching vehicle.

"It's coming here, listen."

"You sure, Chad? Think they've seen us?"

"We're gonna find out."

Sienna watched in dismay as a utility vehicle, much like their own, entered the parking area.

"Goddamn it," hissed the Texan. "Blues."

"Look familiar?" Sienna whispered.

Two troopers cautiously exited their vehicle. She recognised them from the squad that had raided Kirilia.

They eyed Kilo's ute with suspicion. Sienna did not move as the troopers spoke, looking about.

Then they approached the cellar door. One — the corporal — withdrew some keys and made for the door, while the other strolled around the building's perimeter. He passed by metres from their hiding place and she was grateful the rosemary grew thick and healthy.

The man paused to light a cigarette. Sienna held her breath as the trooper exhaled a plume of smoke and rolled his shoulders.

Then he threw down his cigarette. He was staring at a different part of the garden, his hand moving to his pistol. Then he stepped forward.

"Stand up," he demanded. "Drop that weapon."

Vlad slowly emerged from behind some grapevines, still holding his hockey stick.

The trooper drew his sidearm.

Sienna charged. She did not think, it was pure instinct. She threw herself at the man's legs from behind, and his knees buckled.

Before Sienna or the trooper could regain their footing, Vlad was there. The hockey stick found its mark. The man fell to the ground, unmoving.

"Is he dead?" she asked as Vlad helped her up.

"Yous dogs sure are," came a voice from the deck outside the cellar door.

The corporal aimed his pistol. Sienna breathed in and froze as he stared at her.

"You," he tilted his head as he spoke. "I do know you. You're that s—"

Then the man spun around. His eyes bulged as Witek thrust a blade into his gut, driving it up beneath his ribs.

Sienna's heart raced.

Then Kilo was there. "Well done, team. The die is cast. There is no turning back now."

18

Harrison

The wide, open spaces of Farm 1469 were not enough. Harrison felt trapped. Nobody's safety was assured – the demise of Lieutenant Michael had proven that. His world had shrunk to the land within that cursed dog run.

Only the drone helped him retain sanity. It was *his* toy, the one thing that could take him elsewhere, an escape that was his and his alone. Longer power blackouts limited his opportunities to recharge the UAV. He wondered if this was for the best, fearing in time his secret would be exposed, and he dismantled his incriminating "attack mod" at the first opportunity.

Harrison did not stop wondering if there were better places in the zone to stay. He was the only one with a means of reconnaissance. As his nerve returned, he resumed his strolls to a certain patch of shrubbery at the back of the property, near the canal. The dogs rarely ventured into that part of their run and he enjoyed the freedom to launch the drone and explore the land beyond in peace and solitude.

For a big man, Junior was stealthy. Suddenly he appeared, watching, just as Harrison finished charging both drone and controller.

"Harrison. What are you doing? Where did you get that?"

Harrison flushed, his mind racing. The straight shooter's piercing eyes were fixed on the gear he clutched against his chest. Sometimes the most believable lie was a half-truth.

Harrison feigned excitement. "Junior, you won't believe what I found. Did you ever notice that trapdoor back there? Well, today I got the padlock open. Now, I know you're not a drinker but there's wine down there. I found this too. With the power back on I thought I'd see if I could get it charged and working."

Junior said nothing for several seconds, which felt like hours. Harrison's mouth went dry.

"Harrison. All of these things are Jon-Jon's. We should touch nothing. We will give him no excuse to send Amahle away."

He did not have a pre-prepared response for this conversation and could not argue. So much for his plans for further exploration.

Then Arjun and Aditya appeared.

"Hey guys, the ladies are refreshing themselves but will join us soon," said Arjun. "Aradhya is nervous about that smoke to the east. Many are worried more bandits are around. Jon-Jon is inside his house speaking on the radio. He isn't telling us anything. We knocked but Jon-Jon's girlfriends said not to disturb him and sent us away."

The pair noticed what Harrison held.

"Where did you get that?" asked Aditya.

"The basement – Jon-Jon's old wine cellar. There."

An idea formed in Harrison's mind and he continued. "Hey, if something's going on that Jon-Jon won't explain, we could use this. Drones have excellent range these days and this one is fully charged.

We can launch it from somewhere hidden. If there's another serious threat coming, we need to know, right? I mean the truth – not just whatever Jon-Jon chooses to share."

Arjun stepped forward, speaking with enthusiasm. "I completely agree. Jon-Jon is an untrustworthy guy. I am sick and tired of being stuck here without knowing what is going on outside that dog fence."

Aditya nodded. Bingo. Junior was outvoted. Harrison hoped the big man did not argue.

"I do not like this," Junior's deep voice boomed. "We must consider the consequences of playing with a toy that is not ours."

"Agreed, but it's a calculated risk," said Harrison. "There'll be far worse consequences if bandits break in. Look what happened at the gate."

Jon-Jon was paranoid and had spent much of his time indoors since then. That raid may have been stopped but at the cost of two of the Blues' own men. The aircraft had vaporised everything: grass, flesh, even topsoil, leaving the earth scarred. Selvin had arrived the next day to speak with Jon-Jon, inspect the scene and clean up what they could. They commanded everybody to keep working; the Blues would have their back.

Nobody explained the aircraft or where the bandits came from. Jon-Jon stated that automated defence systems were protecting the ag zone but elaborated no further. The uncertainty made people sick with worry.

"We are not soldiers," said Junior, not backing down. "How can we fight, even if we know they are coming?"

"We can hide, Junior."

It was Amahle. She and Aradhya had been following the

discussion from just beyond the doorframe.

"Amahle." Junior's voice was softer and more tender as he turned to face her. "This is so dangerous."

"Everything is dangerous now, my dear. None of us have been truly safe since we left protected accommodation. That smoke: it may be bandits, it may be some kind of accident, it may be nothing to worry about at all. However, if this thing Harrison has found gives us insight, then knowledge is one thing that may keep us alive."

"I will not be able to sleep without knowing what is causing all that smoke," said Aradhya. "It is too close. We must have a look before it gets too dark."

"Very well," said Junior, fixing his gaze upon Harrison. "Discreetly then."

Harrison nodded. "I can think of a less obtrusive part of the farm. Shall we go for a nice evening stroll?"

There were no further protests. Excellent. Harrison concealed the drone and its controller in his pack and they set forth.

Outside their dilapidated residence, others had finished work and gathered in small groups, all speculating about the column of dark smoke. Avoiding them, Harrison led the group to his hiding place.

"There, under that shrubbery. What do you think?" he said, as if discovering the site for the first time. "I'll fly this away low and fast. Others are looking this way. Can't risk them running off to Jon-Jon to report a UFO sighting."

The others watched him in silence but despite their lack of enthusiasm Harrison was having fun. While he had enjoyed numerous flights already, it was kind of exciting to share the adventure.

"You already know how to fly a drone?" asked Junior.

"Raced them with friends in Melbourne. This one looks straight-forward. Let's try a launch from that clear spot."

Harrison placed the drone on a dusty patch of ground then sat cross-legged under a small native tree with grey weeping foliage. The others gathered round. No dogs had followed them along the run. Perfect.

"Well, this is it. Three… two… one." Harrison took the drone up, keeping it mere metres off the ground.

"Eastward ho," he said then shut up, realising no one cared for his random chatter. Harrison often blathered to himself during his flights or even brought his headphones and death growled along to some Urtaxx.

The drones cleared the dog run, the large wide canal behind it, then crossed the weed-strewn flats beyond.

"These fields are untended, like a no man's land next door." Harrison already knew the surrounding farms were uninhabited.

"Can we go higher?" asked Aditya.

"Why not?" said Harrison. "We're well clear. Let's check out the panorama."

The image on the display changed as the drone shot skyward. Harrison took it to 1000 feet, exceeding the legal altitude cap for civilian drone operation, not that anybody would bother enforcing such a law now. Nor had he given a shit during more civilised times. The drone races he had contested were illegal.

"That's us – Farm 1469, beyond the canal," he announced, rotating the drone.

"I cannot see us," said Arjun.

"Good," Harrison replied. "Means we've found a decent hiding spot. Now look off in the distance, past the farm — that must be Budgieweir. Wish we could take a closer look but I doubt the Blues would welcome us snooping round."

"What is that shiny thing, reflecting the sunlight?" asked Junior.

"Solar farm. So much for those engineers Jon-Jon was talking about, what with our glitchy power supply."

Harrison rotated the drone to the right.

"That'd be the railway line and main highway. Looks like it passes that village then runs east, past the hills — that's the way we came into the zone. Wonder if anyone still lives in the village. It's not far off."

Harrison had not yet scouted that area, only daring to fly over land that appeared unpopulated. He already knew the layout of main roads but maintained the pretence of discovery.

"What's that?" said Aradhya.

"Overwatch drone," Harrison said, zooming the display. "Don't worry. It's moving away. Too far off to see us."

"The smoke," demanded Junior. "That is why we are here."

"Yes, well, now we have our bearings. Hmm. The wind is blowing it away from us. We should get a clear view from this side."

Even from a distance, he could see a lot of activity on the ground. Vehicles were moving about. People too, milling around like the meat ants Harrison had observed scurrying about their oval-shaped nest mounds.

"Harrison, can we get closer?" said Amahle.

He nodded, descending, but taking care to remain back from the chaotic scene unfolding on-screen with disturbing clarity.

A once pleasant farmhouse was ablaze, as were its outbuildings, hay shed, even some vehicles. People in hi-vis shirts were being chased around by more plainly dressed armed men. Some of the attackers were on foot, others rode motorcycles. There were twenty figures or more.

Harrison heard gasps in his ear and two of his companions moved away. The others remained transfixed by the horror on screen. Workers were being slaughtered by all manner of weapons.

An axe-wielding maniac hacked away at a man who could not possibly be still alive.

A motorbike passenger, gripping the rider's jerkin with one hand, used his free arm to level a lance at a group of girls trying to flee towards some gum trees. He missed but dismounted and chased one of them on foot, leaping upon her like a predatory beast, then rammed her head into the ground again and again.

The rider spun about, selected a new target, gave chase, then reared up onto one wheel to take down the worker with his bike.

Four large men, shirtless save for their tattoos, were hefting the dead into the back tray of a ute parked beside a larger vehicle containing livestock: a cow, a few sheep – or perhaps goats. Two thin women held a group of workers at gunpoint, forcing them into the back with the animals.

Harrison felt detached. It was odd watching this from a place upwind, where all he could hear was birdsong and the breeze gently whistling through foliage.

"I have seen enough," said Amahle. "God have mercy."

She pressed her face against Junior's chest as he embraced her as Harrison retracted the camera zoom.

"Wait. Down there, beside the field." Arjun jabbed his finger at the screen. "Those two are waving. They see us."

A young couple had gotten clear and were running in the direction of the drone.

"Where the heck are the Blues?" Harrison muttered. "So much for their overwatch drones."

"They will not escape, jumping about like that wearing hi-vis," said Aradhya. "Fly closer, Harrison. Let them know you see them."

And put my drone in danger? That was his first thought, which he refrained from voicing aloud. He had seen enough action and just wanted his drone to stay intact.

However, if he could be seen attempting something heroic it could serve him well in the future. It could even make the others more pliable, trusting and prepared to go along with his schemes.

"OK, going in," he announced before engaging in a descent.

Harrison took the drone down to hover in front of the workers, ten metres or so away. They were young, only around his age, a guy and a girl with skin bronzed from outdoor work, hair in good need of a cut, faces and hi-vis stained with red dust. They were chattering away at the drone and gesticulating, but with no audio detection it was impossible to understand.

"I'll bob up and down, like we're nodding," said Harrison before conducting the manoeuvre. Then he pulled the drone back a few metres, stopped, then bobbed it again. "Come on, follow. Get yourselves out of there."

"Too late," said Aradhya. "Look there, Harrison."

A plume of dust rose from the land behind the workers.

Harrison wished the drone was still weaponised. He was confident in his ability to take something down with precision.

"Motorbike," he stated. "I'll try to distract the rider. Might buy those people some time."

He flew the drone low and fast, directly at the motorcycle, then veered away at the last second, circling for another pass.

When his target came back into view, Harrison saw the rider was alone. The denim-clad man slowed, his attention now on the UAV speeding at him.

"I'll buzz him again."

Too late, Harrison noticed the weapon affixed to the man's fore-arm, some sort of hooked blade extending over and above the man's fist. The man stood tall and swiped and the feed became a blur. His drone tumbled, coming to rest in a tilled field, tilted but more or less upright.

By chance, the drone was facing the rider, who had dismounted and was marching forward. He was a large ugly man, head com-pletely shaved, tattoos worn beneath denim. Some ink even stood in for hair on his bald noggin.

"Shit." Harrison jabbed at the controls. The image on the screen shuddered and he hoped it was just snagged on something. The bald man was running.

Harrison jerked the controls in several directions. The man stopped and squinted, as if looking right through the camera lens, right at *him*. He grinned, showing horrible stained yellow teeth. As a hand snaked forward, Harrison could not wrest his eyes from that nasty hooked blade.

Then, something splashed in the canal nearby. As Harrison reflexively leapt to his feet, something smacked into his head.

19

Sienna

"Would it be safer to wait for the cover of darkness and sneak in on foot?"

Kilo watched the rocket drone fly off in the direction of Budgieweir.

"No, Riku. We must seize this opportunity. A vehicle driven by Blues might remain unchallenged. Do those uniforms fit?"

"These collars are ridiculous," muttered Witek.

"Just my size," said Vlad, adjusting his own popped collar and stroking the chevron stitched upon it. "Hey, why am I just a trooper?"

"You can be the corporal if you prefer your uniform more bloodied," said Witek.

"No thank you, Sir."

"Anyway, my mess, my responsibility. Do you not agree, Trooper Varga?"

Vlad replied with a casual salute.

Sienna thought they looked just the part. She was unsure if Vlad had inflicted a fatal blow on the trooper she had helped bring down, but the overseer had not taken any chances. Both men had been dragged away, Kilo's blade ensuring neither would trouble any farm again. Stripped of weapons and uniforms, their bodies were hidden in a small dark storeroom.

"What was that corporal saying about knowing you, Sindy?" said Vlad.

"You knew him?" asked Kilo, rubbing his chin as he turned to her.

"No. Only time we met was at Kirilia, during their raid."

"Sindy stepped up to speak her mind to that asshole," said Chad. "They sure as hell weren't the kind who appreciated anyone challenging their authority."

"Hmm, well, they are going to have to get used to much more of that," said Kilo.

Sienna was bothered by the suspicion there was something more to the corporal's particular interest. Not wanting to contemplate this now, she shook the side of the tarp stretched over the back tray of the Blues' ute.

"Speaking of their raiding, think they planned to fill this with wine? Thought the cellar door would have been cleared out by now. Can we do the honours? Taste the local vintage?"

"Later," said Kilo. "We are seeking provisions of far greater value. Time to move out."

Witek and Vlad took the driver and passenger seats, while Kilo crouched low in the cramped back seat, covering himself with a blanket.

Sienna piled into the back tray with the others, hidden beneath the tarp.

As they approached the village, she had to remain confident in

Kilo's judgement. He claimed to know the layout of streets, as the village was over 100 years old and had changed little. Kilo said his uncle hated shopping in Budgieweir, being too "crowded, noisy and full of ferals", and preferred to support the small businesses of Brewerton, which had retained its post office, pub, butcher, community bank, supermarket, ag supply store and even a tiny police station.

Peering out from under the tarp, Sienna saw they had reached the main highway, where a sign indicated the way to Budgieweir. Another sign, erected beside a railway crossing, declared: "No access to Brewerton without authorisation. Trespassers and looters will be arrested."

Beyond this were deserted suburban streets, the homes and gardens empty and abandoned. She spied a trampoline and swing set beside one of the houses and she wondered about the fate of the kids who not so long ago would have bounced around there with joy.

They came to a halt in a laneway. As they disembarked, Kilo explained he did not wish to drive into the open village square. It would be safer to scout the area on foot.

Everything was silent save for the sound of wind whistling through the long, thin foliage of a nearby casuarina. Eddies of dust stirred in the empty street at the end of the lane.

"Look there," said Chad. "Isn't that what we saw?"

There was a carving on a fence post, not unlike the one near Witek's tree house.

"Ah, shit, man. Anyone have the photo?" Chad continued, jabbing at his screen with futility. "My battery's flat already."

"So is mine," said Sameera.

"Witek." Vlad nudged his friend. The friends checked their photo galleries. "Witek and I have Marekteks. Fully manufactured in Poland for the European market. Longer lifespan, better battery charge, no need for constant updates, no cheap components made in sweatshops."

Kilo strained forward to see. "I liked the idea of owning a Marektek. Read about their founder and the quality of his products in an airline magazine. Pity this crisis came before they expanded to a global market."

Sienna took a photo and compared the two carvings. There were strong similarities, although the part resembling a question mark was doubled on this new carving and two arrow-like symbols were also at the top of the glyph.

"Come on. Keep moving," said Kilo. "Hold on – movement. Just a fox… or a vixen. Yes, with kits in tow, look."

Sienna watched the red fox family trotting out of sight into an overgrown garden. She hoped the confident daytime appearance of the feral animal indicated an absence of humans.

They picked their way along a silent street and nobody spoke.

A commotion erupted in a garden. Almost in unison, hands gripped weapons. It was birds, squawking loudly, raising an alarm.

"Is someone over there?" Riku whispered.

Then Sienna saw. She exhaled a little and put her hand on Riku's shoulder, pointing. The birds making the fuss were vocal honeyeaters, feeding on nectar in a grevillea bush boasting gaudy red-orange flowers. Larger birds sporting blue faces had shown up and settled on the curved metal light pole overlooking the garden, peering down.

"Australian noisy miners don't like sharing," she whispered as several honeyeaters stopped feeding and took wing to challenge the interlopers.

Kilo twirled his finger, directing them into the village square. It was devoid of life, fringed by old crumbling shops with faded signs that looked to Sienna like they had been painted decades before her parents were born. Broken glass and scattered cardboard boxes suggested recent looting.

There was a park in the centre of the square, with a small war memorial, playground, public toilets and a couple of tennis courts.

On the far side was an old pub, just as ancient as the deserted shops, but still standing proud. Sienna knew pubs like this were the beating heart of every small Aussie community and had the villagers not been sent away, she wondered if the place would have been lively even now.

"It is creepy here," said Karmen. "No families, no kids playing. When was the last time anybody saw kids around?"

She had raised a good point. Sienna wondered if they were the youngest people left alive, perhaps due to high attrition among the young during the pandemic.

"There," said Kilo, producing the key ring she had found, and made for a large building with a dark-green number eight painted above the door.

It was an agricultural supply store. Sienna now understood what Kilo had figured out the moment he saw the key ring's tag. Number 8 Yarrantree — that was the name of the square. She assumed the yarran was a tree indigenous to the area.

Kilo studied the building, which had security bars on its windows and doors. After peering inside for several moments, the overseer turned, his usual morose countenance morphing into an expression of maniacal glee.

"It's untouched," he announced.

Then, looking serious again, Kilo checked the square with a few furtive glances and tried the keys. One turned.

"Bolted from the inside," he huffed.

He rattled the door then wheeled away.

"Right then. We will try the back. The old police station is just down that street leading west from the square. If there are Blues about, that is where they will likely be based… unless they decided the pub is more comfortable. Either way, someone should watch over the square – any volunteers? Two perhaps?"

"I will," Sienna blurted.

Even though she was curious about the contents of the supply store, she felt more comfortable outdoors where her senses were sharper than confined within an unknown building.

"Me too," said Sameera and shook the handheld radio she carried. "If anyone comes…"

"Good," said Kilo. "Stay out of sight somewhere you can watch all approaches to the square. The park perhaps."

"Cool beans," said Sienna.

Kilo led the others around the back while Sienna strode into the park, Sameera at her heels.

The pair lingered beneath a stand of Norfolk Island pines, neither speaking. A crow wailed somewhere in the distance. It was not long before boredom set in and Sienna began to regret volunteering for sentry duty.

She saw an overwatch drone gliding far off to the east.

Sameera cracked her neck and broke the silence. "We need not worry about that. It is too far off."

"At least that rocket drone is not around."

"I just hope Kilo finishes his business before it comes back," Sameera replied, scanning the sky in other directions. "We need our own blue uniforms, being stuck out in the open like this. Nice tackle back there, by the way."

"Thanks, sis."

More time passed in silence. Sienna kept contemplating potential repercussions of their actions at the winery. Her companion appeared restless too, first shuffling her feet, then progressing to some sort of fast footwork that resembled dance steps.

"Is that some sort of traditional routine?"

"No, just my own steps," said Sameera.

Sienna did not know much about Sameera's background, only that she was from South Africa.

"Sameera, when I last heard real news, they said nothing about the African continent. Hope some countries there dodged the pandemic. Think they kept it out of your old neighbourhood?"

Sameera scowled. "They can rot for all I care."

Sienna was lost for words and closed her mouth when she realised it was hanging open, not expecting the outburst.

"Sorry if I snapped. I am a stranger to you Aussies, which is exactly why I am here. Back home, I am much more well known. More infamous than famous I suppose."

Sienna was intrigued and nodded, waiting for Sameera to continue.

"I was on a reality dating show. The producers got it in their heads to cast me as one of the villains. Naturally they had to pick on a woman of mixed background who freely speaks her mind; they would not dare pick on one of the girls who was completely black or completely white. They aired less than ten per cent of my dialogue, only selected cuts of things I said, which were taken completely out of context by the public.

"They kept me in it almost to the end and should have thanked me for boosting ratings. Didn't win a damned thing. After it finished airing, I was still abused on the street, bullied by trolls online, criticised by those I thought were friends. I could not even get a decent job. So, I told them all to go to hell and left the country."

"Freakin' trolls. One reason I steer clear of social media. People who know nothing have the biggest opinions. Even at Kirilia I overheard someone bitching about our group being Kilo's 'cult enforcers'. But your story is like next level. Did you consider trying to sue anyone for basically ruining your life?"

"No. The bastards had me sign contracts, which covered their backsides from the beginning. Anyway, I do not wish to speak about it anymore. It makes me angry thinking about the whole situation. So, let us change the subject – Chad. What do you think of him?"

Sameera tugged on one of her tight ringlets of hair. "You two seem to be getting along very well."

Sienna flushed.

"Chad, he's just, well, he's easy to be around. Funny too."

Perhaps she could change a subject too.

"Mum was from the States, too. Oregon. My parents met when Dad went there for work."

"Wait, why do you not call her 'Mom'?"

"She said she would've liked me to call her 'Mom' but 'Mum' is what came out. People say I take after my father. My height sure comes from his side. Anyway, I guess she accepted folks speaking differently was part of life when she moved here."

"So, back to Chad then."

Then Sameera whirled.

"Huh?"

"Over there – listen."

Sienna cursed herself. The conversation had been a welcome distraction from boredom and anxiety but she had let her vigilance lapse. She followed Sameera's gaze, which was fixed on the pub's beer garden.

Sienna glimpsed a group of people disappear behind the crumbling building. She crouched, tensing. The figures reappeared, dashing across a lane beside the pub before vaulting over a fence, one at a time, each with effortless agility.

"Still kids around after all," she said.

All were slightly built and wore large hoodies.

The last of them paused and turned. Sienna could make out no face save for a pair of large eyes. They locked with her own. She felt a tingle in her neck and shoulders as she stared back, unmoving. Then the stranger followed the others, hurrying from sight.

"Did you count five or six?" Sameera whispered.

Sienna shook her head, listening, eyes still fixed on the lane. It remained empty. Then, much further to the right, somewhere behind the shops, came the sound of startled chickens.

"See ya, sis," said Sienna. "Something's up and I've gotta check it out. Wait here."

She moved off in a low crouch and Sameera hurried after her.

"Sindy, wait, we should report first." Sameera then spoke into her radio. "Hey, it's me. There are others out here, a bunch of kids running behind the shops. We're going to take a closer look."

Sienna ducked into an alcove at an old shop entrance.

Chad's voice crackled over the radio. "Hey, we're in. You should see the great stuff…"

There was a pause.

"Sorry. Boss man says go ahead but be careful. Don't go far, watch, but don't engage. Have a quick look, then come back. Keep us in the loop."

"OK, out," Sameera replied, then fiddled with the radio. "Best turn the volume down a bit, right?"

Sienna nodded then moved off along the footpath, pausing at the sheltered entry to each shop.

"Not too far, Sindy. Remember the police station is down that way."

"Just a little further, we can always run back."

They reached the last shopfront, a two-storey building in a corner of Yarrantree Square. Sienna could see the police station a short distance down a long, straight street.

"Blues," Sienna whispered, spotting an armed uniformed man at the kerbside.

Something shattered beside her ear. Sienna whirled, her eyes flicking from the broken glass at her feet to the window. She expected to see a gun-toting figure in the shop but it was empty.

"We are under attack," Sameera radioed, flattening herself against a wall.

Then Sienna heard their attacker. A small drone sped across the square, coming straight at them. Her head snapped about. There was no cover at the shopfront.

"Run this way," she yelled as a faint reply came through the radio.

Sienna sprinted down a lane beside the shop while the drone whizzed up and over the rooftop.

After several metres, she halted.

"Wait, Sameera. Stop. We might be ambushed back there, behind the shops."

"Fine, let's run back."

"No, the square's too open. Over here."

Sienna ducked under a metal fire stair leading down the side of the building from the upper level. There was a large rubbish dumpster right beside the stair. Sameera threw herself down to join her and the pair squatted. This cover was far from perfect but it allowed a moment to think.

Sienna heard muffled gunfire. Several shots. Then the drone whirred somewhere further down the lane and they heard the crack of its weapon firing, which sounded different to the other shots.

"The others?" asked Sameera.

"Wrong direction. Those shots sound like they're coming from down the lane and near the police station too. Better check on our mates though… Wait, someone's coming."

Sienna heard footsteps running down the lane and flattened herself against the dumpster, gripped her weapon and crouched, ready to spring.

Then they swung into view. One was dressed wholly in black, his face covered by a ski mask. He had a pistol in one hand. His other dragged a slightly built young woman behind him.

Sienna raised her blade, while the man lifted his firearm, waving it about with an unsteady hand.

"Back away or I'll shoot." His voice sounded rather young, and dark eyes blinked at her.

The drone buzzed again and everyone looked up and about.

Sienna turned her attention to the young woman, who she recognised from the other bus from Canberra.

"Aren't you the sister of that quiet one… Duc?"

The young woman nodded vigorously, a tear streaming down her face.

"Yes, I am Foo. Where's Duc? Is he with you? Is he all right?"

"He's fine. Doesn't say much, keeps to himself. He's back at our farm. Your bus – where did you go? How did you get here? Are you staying close by?"

"Wait, you know these two?" said the masked man.

"Yes. Yes. They're OK. Trust me."

Sienna lowered her weapon in unison with the man.

"We were checking on some kids jumping fences over this way," said Sameera. "Did you see them?"

The masked man nodded.

"Yeah, I seen 'em too. Total weirdos. Ran off when they seen me looking. We didn't get a real good close look but their costumes were… something kinda strange."

"Yes," Sienna nodded. "They were not quite…"

She wished she had paid more attention to their outfits but all she could remember was that pair of eyes. Sienna turned back to the young woman.

"Anyway, Foo. Is everyone all right in your group?"

"We were sent to Farm 1469," she replied, speaking fast. "Overseer Jon-Jon and his friends are right in with the Blues. They're a law unto themselves. They are taking some of the girls away and using them… those men are monsters. Please. You have to help. I managed to get away from –"

Everyone froze at the sound of incoming fast footfalls. A trooper jogged into the lane, a young clean-shaven man. Sienna did not recognise him from the group of Blues that had raided Kirilia.

So fixed was his attention upon a control tablet he failed to notice he was not alone until he was mere metres away, then swore. The trooper jabbed furiously at his device and the drone reappeared.

Sienna's eyes narrowed, mouth twisting into a snarl as she launched into a charge, slamming into the man with her shoulder. While not large, the trooper was heavier than Sienna. Both parties staggered from the impact. Sienna regained her footing and circled the man, closing in.

The drone veered sideways in an arc, crashing into the building.

Sienna raised her blade, feeling charged by fury. The trooper paused and raised his control tablet like a shield. Sienna swung down her weapon with full force, cleaving the tablet in two.

The trooper stumbled backwards, lowering his hand as he remembered his sidearm, fingers fumbling at the holster.

Now it was Sienna's turn to hesitate. Disarming someone or crash-tackling was one thing. Smiting someone with a weapon though, even in self-defence…

A loud gunshot rang out and the trooper was knocked off his feet.

Another masked man in dark clothing appeared, rifle in hand. He strode to the fallen trooper, who was writhing on the ground, clutching his thigh, trying to stop the gushing blood.

"Pig bastard," the newcomer spat, stepping on the terrible wound. The trooper's scream was cut short as a second shot was fired into his chest.

A luxury four-wheel drive vehicle appeared at the end of the lane, two more masked men within. The rifleman turned to the young man beside Foo.

"That's how it's done."

The youngster nodded, holstered his pistol, took Foo's hand again and jogged over to the vehicle. The girl did not resist as he helped her inside.

Sienna looked at the fallen trooper, wondering if he was another arsehole or a dutiful young man following orders.

The tall man with the rifle regarded her awhile, turning to the shattered drone and down to the smashed control tablet at his feet. Then he faced her again, inclining his head. He reached into a pocket with his free hand and withdrew a piece of paper, which he studied for a moment before stepping forward to hand it to her.

"What do these dogs want with you then?" he said, before striding off without another word to join the others in the vehicle, which sped away.

Sienna looked at the paper. It was a wanted poster with her name and likeness. Hand drawn but a good representation.

It made no sense anyone out here would give a damn about her. She knew her parents were critical of the government but doubted they had ever committed any serious crime. If they had, she knew less about it than the Blues. That corporal's words and the strange looks now made more sense. She would henceforth wear a mask when venturing outside Kirilia.

A faint voice came through the radio. Sameera turned up the volume.

"Sorry, say again."

It was Kilo. "Stay where you are; I'm on my way."

"We will," said Sameera.

Sienna sighed. "What just happened?"

"Wow," said Sameera. "Those men in masks – think they are also workers from the other bus?"

"Probably not. Foo said, 'I got away' not 'we'. I think they're a different group entirely."

"Lucky Dragons?"

Sienna shrugged. "Their workers wear white uniforms but who knows?"

"Think Foo is their prisoner? Should we have tried to keep her with us?"

"Not sure if they'd have allowed it, though she didn't look too stressed about leaving with them."

"She was probably too terrified to resist," Sameera insisted.

"I don't know. I mean, Foo did ask for help, but her issue wasn't with these guys. She seemed to know that young fella."

Another vehicle arrived, comfortable looking, not unlike the luxury 4x4 that had just departed. More masked men were within. One jumped out – accompanied by Kilo.

Kilo shook hands with the other man, who was significantly shorter than Kirilia's overseer. Broader too. The stocky man turned to the girls in the alley and waved, before departing with his companions.

The overseer watched them depart, then walked forward, removing his sunglasses. Crouching, he searched the dead man methodically, retrieving his firearm and checking each pocket. It seemed to Sienna that Kilo was unbothered by death and she wondered about the events of his life before Kirilia. Satisfied he had found everything of value, he turned to her.

"We have much to discuss. That can wait though. Come. We have loot to load."

Kilo moved to depart then paused, looking into Sienna's eyes. There was no emotion in those eyes now: no joy, no sadness, no rage. Just emptiness. Without a word, he offered her the pistol.

20

Phuong

Her feet felt wet. It was strange for Phuong to dream of such a thing. It felt so real. She sat bolt upright, awake. A huge mastiff was watching her, tongue hanging out, panting. Drool dripped from its huge jowls and she was certain the dog was highly amused, having done a thorough job of drowning her right foot in slobber.

"She likes you so much she could not resist giving you nice wet sloppy kisses," came a teasing voice behind her.

Phuong blinked. The day was warm and sunny but much brighter still was the white opulence surrounding her. The balcony's day bed on which she reclined was so comfortable. Sitting up, stretching and looking around at the opulence of the Rossi family's mansion, she could not believe she was recuperating at the nicest residence she had ever seen.

Samantha, who often commented on styling, would have been amused by the mansion's clichés. Every portal was in the shape of an arch: garage access, doorways, windows, even the entrances to all the sheds and outbuildings. White pre-cast concrete balustrades were everywhere from the balconies, encircling the pool, along every stairway, even framing the property's front gates, which also boasted two huge white lion statues atop large brick pedestals. All of the exterior brickwork was of a shade of brown, testament to the property's age. It was not so unlike 1970s or '80s-era houses she had seen in suburban Sydney, except this one was huge.

The interior fixtures were modern. The tiles all had tasteful modern hues and the granite benches were magnificent, although she felt the number of grand chandeliers was excessive.

Most welcome was the hospitality of the family. When she had broken into Nonna Rossi's abandoned house in Brewerton and been discovered, she thought she would be shot. However, they let her explain her story and when she finished, Rosario Rossi, the barrel-chested head of the family, had laughed and called her "a Goldilocks of the Apocalypse".

All was forgiven on the condition that she came to the mansion to meet Rosario's mother, short in stature like Phuong but loud and vibrant. The matriarch had set about catering for her guest, with portions she could not finish, in spite of her appetite.

A massive bowl of fettuccine smothered in homemade passata and generous-sized meatballs, topped with freshly grated pecorino, was just the beginning. The family made their own pizzas, thin bases adorned with simple but delicious toppings, far better than the thick tasteless franchise pizzas she had eaten in the city.

There were sides too: vegetable fritters, eggplants topped with some kind of mince, a leafy green side salad, bread served with chunks of cheese and spicy salami. It was different to the traditional Vietnamese cuisine she would have shared with her own family, but sensational.

Phuong wondered where the family obtained their provisions. They had large, productive vegetable gardens, but staples like flour were unattainable unless one was prepared to scavenge. The Rossis had being doing just that in Brewerton, along with recovering family valuables. With no international trade or local manufacturing, Rosario explained they were trying to collect what conveniences they could before they were gone for good.

The whole family resided here now. Aside from Rosario and his mother there were his three daughters, his youngest and only son Giuseppe, his three brothers, their wives and children. They had rescued Nonna from her home in Brewerton before the village residents were relocated. Phuong hoped her family in Sydney were together too, doing their best to ride out the crisis.

On Giuseppe's insistence, they also brought home the hungry mastiff, who took a liking to Phuong, the biscuits perhaps having made a lasting impression.

"Now you're wide awake, what are we gonna call her?" said Giuseppe, sitting on another day bed.

Giuseppe had taken a liking to her too. He was a teenager, cocky, confident and immature. She was grateful that he had stuck by her side in Brewerton. He was the first to lift his mask, revealing he was just a kid, not some faceless freak.

Phuong was still unsure about the others, who could inflict murderous violence on anyone who challenged them and carried it out with comfortable ease.

"So, *Mastina*," said Giuseppe, rubbing the mastiff's neck. She closed her eyes and panted, enjoying all the attention. "What we gonna call you? Piggy? I've never seen a dog eat so much."

"Mastina?" said Phuong. "What about Tina? Tiny Tina."

"Hey, I like that," Giuseppe replied. It sounded like he was trying too hard to be agreeable. She wondered if he had a crush on her or if it was youthful excitement at having a guest close to his own age.

At least none of the Rossi men gave off sleazy vibes. Killers, yes, but polite ones.

Giuseppe's sisters and female cousins, all with immaculate straight hair and flawless – if excessive – make-up, were more aloof and she was yet to connect with any of them.

If she was to learn anything, Giuseppe was the one to ask. She remembered a scene from an old movie where the matriarch imparted wisdom along the lines of, "If you want to know a family's secrets, ask the little children". Giuseppe was among the youngest in the mansion.

The residence's imposing hilltop position offered fine views west and east. They were presently relaxing on a west-facing balcony overlooking the pool, orchards, olive grove and vegetable gardens.

"The land is so flat that way. Is anything out there?" she asked, pointing at the plain stretching from the foot of the hill to the horizon, coloured with a palette of dusty red earth and dry grass.

"I've never been out west. Dad said there's not much out there. This here is the last range of hills and there's nothing but flat land for hundreds of k's. Not many towns, no irrigation, hardly any trees."

"Who owns it all? I mean, what kind of farms are there?"

"It's all dry-area farming. Used to be big sheep stations. Dad said the old families left because of droughts and it's owned by companies now."

"Lucky Dragons?"

"Yeah, probably them. Other ones too. I dunno, I don't really get into that sort of thing."

"Can we have a look back east?"

"Yeah, all good," said Giuseppe. "We'll have to leave Tina here. They'll kill me if she comes inside. Come on, girl."

He led the mastiff down to the pool area, then returned. Tina whined from behind the gate.

"It's OK, girl," said Phuong. "We'll play later. Yes?"

Though big and scary in appearance, the mastiff had quite a sweet temperament and no doubt was far happier now she was enjoying regular meals.

As they crossed through the house to the other side, they passed Rosario.

"Hey, how are you feeling?" he asked.

"Good thanks," Phuong replied. "Think I've slept so much these past days I won't need any more for a week."

"Very good, maybe we –"

His sentence was cut off by shouting from downstairs.

"OK, OK Mamma," he shouted back, then explained. "Mamma's got a snack for us. I'll bring it up."

Rosario hurried downstairs while Phuong and Giuseppe ventured onto an east-facing balcony. The wide irrigated valley on this side was greener than the western plains.

"There's Brewerton and that's the Cooper Hills over there," said Giuseppe, following her line of sight.

"What are these hills right here called?"

"Umm... McIntosh Range or something like that? It's like one really long narrow hill. It just keeps going on for k's and k's that way, up near Bimblebox Springs," Giuseppe explained, pointing north then spinning around, "and down that way it goes to Budgieweir. The road outside our place runs along the hill all the way there. I went to school there."

"Good school? Did you have fun?"

"We mucked around a lot. Couldn't stand it though. Glad I don't have to go back now."

Phuong could see Budgieweir in the distance, sprawling below the hillside. There was no sign of activity. She turned back to the valley, trying to spot Farm 1469, wondering if her friends were OK.

"Giuseppe, who do you think those people in hoodies were? Thieves? Local kids who dodged the Blues when they cleared out everyone else?"

"Dunno. They were a bit different. Two of them looked right at me. They looked like people who do cosplay or bank robbers with silly masks. Strange stuff's going down. A couple of weeks ago I seen weird lights too."

She recalled her own strange sighting, wondering if she had imagined it.

"What kind of lights?"

"I got up for a drink and seen three lights out in the valley. Thought it was workers but one flew up in the air in a circle. So, then I was thinking drones. Then it got weird — they came up here, right past the house, low and fast, but made no noise. So, I run out the back, thought I'd lost them but they were going off real fast over the plain until I couldn't see them. Dad said I was dreaming."

"No. I believe you, Giuseppe. I... out there in one of the farms near Brewerton, before I found your nonna's house, I saw them.

Dead silent, just like you said."

"Who's silent?" said Rosario, joining them on the patio with a smile. He carried a tray laden with bread, chunks of cheese and homemade charcuterie. Phuong had been shown the impressive curing shed for the latter.

"Those lights. Your son wasn't dreaming."

"Lights? Ah."

Rosario squinted at the valley. "When you're tired, the mind can play tricks. When I was young, I'd stay up partying all night and saw all sorts of crazy stuff. There was one time after a wedding when I swore my cousin Pat's shoes had grown teeth and tried to bite everyone."

"Dad, I wasn't partying – no drugs, no wine, no nothing," Giuseppe protested.

Phuong backed him up. "Sir, had I stayed another day at that horrible man's farm, I might have consumed spiked party drinks, but I got away sober. The lights I saw were real as anything."

"Well, the people in charge of this so-called ag zone brought in all these new types of drones."

"That crossed my mind," said Phuong. "It's true they have exper-imental technology, prototypes..."

"That thing you rode on to get away," said Rosario, smiling. "I never heard such a story. One to tell your grandkids."

"My job was to test these. I'd never have volunteered had I known how much trouble I'd get myself into."

"Hey, it's not your fault, Foo," said Giuseppe. "Those men are total dogs."

Rosario clapped his large hand on Giuseppe's shoulder.

"My son is right. I've never known such self-serving corrupt sons of bitches. They answer only to themselves, especially now we're cut off from Canberra."

"Cut off?" Phuong blurted. "What else have I missed? It's been a while since I was anywhere you can get news."

"I keep in touch with old families still in the valley. Word is the supply convoys can't get through. Whoever these highway raiders are, they either have serious weapons or there are a bloody lot of them.

"Wonder why the Blues aren't using their high-tech gear to break through or even talk to Canberra. You'd think they'd have retro communications gear as backup – they don't even have shortwave radio."

"What about satellite phones?" asked Phuong. "Surely their officers have those. The satellites up there should be fine. Not like our problems down here can affect them."

Rosario shrugged his broad shoulders. "Giuseppe, we should have bought some of them when we had the chance.

"Anyway, if Canberra knows what's going on, I wonder if they care. They might have their own hands full. Maybe ag zones closer to the city are easier to protect. They might have written us off as an acceptable loss.

"Now we only see supply trucks on two roads and one of those is the main drag into Budgie. Blues are grabbing produce for themselves. Sticking their noses in the pig trough and stuffing their fat faces. Instead of watching our arses, they let raiders burn our farms. Typical state cops, hitting soft targets. They break balls if you signal too late at an intersection or you drive a few k's over the speed limit but can't be arsed lifting a finger to help your nonno if he gets bashed and robbed by a meth-head."

Having finished his rant, Rosario stuffed a sizeable portion of bread, cheese and salami into his mouth, chewed a few times then gulped it down. Phuong suspected Rosario and his family had been in trouble with the law for more than mere traffic offences.

"What became of the good cops?" she asked. "I heard most of the Blues are not even ex-police but what of those who were dedicated to their work, back before all this?"

"Good cops? Like ones who were actually human, who you could reason with? Most of them died out long ago. Seriously though, Blues are worse than the worst of the bad cops."

"The supply trucks – you mentioned two roads. What about those not going to Budgieweir?"

"West. Out across the plains. There's a rough-as-guts road, full of pot holes and unsealed patches – Budgie City Council reckon they couldn't justify the expense of an upgrade. You can see part of it from the back balcony. I've seen several trucks heading out and have no idea why. There's bugger all out there.

"The land is foreign-owned and unproductive so I guess corporate staff are doing a bit of hoarding too. Probably have a deal with the Blues."

"Is it possible the Blues are sharing supplies with the people of Budgieweir?" Phuong asked.

"Maybe, to keep them onside. Not many mouths left to feed. Most were wiped out within weeks. Teams in HAZMAT gear went in to remove the bodies and that was the end of it. No one's heard of new cases in months. I won't go back – don't want to, don't need to. Too spooky. Budgie's probably one big ghost town.

"Anyway, we're playing this our way now. The remaining local overseers I've spoken to agree nobody has our backs. It's time to take charge of our own land. We can barter and share resources amongst ourselves. Take the blue factor out of the equation and we're looking at a free and independent valley."

"Can we do it? The Blues have weapons and drones."

Phuong liked the concept of free farms, less so the idea of an impossible war.

Rosario winked. "Not all of them. I'm not talking about going toe to toe. We need to think smarter. We can take them apart one piece at a time. With the constant power blackouts, they cannot keep their electric drones fully charged. It is all about seizing opportunities.

"This is something that can wait though. Tomorrow, you will be reunited with your brother, but you will always be a welcome guest here."

Phuong's heart jumped and she could not help but grin from ear to ear.

"However, there is one last thing. I need help with a drone."

Another drone? Again?

"It would be my pleasure," Phuong replied with sincerity. It was the least she could do to repay their kind hospitality. She was on their good side and that was where she wanted to stay.

The UAV in question was a Lite Shot security and support drone, which the family had found at the old police station in Brewerton. Phuong had never flown an armed drone before.

First, everyone enjoyed coffee, a rare treat, and Nonna Rossi's homemade biscuits, which were enhanced by the inclusion of slivers of fruit and almond.

Then she was free to set about her task – setting up security exceptions for all Rossi family members with the drone's facial recognition software. She estimated the drone could handle over a hundred such exceptions before its memory was full. In theory, when programmed and set to sentry mode, its AI would disregard "friendly faces" and ignore them.

She figured this was what the Blues had done when they had scanned the convoy en route to the ag zone.

Phuong also took the precaution of storing her own face in the database.

"Hey, store Tina's face too. Can you?" Giuseppe insisted when the human scans were done.

"Hmm. I wonder if it is already set to ignore animals. Let's try. No need for Tina to cop a loose bullet."

Giuseppe managed to keep the mastiff in place by giving her back and neck a good rub. Phuong held the drone in front of her and attempted to scan the large face.

"I'm glad we don't have to fly the drone to do this – she might think it's a frisbee," said Phuong.

Giuseppe struggled to keep Tina's excitable head still but eventually the program accepted the new entry.

"She's getting restless," said Giuseppe as Tina lurched away and ran around the pool.

"What's up, girl?" asked Phuong. "What do you smell?"

The mastiff sniffed the air and stared at the hillside.

"Ah, it's probably just a roo or something," said Giuseppe.

"There's feral goats around too. She'll enjoy chasing them."

Tina started baying.

"Forget what I said about goats. With a voice like that, bandits won't come near the place."

"Giuseppe, something's up. Can you hear that? What is it, Tina?"

Shouting came from inside the mansion. Tina barked again. The mastiff kept staring at the wooded hillside.

"Let's find Dad," said Giuseppe.

The pair bolted back up the stairs to the balcony. Giuseppe's uncle, Tony, was there, armed with a large military-style rifle, the kind Phuong had seen only in movies.

"Find your dad. Move it. He's inside. Someone's coming."

Tony squinted at the hills, the western plains, the sky, searching for something nobody could see.

Phuong swore she heard something.

They found Rosario on the eastern balcony with his other two brothers. He was speaking into a radio. All men were heavily armed.

Rosario turned to his son. "Trouble's coming."

He picked up another rifle and passed it to Giuseppe. Phuong did not know what kind it was but it had a very large curved maga-zine. That bothered her.

"Brace yourselves for anything. If we can't talk our way out of this, forget what I said about not going toe to toe. I have a feeling we're going to see a lot of blood before this day's out."

21

Harrison

Harrison rubbed his sore head with his free hand and felt himself flush. He had forgotten the low branch hanging above where he was seated. That splash had been no doubt just a diving bird or fish and he felt foolish but grateful the others did not laugh at his discomfort. Everyone around him wore sombre expressions. Understandable, given what they had just witnessed on the farm.

He blinked and looked back at the screen. Somehow, his drone was free, gaining altitude with speed. Harrison fought to regain control and stop the dizzying image of a spinning horizon, amazed the UAV remained upright. He used the dark silhouette of hills as a reference to stabilise the view.

"I think we are well out of reach of that freaky guy," said Aditya.

Harrison nodded and checked the altitude — it passed 1200 feet and he stopped the climb.

The sky was changing to hues of evening. Tail lights and dust trails suggested the raiders were leaving the burning farm, down a back road. Harrison saw another bike speeding to catch up with the others and assumed it was the big man with the hooked blade.

"Lucky this canal is between us and them," Harrison commented. "I didn't see any bridges."

"Those two workers," Junior cut him off. "Can you see them?"

"No sign. Not from this height. Maybe they hid in a ditch or among that crop."

"You should go back down and check," said Junior. "We could lead them here."

Perhaps. They would be indebted to him for saving their arses. However, it would take time to lead them here on foot. Night would fall fast.

"Wait," said Arjun. "You said that is the main highway over there. It goes through the bushland near those hills, yes?"

Harrison nodded. "Sure, then past that village then southwest down to Budgieweir. Why?"

"Those are other lights, right?" Arjun continued. "There, heading for the hills."

"Er… yes. You're right. You have a good eye. That's the way we came into the zone."

Harrison felt anxiety welling as it dawned on him where Arjun was going with this.

"The raiders are going the opposite way. Think this is another group?"

Arjun shrugged. "People trying to escape? Blues on patrol?"

"I really hope so," said Harrison. "Are you thinking they might turn down the road that brought us here?"

Arjun nodded.

Harrison jumped again as another splash came from the canal but was mindful of his head this time. He stared at the ripples on the surface but saw nothing more.

"What is that?" whispered Aditya.

"Well, these inland waterways have been overrun with carp since forever."

Harrison tried to sound hopeful with this explanation, wanting to believe it himself. He could not understand why the noise unnerved him more than the raid.

"Must be very large carp," Junior stated.

Harrison knew a whole person could jump into that canal and make less of a splash.

"We should get back," said Aditya. "If those other lights are bandits coming here, the others must know."

Nobody protested. If the two workers had survived the raid, for now they would have to fend for themselves. Harrison had no desire to remain back here any longer, though he knew it was a safer place should raiders attack Farm 1469's main buildings.

The group started to hurry back across the fields and Harrison set the drone to home in on his location as he rushed after them.

Arjun fell back and checked the controller screen.

"We need to monitor those lights."

Harrison nodded, wishing his drone was closer, not kilometres behind, where there was nothing more to see. There was no indication the Blues were sending aid to the burning farm, but if their farm was under threat too, he hoped their arses would be saved by Jon-Jon's amicable relations with the likes of Sergeant Selvin.

Crossing the field was taking forever.

"Let me see," Junior demanded, and Harrison tilted the controller tablet his way.

"It will catch up with us, Junior. Look there, that's the canal."

"Check the highway."

"I can't see anything. Hang on, was that a flicker below that hill? Yes. They're in that stretch of highway that goes through the forest. Soon we'll know if they take the turnoff and come this way or head for that village – or on to Budgieweir."

"Someone is driving the other way," said Junior, just as Harrison spotted a new light, much brighter, eastbound.

"Looks like they're going to meet up."

Without warning, the brighter light vanished. In its place came a flash of red.

"They are braking," said Junior.

It was now too dark to see the roads but Harrison knew what this meant.

"It is turning – that vehicle is coming this way," said Junior. "We are moving too slow. We must warn the others... Amahle."

Amahle nodded and without another word, the pair bolted. Harrison knew he could never keep up with the athletic pair and feared the rest of the group would run after them, leaving him behind, alone in the evening gloom, and spoke fast.

"We should hang back and monitor the situation. If we run right into the middle of an attack and die, we will be no good to anyone. Listen. I think I can hear our drone."

"We can handle ourselves, Harrison," said Arjun. "We are not afraid to fight. We know how."

"I know, I know and I think you are very impressive fighters indeed. If it comes to that, don't you think it more prudent to attack from ambush rather than charge straight in? Let us keep the upper hand by seeing what we are facing."

Then Harrison felt too puffed to keep talking and tapped the controller screen, trying to keep Arjun's attention there.

He looked up and saw the light of the fire pit ahead. None of the buildings were lit up. Either the electricity was off again or Jon-Jon had been forewarned in time to kill the lights.

Harrison heard the buzz of the UAV behind him. The screen said it was already below 100 feet. He cancelled the homing function and maintained the low altitude, manually flying the drone right past them, then over the dog run.

"Let's see what's on the road."

He saw two sets of headlights approaching.

"Arjun, Harrison, keep up," Aditya called back with urgency.

Jon-Jon's dogs barked with fury.

"Wait," Harrison protested. "Let's keep together – the drone's almost there. Look at this, guys. A truck. I think it's being tailed."

He flew over the vehicle, a small tip truck, the kind that he had seen deliver mulch and other landscaping supplies. They were travelling without headlights, driving by the fading natural light alone or perhaps the illumination coming from behind.

Two utes were closing in on the truck, driving side by side, their headlights on high beam.

The vehicles did not seem to be moving at speed – when he made a sharp turn and reversed the drone's course, Harrison was able to ensure it fell in behind them, keeping pace.

In the back of one ute stood a brute wielding a firearm. The other ute had its own passenger – a skinhead holding a kind of lance. Harrison could not see the drivers.

"Must be from the same raider group," said Arjun. "They like using those spears."

Harrison winced, remembering the fate of Trooper Garcia.

"Yes, but I wonder if that truck is with them."

He heard voices in the darkness ahead and looked up from the screen, realising they had reached the farm buildings.

"We should hide back behind there," said Harrison, indicating a metal shed nearby. "Let's keep away from the fire pit... or any building that looks like a good target."

He looked about for Junior and Amahle but could not see them anywhere. Then a shadow appeared in the gloom. Harrison yelped and fumbled, almost dropping the controller.

Arjun leapt forward, ready to fight.

"Stop there," said Aradhya.

"It's just me. It's just me," cried a familiar voice.

"Jacko?" said Aditya from the darkness behind him. "What are you doing back here?"

"Hiding. Everyone's saying we're being attacked by mad killers. Jon-Jon said not to worry and just stay together while we wait for the Blues. Uh-uh. Not me. I'm staying out of sight."

"If you want to see what's coming, take a look," said Harrison.

"Do I really want to know?" said Jacko.

Harrison showed him the drone's camera feed.

The utes had caught up with the tip truck. Red lights flashed as the truck braked and three shadowy figures suddenly emerged from its back. The firearm-wielding thug clutched his chest and tumbled out onto the road moments later. The vehicle in which he had been riding veered off the road, smashing headlong into the trunk of a small but sturdy tree.

Undeterred, the second vehicle drew beside the truck, to its left. The lancer sought a target, though against the bulky truck his weapon appeared rather pathetic to Harrison.

He flew the drone in closer. Another figure riding in the truck leaned out, taking aim at the lancer with a handgun. Harrison noticed the figure's face was covered by some kind of mask.

The lancer attempted to strike first, but his lunge was cut short when the masked figure fired. The man dropped his weapon and collapsed to his knees in the back of the ute.

Someone emerged from the truck's passenger side, literally riding shotgun. He discharged his weapon into the cabin of the ute, which slowed and fell behind.

"What is this, rival gangs?" Harrison mused aloud. "Oh crap, they've seen us."

Another figure in the back of the truck, face obscured by a bandanna, raised a firearm at the drone.

Harrison jabbed the controls, sending the UAV veering off over some trees. He flew it low and fast across the field just outside the dog run.

"Hope we're out of their firing line."

"Listen," said Arjun. "I can hear the truck coming."

"They're braking — I can see the lights through the trees," said Jacko. "Oh my god, they're really coming here."

"I'm bringing the drone back," Harrison announced, resetting the homing function. Moments later it arrived, hovering nearby. He set it down to land on the ground before him, shutting it down and killing the light of the controller.

He picked up the UAV and checked it over. It was too dark for a proper inspection but it was clear one of the landing struts had been cleaved off. It felt otherwise intact.

"Look," said Jacko. "Is the truck stopping? What do you think they're doing?"

Then, without warning, it lit up, headlights on high beam, engine roaring as it lurched forward. At the gates, Harrison could hear Jon-Jon's dogs going berserk.

They peered from their darkened hiding place as the truck swerved off the road and into the driveway, smashing through the gates with its bull-bar.

"Shit, the dogs," Harrison cursed.

The beasts poured out of their run, their dark forms giving chase as the truck made its way into the grounds. The attackers riding in the back of the truck emerged once more, unleashing volleys of gunfire at the pursuing dogs from the safety of their mobile castle. Though in no danger of a mauling, they kept up the slaughter.

The truck made straight for the overseer's house, where Jon-Jon must have just hit all the light switches, as the area was flooded with illumination. Harrison blinked, trying to get his eyes to adjust but realised his glasses were dusty too. He removed them for a quick polish with the hem of his shirt.

Putting them back on, he spied Jon-Jon's distinctive silhouette running around outside his house, carrying a rifle.

The overseer whistled to his dogs and shouted, "Come here. To me. To me."

Then Jon-Jon aimed his weapon and fired a couple of rounds at the truck as it smashed through his garden. The vehicle began to circle his house.

"Look, they're torching the place," said Jacko.

Harrison felt his heart rate rise as he watched flickering incendiaries hurled from the truck explode against the walls. He heard Jon-Jon's concubines squealing and wondered if they had the sense to get out before it was too late. The Molotov cocktails – or whatever they were – were effective, plumes of flame rising wherever they struck.

Jon-Jon fired again as the truck rounded the corner of the house, the bandits driving straight at him. He threw himself to one side – the wrong side.

Harrison saw the gunner lean out the side window and fire his shotgun twice. Jon-Jon swung about, trying to keep his feet, his weapon flying. Then he stumbled and fell.

The truck stopped suddenly and the attacker leapt from the passenger side door, running straight at the fallen overseer.

The killer was dressed in dark clothing, hooded and masked. He stood over Jon-Jon's convulsing body as it lay disarmed, helpless and prone. The Harrison saw the overseer attempt one last show of resistance – he had managed to detach his wrench but the action looked pathetic; he struggled to lift the tool.

The attacker stepped on the defiant arm, pinning it to the ground, and shouted something about "acceptable conduct". Then he pointed his weapon down, pumped another shell into the chamber and pulled the trigger.

"Farm 1469's going to need a new boss," Harrison murmured. "That guy was a slime-ball but he was our last line of defence. We'd better get out of here."

"Wait," said Aradhya. "What's he saying?"

The attacker pulled down his mask though Harrison could not make out his face. The man strode forth, moved to stand in front of the truck, a dark silhouette against the headlights. Harrison strained forward to listen to the man's words.

"It's all over, it's all over," the man cried. "The crimes of that man and his friends are finished."

One of the dogs emerged from the shadows, running straight at him. He raised his shotgun but it jammed and the dog leapt, tearing at the man's coat. Undeterred, the stranger slammed the butt of his gun into the dog's head then kicked it away.

The dog regathered itself, preparing to attack again. As the beast lunged, the man spun, but it gripped the hem of his coat. The man righted his weapon and fired. The dog collapsed, dead at his feet.

Then the man walked to a ladder affixed to the truck's side and climbed it. He joined the other attackers in the back and stood tall, looking around as the truck drove on, circling the other buildings.

Harrison could see the attackers in the back had pulled back hoods and lowered their cloth face masks though he could not make out any faces.

Jon-Jon's colourful concubines had fled their flaming home and were now collapsing all over their fallen lover in tears. One threw a shoe at the truck and screamed something unintelligible. The attackers paid her no heed.

Then a female voice began shouting. "We are workers just like you, we came here on a bus just like you. We came with you… here to this ag zone. You were sent here, while we went somewhere better. Come join us, while you still can."

"I think I know her," said Arjun, walking forward. His two countrymen followed.

"Wait, it might be a trap," Harrison urged. "We could be shipped off anywhere, just like those others we saw today."

The trio were undeterred but Jacko remained at his side in the shadows.

"You are free to choose your own destinies but choose fast," shouted Jon-Jon's murderer. "Grab all your gear now if you want to come with us. We will be leaving in five minutes."

"It sounds kinda fair dinkum," said Jacko. "Look, there's Junior and Amahle."

Junior was already on the ladder, its occupants helping him up and into the back of the truck. Then he turned and reached down to assist Amahle before climbing back out to sprint over to their lodgings.

"They didn't waste any time deciding. I must confess Junior has a good nose for sniffing out bullshit. Maybe you're right, Jacko."

Then they heard a growl somewhere in the darkness behind them, followed by a deep *Wwwwooof*. It was hard to tell how close the dog lurked but Harrison knew how fast the distance between them could be closed.

"Run," whispered Jacko.

They sprinted. Neither was particularly athletic and soon Harrison could hear the beast, its panting, growly sounds getting louder by the second. He chanced a look over his shoulder as he burst from the shadows into the lit-up area. Fortunately for him, Jacko was slower and fell behind.

Then Jacko veered away, making for one of the buildings. The beast chose to pursue Harrison. He was unable to find his voice to cry for help. He could hear it almost upon him. Glancing behind a second time, he saw it was that horrid white bitch with pink piggy eyes, the one who had wanted to eat him from the beginning.

Looking back was a mistake. Harrison tripped and fell forward, his glasses flying.

A gunshot rang out, then another. He pushed himself up a little, shaking, then turned and squinted at the twitching white heap on the ground behind him. Then he looked at the blurred figures in front, who he guessed he now owed a favour.

He was glad he had already stashed the drone and controller in his backpack – falling on his face, he hoped it remained undamaged.

One of the newcomers, a blonde with a high ponytail, holstered her pistol and approached as he struggled to his knees, checking his body was intact. She handed him his glasses.

As he put them on, he thanked the girl, then his mouth hung agape.

Harrison knew the face. The hair was wrong but the eyes, the freckles on her nose, the face shape were unmistakable. He had studied that sketch over and over.

He would join these people – because right in front of him, helping him to his feet, was the mysterious Sienna Jones.

22

Witek

So, he was "that boring, average guy who's in charge". As he lay in the still, silent darkness, reflecting on their achievements and unable to sleep, he decided he did not care, doubting whether the workers with loose tongues were capable of doing whatever was necessary to survive. They were like children.

The new arrivals were respectful. Witek noticed a quieter demeanour in most of them, guarded but alert – understandable given their relocation to an unknown environment and a very different kind of overseer to come to terms with.

What did matter to Witek was doing right by his team. He had agreed to do his duty and would see it through. He was only vexed by the fact the others were undisciplined. Missions had been successful so far but he saw the potential for problems and did not want mishaps on his watch.

Riku was hesitant, Chad was too loud and Sindy was reckless, at least when she was not preoccupied with her silly theories about paranormal things being responsible for everything. At least they had demonstrated a willingness to fight. Witek just had to keep them all alive.

After liberating Farm 1469, Kilo set about organising new groups, as proposed. Defences were upgraded and attempts were made to ensure everyone at Kirilia was familiar and comfortable with weapons. Defence drills were conducted. Witek agreed with Kilo that this life would be the new normal.

Raids by either Blues or desperados had taken place on other farms but Kirilia had been spared further unwanted visits, buying time for the recon team to scavenge more supplies. Kilo began net-working with the overseers of a few other farms, plotting how to overcome the Blues' air power. He was also securing new and better firearms via a trade deal with a wealthy local family across the valley.

The haul from the supply store in Brewerton was a great boon. Kilo knew that a manager once lived on the small farm next door and the key Sindy had found had made access easy.

They had broken into the gun cabinets and taken several rifles and a lot of ammunition. Their raid also equipped Kirilia with a plethora of useful gear: air compressors, fuel-powered generators, a couple of AdSoS solar generators, camping supplies and a lot of durable work clothing.

In the rear yard there had been vehicles too. Vlad had hotwired a small truck – only later had they found the spare key hidden within. The vehicle had proven an effective mobile platform from which to attack, or to transport people or goods.

Thinking of these gains did not help Witek relax. In time, he fell asleep but slipped into an odd, nonsensical dream. Karmen presented him with a plate laden with pierogi. He took one, hoping to taste a delectable savoury filling. Instead, to his horror, the dumpling dissolved in his hand, revealing a bloodshot eyeball staring up at him.

Witek woke with a curse, feeling only minutes of sleep had passed.

He hoped Karmen enjoyed better rest in her room within the shearers' quarters, her dreams more pleasant. He could not deny his fondness for her extended beyond physical attraction, though he took pains to ensure that she remained in the friend zone.

Then his thoughts were distracted by a commotion in the cattle yard. The herd sounded distressed and was moving about. It was otherwise too quiet, neither frog nor insect lending a voice to the usual chorus.

Witek grabbed his new rifle and crawled from his swag. Outside the shed, thick fog had settled. There was a little light though it was unclear if dawn had come.

The large forms of Nestor and Kyle from the security team jogged out of the mist and Witek hurried after them.

Kilo stood by the kitchen, awaiting their report.

"Two cattle mauled," Nestor explained. "Whatever did that, it left behind a mess."

"And pawprints," added Kyle. "They crisscross the pasture but are hard to track among all the hoofprints left by the cows."

Kilo nodded. "Follow me."

The overseer walked just a few metres then pointed at the ground. A trail of pawprints meandered around the buildings. Witek did not need to check the images on his Marektek to know they were the same. The spoor indicated the beast had wandered past the very buildings in which they slept.

"People are on edge, especially the newcomers," said Kilo. "For now, we will have to put aside our concerns about raiders and Blues. Someone at Kirilia might be mauled if we fail to deal with this creature first."

"I will gather my team and patrol the grounds," said Nestor.

"Go ahead," said Kilo.

The others vanished into the fog and Witek turned to Kilo.

"I want to see the cattle."

"Fine, but do not go alone," Kilo replied. "We have a trail so this thing can be tracked. Meet back at the armoury. Rocky has been busy."

Witek turned and ran back to Vlad, shook him awake and dragged him off to the cattle yard.

The herd huddled in one corner, while the bloody mess Nestor had described was on the opposite side. The carcasses' abdomens were torn open, their contents strewn about, but little flesh had been devoured.

"I think your friend is killing for sport, Witek," said Vlad with a yawn.

Witek checked his rifle and glanced around the mist. There was no sign of the beast.

"Perhaps, Vlad. Look at that that cow's throat. The jaws that did that must be large and powerful."

He walked along the enclosure's perimeter for a few minutes.

"Think it jumped over this corner post on its way out."

"And checked us out next," said Vlad.

The spoor did not lead away into bushland, but rather back to Kirilia.

"No more to see here," said Witek. "We must hurry to the armoury."

His team had gathered outside the shed, eating. Chad was having a lively conversation with Sindy. Her true identity had come into question, though Kilo insisted that they continue calling her "Sindy Mason" for now. She had changed her hairstyle, the usual twin braids replaced by a simple high ponytail.

"Our task today is to hunt whatever has been stalking us," Witek stated. "Any objections?"

Heads shook. Chad thumbed in the direction of the hills.

"If we pull this off, suppose we won't have to worry about the threat on that front. One less thing to keep us awake at night. Let's do this."

Rocky waved for them to enter the shed.

"You hunting? Uniforms, cloaks, masks, hoods no good. See what Rocky and Agus make for you."

Witek understood. The gear they had worn while scavenging and during the liberation of Farm 1469 was fine for concealing them from human eyes without impeding freedom of movement, but less practical in the bush.

Their all-purpose base apparel consisted of drab-coloured durable workwear, the kind worn by farmers and tradespeople. Kilo had prohibited hi-vis shirts.

"Choose your patrol armour," said Rocky. "Boss says maybe hot in Aussie sun, yesss, but extra protection to keep you alive."

Rocky had enhanced a lot of existing clothing. Jackets and vests made from leather, denim or workwear were ideal for modification and Witek's team had scavenged such garments from Brewerton.

In addition, a few wholly custom-made armours were also made – these took the form of a kind of harness protecting the front and back of the torso, which could be easily slipped over the head.

Rocky grinned and lit a cigarette, then nodded at the benches inside the shed where garments were laid out on display.

"These look good," said Witek. "Uncomplicated, quick and easy to equip. These would have taken time to make. Thank you both."

"Choose," said Rocky.

"No helmets or special pants, not yet, sorry," said Agus. "Maybe soon we make protection for knees, front of legs…"

"That's OK," said Sameera. "I think the right words are a very big *terima kasih* – these are amazing."

Riku rushed to the nearest bench and stopped by a denim jacket, which had some kind of embroidery on it visible between strips of rubber padding.

"These colours could work for me. Wait, what's this? Were these once part of metal signs? Very cool. Hey guys, there's even more at the back."

Witek joined him, perusing the diverse outfits. Nearest was a long plain black leather coat, tailored, smart and adorned with simple silver buttons. It lacked any protective enhancements and its sleeves and overall length were too long for his arms.

A shorter leather jacket looked promising.

"Too busy, too noisy," said Karmen, following his line of sight. "All those metal bits they've added will jingle more than Christmas. They will catch on all the bushes and branches too."

"You are right."

"We all know how obsessed you are with silence," Karmen added with a wink. "You never let us speak out there."

Witek smirked at her correct assessment. He wanted a team of scavenging ghosts. Avoiding possible conflict was how he ensured everyone kept returning unscathed.

"What about one of these?" said Karmen, lifting a vest. "You will feel more freedom of movement. Trust me."

She selected a biker-style leather vest and helped him into it. It was reinforced with strips of rubber cut from old car tyres. Two thicker chunks of rubber had also been affixed to the top of the garment, one on each side, to help protect the neck and shoulders.

"There," she said, tapping the front of the vest with her forefinger. "This will protect your heart and vitals."

"Thank you," he said, looking Karmen in the eye, feeling his face flushed but smiling, without even having to force the expression.

"Good deep interior pockets," he observed, checking the vest's inner lining. "Could be useful."

"It isn't fair. Do you realise that guys always get bigger, better pockets compared to those in ladies' clothing?" said Karmen.

He twisted about. Witek had once worn proper military body armour and this custom-made garment's balance was off. The weight of the rubber pieces on his shoulders felt cumbersome but unrestrictive.

Karmen watched him squirm awhile, then reached out with both hands and buttoned the front.

"Better?"

"Yes. More stable."

Witek rocked from side to side then nodded as Karmen patted and pulled at its sides.

He knew none of the garments would make them bullet-proof, despite their rubber and metal reinforcements. There was a reason modern soldiers did not suit up like mediaeval knights. However, it was feasible the patrol armour could deflect blows from hand weapons or low-velocity projectiles.

Karmen moved away, seeking something for herself. Witek exhaled, realising he had been holding his breath while she stood so close, then looked at his team.

"This one, oh yes, this is the one," said Riku, donning a harness comprised of miscellaneous metal plates. Its central chest piece was a large dark-blue metal toolbox lid, handle still attached, with a comical koala character printed on it.

"Make sure the metal pieces do not rub together and make too much noise," Witek instructed.

Riku danced about. Most of the plates had sufficient spacing that Witek was satisfied there was little risk of people hearing his team coming from kilometres away.

Vlad selected a light-brown World War II-style leather airman's jacket, complete with faded leather patches, then stepped forward and clapped Witek on the back, inclining his head at Chad.

The American was presenting Sindy with a charcoal-coloured jacket with a large red rose emblazoned on the back, complete with several thick leather pads stitched in place with care, to reinforce the shoulders and upper arms. Additional black leather padding had been added to the ends of the sleeves, serving as bracers to protect the forearms. She beamed at the Texan.

"That is one way to give a girl flowers," said Witek.

Vlad winked. "Chad found it in the back office of that supply store. He kept it hidden and gave it to Rocky to work on as soon as we got back."

Witek watched her put it on.

"A perfect fit. Those large pockets on the front look good for additional storage."

Vlad rolled his eyes.

"Witek. Hashtag mister practical. You should see romance in this gesture. But no. Immediately you go and be utilitarian."

"Somebody must be sensible, boring... and average... and focused on our mission." Witek raised his voice. "Is everybody happy with their selections? We must head out."

"Hey look at y'all," said Chad. "Now we got our cosplay sorted we can all head out to the nearest apocalypse convention."

"Except this gear might actually work," said Sameera. "At those conventions or on dystopian TV shows you always see girls wearing ridiculous sexy outfits that show off far too much flesh and therefore offer little to no protection."

"Excellent point," said Witek, "I am glad you have the sense to see that. Rocky, Agus, thank you."

Kilo was waiting outside. He studied each of them, then nodded curtly.

"Look the part and your battle is half won," Kilo said. "We will work on some freaky-looking face masks so you look even more intimidating. Of course, that does not apply to today's target. I would prefer waiting until we get our high-calibre weapons but fear there is no time. This predator must die before it kills again. If you find it and have a clear shot, take it.

"Stay together. Stay alert. Use the land to your advantage. Cover each other. Remember our tactical retreat drills. Follow your team leader's directions.

"That is all. Good luck. Hurry, while the trail is still fresh. Nestor learned where it left Kirilia – it made for the bush that way, between those two trees."

"So, you are not coming with us?" asked Riku.

"Something is up. Word just came in that the Blues are up early and moving about the valley. I doubt they have learned of our actions at Farm 1469, yet I will stay here, just in case. Now go."

Witek nodded and led his team out, eyes fixed on the ground. He felt his nose become wet – if he believed such nonsense, he would assume he was a hound in a previous life.

The spoor led them north along the old stock route trail, then veered east, on rising ground to the national park's fence line.

Riku stepped out in front.

"Guys, guys, hang on. Before we climb over... do you think the boss considers us expendable?"

Witek exhaled, perhaps with too much force.

"Why? What's on your mind, Riku?"

"We follow his tasks but know nothing of his life before Kirilia. What about that amulet he wears? Maybe he is a fanatical follower of Zach and Aree, or the leader of some strange cult of his own... and in his mind, we are his new disciples."

"The ankh he wears around his neck?" said Chad, laughing. "It's just an ancient symbol of life, man. Don't think I've seen Zach, Aree or their CHAPs wear one of those. They're not his style of music anyway – I've heard the boss man listening to '80s rock bands. Hell, he might have been a New Age hippie stoner all his life for all we know. Hey, check out what I wear.”

Chad revealed a tooth worn on a necklace threaded with little cylinders of painted wood and many beads, then deepened his voice.

“Tonight, I will be sacrificing y'all to Maxine, the mako shark demon. Come on, it's just his bling, man. We'll ask the boss straight up about it later on.”

Riku folded his arms.

“Well, for someone who honours life, he is comfortable with killing people. Is everyone happy killing for him?”

“I kill so we can live,” Witek replied. “In the truck, we were under attack. We defended ourselves so we could rescue those workers.”

“Yeah man, those freaks were coming for our blood,” said Chad.

Witek realised everyone in the squad except Riku and Karmen had killed a person now. Those two had helped clear the dogs from Farm 1469.

“We did what we had to,” said Sindy.

“Including firebombing that overseer's house?” Riku pressed.

Witek rubbed the back of his neck.

“Kilo's plan was to flush out the overseer and take him down. The plan worked.”

“I know, Witek, but we were lucky no workers were in the house,” said Karmen.

“But there weren't,” said Sindy. “We got every worker safely back to Kirilia. Kilo could have killed the wives too. They were obviously loyal to that horrid man. Look how they carried on when he died. Even so, Kilo left them to live.”

“Left them to their fates, you mean,” said Karmen. “Left them behind to die.”

"The wives were not our responsibility," said Sameera. "The workers were. We could have easily been the ones sent to that farm. Duc's sister said that overseer was a monster. Our actions probably saved many from an awful fate."

"Probably," said Karmen. "How much longer will we be expected to kill for our overseer? He calls it justice but —"

Vlad cut her off. "Kilo has no issue with any of us leaving Kirilia at any time, remember? If your conscience cannot handle things, well…"

"And go where?" said Riku. "We should consider moving, if we find a more peaceful place."

"Buddy, I hate to break it to you but the world ain't rainbows and unicorns anymore," said Chad. "Now, I am real sorry if that sounds insensitive to y'all but I have no doubt this is how the whole planet is now. People sometimes have to do ugly things for the greater good. That overseer and those bandits are not the last monsters we're gonna see."

Witek felt he was losing control. He regretted allowing so much time for his team to air their grievances. They were fracturing just when he needed them working together, focused. This was not the time for this discussion.

"Is everyone still happy to go on this hunt?" he said, almost shouting. "Nobody will think less of you if you turn back. It will be dangerous."

"I am cool," said Riku. "We stick to the plan, back each other up, right?"

Witek was relieved to see quiet nods all round but the cracks in their unity made him uncertain. Doubt would not help. Action would.

So, Witek strode to the fence line.

"Look, it jumped over here," said Chad. "Check out that big corner post. Are those scratches? Hey Sindy, what if it's a yowie, marking its territory."

"A what?" said Witek, tilting his head.

"A yowie, man. Like an Australian bigfoot, right? Those other marks we saw were yowie runes."

"Right, dude," Sindy laughed. "I thought yowies lived up north, in the Pilliga Scrub. Guess a few got cut off from their mates when the land was carved up by settlers in the old days. Maybe a small group has been living in these very hills ever since."

"They have no idea what are they talking about, eh Witek?" said Vlad. "Those scratches were clearly made by the feet of the house of Baba Yaga."

"Yes, Vlad, just as this whole situation was caused by *morowa dziewica* – the plague maiden. These are all just folk stories. Enough nonsense. We must keep our heads clear. This is a natural creature. Did you ever see lion footprints in Africa, Sameera?"

"I was a city girl. I never went on safari and we do not have lions roaming all over South Africa."

"OK. Fine. Well, I see nothing unusual about these marks. Regular animals do that to sharpen their claws. Come on."

Witek climbed the corner post and jumped over, then turned to help the others.

The spoor was easy to follow in the dusty red earth. It led them along a natural animal trail amid eucalypts, wattles and stands of small conifers, all sparse enough there was little risk of ambush. Other animals had used the trail: kangaroos or perhaps wallabies, something with a cloven hoof as well.

The fog was lifting, the morning now full of birdsong. The path took them around a hill then down into a wide valley. Witek remembered the drone flying over this area before it attacked. He could see the peak Kilo called a "camel's hump" off to the right. The sandy bed of an ephemeral creek bed meandered across the valley floor.

He was about to cross over when Sindy pointed at some different tracks – worn by somebody with small shoes.

"Think those weird Brewerton kids hang out here too?" said Sameera.

"Something feels off about them," said Sindy.

"Normal human footprints," Witek said with a sigh. "We are not the very first people to ever hike here. We do not need to figure out what brand of shoes they wore or where they went. Hurry on."

The footprints did remind him of those he had seen near the bodies in that rock cleft but now was not the time for distraction by other riddles.

"Nah. Baby yowies for sure, man," Chad murmured, eliciting a giggle from Sindy.

Witek ignored them and pushed on across the valley then up a hillside.

"The bush is getting thicker here," Sameera whispered.

Witek nodded and slowed his pace.

"Be on guard. Listen."

"I can't hear anything but got a whiff of something nasty," said Karmen.

"Keep moving," Witek instructed, then sniffed. "You are right. There is something dead."

Minutes later, he found the source. A pair of crows took to the air. They had been feasting on the remains of a goat. Its head was twisted backward, throat torn open. A fresh kill. The foul smell was not that of rotting flesh – it was more to do with the fact that its stomach chambers had been breached, their semi-digested contents scattered about the area. A leg was missing.

"Look familiar, Witek?" said Vlad.

"Classic yowie kill, Chad," Sindy whispered.

"Looks like our shaggy friend had breakfast and saved the leg to snack on later," the Texan replied.

"It must be close by," said Riku, eyeing the undergrowth. "A predator would not leave its kill unfinished."

"I feel we are not dealing with a normal hunter," said Sindy.

Witek noted her tone was serious now.

"I admit this seems odd," he said. "It was the same with the cattle. We probably spooked it. The prints continue along the trail here. Keep moving but remain vigilant."

The path circled around the next hillside and the bush began to thin out. The trail became rockier underfoot, making it hard to tell if their quarry had wandered off a different away.

Then the path split and Witek cursed under his breath. He saw a ravine ahead and held up his arm, pausing to scan the area. A thin animal trail led off to the right on the stony ground overlooking the chasm, while the wider left path wound down around several boulders, providing access to the valley floor.

"We will take the high ground and check what is down there from the top," said Witek. "Move low and quiet. We have less cover now."

Minutes later, the animal trail petered out. There was nothing but exposed rock underfoot, crowned in patches by dead moss and silvery-white lichen. Pellets of faecal matter scattered all about indicated recent animal activity.

Witek led his team single file, close to the edge of the ravine, taking care where to place each slow step. Somewhere ahead, across the ravine, he heard the cracking echoes of a stone bounce down to the bottom. He held his breath, raised his rifle and squinted. There was no movement visible along the rim of the chasm or among the weather-stained rocks forming its steep opposite slope.

He lowered his aim, scanning the base of the valley. There was just stone, vegetation and a few muddy patches. After several seconds, Witek exhaled and moved on.

Soon the head of the gorge came into view. There, the gradient of the drop was vertical, and Witek saw many streak marks blacken the rockface there, which became even darker further down. He wondered how long it had been since it had rained enough for water to cascade there and resurrect a creek at the bottom of the ravine.

He paused, wiping his wet nose. A breeze whistled through the small conifers. It almost sounded musical to Witek, as if someone was playing some kind of reed instrument, its notes floating to him on the breeze. Something did not feel quite right.

"Witek," Vlad whispered, clamping a hand on his shoulder, making him jump. He followed his friend's gaze, which was fixed on the bottom of the ravine.

Witek steadied his breathing and watched. Then he saw something – a large dark form slipped between boulders and vegetation, moving up the gorge.

He fixed his eyes on a gap and waited. Then it came into full view.

An enormous black cat was prowling along the valley floor. Witek could see it was unmistakably feline and no regular feral. So, the legend of Australia's big cats was true. The threat came from an ordinary creature, which could be neutralised. Timing would be crucial. The beast slipped from sight behind a vine-covered boulder.

"There is your yowie," Witek whispered. "Nothing unnatural. We have no clear shot. We will track it from up here and fire when it reaches the next open space. Do not shoot until I say… and watch your step."

Witek did his best not to kick pebbles into the ravine as he moved on in a half-crouch.

Near the rockface at the head of the ravine was a large open area, a kind of rocky amphitheatre. Witek was no geologist but it almost looked like a narrow volcanic intrusion had pushed through the surrounding red-brown conglomerate at the base of the ephemeral waterfall, as it was much darker than any of the water streaks staining the rockface higher up.

If the beast moved up to that dead end, there would be a chance for two or three volleys of gunfire. Witek raised his rifle, waiting for the cat to appear. Then he saw the head emerge from behind its cover, a stack of ancient boulders forming a column.

"Hold," he whispered.

The cat twisted its big pointy ears back. What was it waiting for?

"Look back there – is that Sindy?" whispered Karmen.

The blonde Australian was at the bottom of the gorge, stalking through vines along a dry watercourse, handgun drawn, following the cat's path.

Witek exhaled and gritted his teeth. He was the one responsible for keeping the team together. A lost chance for a kill was annoying. Sindy placing her own life in danger was something he could not accept.

The cat bolted across the natural amphitheatre with extraordinary speed towards the darker rock on the far side. It appeared to him the foolish girl had decided to corner the beast there. He knew if they missed, it might turn and be upon her in seconds.

"Hold," Witek hissed. "Wait until it slows."

The cat halted by the rockface and looked over its shoulder. Witek took aim at its chest. Then the beast lowered its head and trotted forward, into the stone.

"What? Where did it just go?" said Sameera.

"There must be a crack or cave we cannot see," said Witek.

"No, Witek. That is a solid rock wall," said Vlad.

His friend was right. There was no cleft, rock shelter or cave. This could only be some kind of optical illusion.

"I am climbing down," Witek announced. "It is hiding. I must stop Sindy before she gets too close. Remember, do not fire until I say."

The slope was steep below his position but not so much that he was unable to descend. He hit a pebbly section and slid, gripping his rifle hard.

Witek detected movement in his peripheral vision and tried to slow his descent. He raised his head in time to glimpse the cat dashing back the way it had come. By the time he regained control of his slide it was out of sight, behind the rock column in the middle of the canyon. Nobody had fired a shot from above.

Sindy was directly below now, on the near side of the same rock column, oblivious to the danger as she paused to look up at him. Witek hurried down to join her. She looked sheepish but there was a defiant glint in her eye and she did not stop striding with determination across the amphitheatre to the waterfall.

"What are you doing?" Witek whispered. "It is right there behind that rock."

He kept his weapon trained on the place where he had lost sight of the beast and was forced to walk backwards to keep up with Sindy.

"I saw something here, Witek."

"Correct, the beast was here but I saw it run back. You cannot sneak away from the group like this because of some… impulse."

"Look," the girl said, twirling her pendant with her free hand, irritation on her face. "If I get myself killed it's on me. Kilo said we are each responsible for ourselves. Remember?"

"No. I cannot accept this. Kilo commanded us to watch each other's back. Work together. We are not a team if we do not communicate. You did not tell any of us you were leaving. Why would you think hunting alone is a better idea?"

"I… I don't know. I had to come down here. For a moment, that was all I could think of. There is something here, other than the beast. Right here. I need to… understand."

While Witek gazed back down the ravine, he realised Sindy's attention was fixed on the waterfall. He glanced over his shoulder and was astonished to find no gaps in the rock wall. They had witnessed the cat vanish here but there was no space large enough to accommodate anything.

He realised Sindy's speech was slow. Maybe she had found some kind of drug while scavenging. If so, she – and anyone else partaking – were liabilities. He would have a discussion with Kilo about making some adjustments to his group.

"I am responsible for this team and everybody in it and I cannot – will not – lose anyone."

He glanced up at the others far above for some indication as to where the predator went. Everyone was shaking their heads.

Sindy looked Witek dead in the eye as her hand reached for the dark rock wall, where a tiny trickle of water dribbled down from above. Unlike the surrounding knobbly conglomerate, the small intrusion of darker rock was comprised of a series of interlocking vertical geometric columns, their exposed surfaces smooth. The formation triggered a childhood memory of a family visit to Gdańsk, where a nine-year-old Witek had gawped at the Oliwa Cathedral's incredible pipe organ.

The girl withdrew her hand and studied Witek's face, measuring him before speaking, her voice normal again.

"What is your problem? I appreciate your concern about our welfare but there's more to it, isn't there?"

Witek flushed and involuntarily averted his eyes.

"I knew it. Spill the tea. What's eating you?"

"A man is entitled to his privacy," he muttered. "What about you? You have been using an alias all this time, no? Why? What is your big secret? We do not even know what to call you."

She studied the rock wall for several seconds.

"Time for truths?"

"I see no other way we can continue working as a team," he admitted and sighed.

"Very well. My real name is Sienna. Sienna Jones."

She stroked the rock wall.

"The authorities took away my family and now they are after me. My parents did not like the way our country was going and were critical of the new government but I can't believe any of them ever did something treasonous. They just wanted to break away and make sure we could still live a good and free life, like Aussies did in the past.

"Mum and Dad had friends down south in a remote part of Victoria, living off-grid in an area that still gets enough rainfall. Not full-on preppers or anything but Dad said they were our best chance at surviving the pandemic. We hit the road before things got bad."

"And this name thing?" asked Witek.

"Sindy Mason is just my travelling name – close to my real name, easy to remember. We pretended we were unrelated. Somehow, I was the only one who fooled the government goons but now they know they made a mistake.

"I don't get why. I'm no threat. I know nothing but sure as hell don't want to be arrested for stuff I'm not even involved in."

"Wow. OK then, Sin… or… Sienna. Do you think they want to use you, perhaps to extract information from your parents?"

This was intriguing. Witek knew he was ignorant about Australia's recent political turmoil. He supposed just like in Poland and elsewhere there were different factions, each with their own vision for the future of their nation.

"That's what I'm afraid of, Witek. This is why I've tried to act like just another random lost kid. So, that's my story. Your turn."

The tall girl — Sienna — continued studying the rock with her large dark eyes and Witek could not fathom why it fascinated her.

"You were a soldier, right?" she pressed. "I feel... something happened then, back in Poland. Yes?"

Witek took a step back, wondering whether this Sienna was simply good at reading people or possessed some deeper intuition. Perhaps it could ease his burden speaking to somebody less likely to be critical. He took a deep breath, keeping his eyes fixed on the ravine, then spoke.

"You are right. Did you know national service was reintroduced for young men and women in Poland due to political instability in eastern Europe?"

"Political insta...? Hmph. Dad used to say our media's more likely to make a headline of some random house fire in Sydney, where nobody was even killed, than report on important stuff that's really going on. What was it like?"

"The service was fine. I loved the challenge, until the time I... I made a... poor choice that cost the lives of everyone in my squad. It is a miracle I am not in a military prison. My father and grandfather were disgusted at the shame I brought to the Zabrewski family name. I did not care about that. I did not even care what punishment I received. All that mattered was my friends. They were the people I failed and they were the ones... dear to me.

"I was formally disciplined and sent home and that was the end of my military career. I had no idea what I was going to do with my life."

"Oh man. This is... how you came to be here?"

"Marcelina was already working here. She did not judge me. She suggested I go abroad too. So, I did, and she was right. I worked hard and I met Vlad and tried to have fun. Before I could meet up with Marcelina... pandemic, lockdown, you know the rest."

"Wow. Dude, that is so intense. I am sorry, Witek. Does Vlad know?"

Witek shook his head. "Not so much. He may suspect something; I am happy if people like him just think me moody."

"If this is too much, you can step down as team leader. You don't have to be responsible for us. Walk away, pick up the trail of your cousin. Check every farm in the zone if you have to. Kilo will understand. Witek, you don't have to put yourself through this to somehow redeem yourself."

"I can never redeem myself. It is true I never wanted this task, but am the only one out of the seven of us with proper military training. I have no choice."

"Well, remember we're all in a different world now. We can't control everything that happens, just do our best to survive and, well, you and Kilo were right... back each other up. So, if I die because of my own stupidity, it's all on me. Mum used to say I was an impulsive, wilful child. I guess I still am and I'm OK with that."

They were silent for a time.

"What the –" Sienna blurted out.

Witek whirled in time to see her arm *inside* the rock wall. She withdrew it and stepped backwards. She had found no hole but for just a moment, there was a black patch, far darker than the wall itself, left in her arm's wake. Then the rock returned to its natural hue.

Perhaps he was the one under the influence of something.

"W–What just happened?" he stammered.

Sienna was flicking her arm at the rock, as if shaking something off, then backed away, raising her pistol.

"If my arm can go in and come back out, so can… anything."

"Impossible. That is solid rock."

"Told you there was something odd out here."

"Witek," Vlad yelled down from above.

All five were gesticulating back down the ravine. There was some kind of disturbance. The sound was indistinct, a long way off, perhaps back near the mouth of the gorge.

The pair advanced down the creek bed. Witek glanced back at the volcanic rock wall one more time before crossing the open space. He slowed as they approached the rock column, wary of the foliage cascading down its face.

"It's too big to hide in those wonga wonga vines, Witek."

He nodded and the pair moved on, the rest of the team keeping pace back up top.

The canyon widened near its mouth and the slopes to either side were much less steep.

Some birds squawked in alarm and took flight.

"Australian noisy miners," said Sienna, watching them scatter. "Gotta feeling they're not just defending their turf like that lot in Brewerton."

Suddenly there was another commotion ahead, the crack of stone on stone. Witek held up one hand then raised his rifle, Sienna standing her ground at his side, pistol raised.

Someone burst into view momentarily, a slim figure sprinting between two boulders.

"Hold your fire," Witek commanded. "Don't shoot until I do. OK?"

"OK."

The figure dashed out from a boulder into plain view. The new-comer was hooded, lean, lanky, perhaps a little shorter than Witek although it was hard to tell because upon sighting them, it ran to one side of the ravine, ducked under a large fallen log then pushed behind another curtain of wonga wonga vines and remained there.

Witek stepped forward, hearing a rustle in the vines as he advanced.

"Careful," Sienna whispered. "I saw a weapon."

Witek heard someone else approaching, in the wake of the first figure. He recalled the girls' chatter about kids wearing hoods in Brewerton. Perhaps a gang of youngsters really did have a hideout in these hills. There was supposed to be an old copper mine some-where out here – a logical place to seek shelter.

However, the second figure to emerge was no child. It was the cat. Witek could hear his heartbeat as he locked eyes with the beast. It was wholly black save for its large green eyes and a little patch of white fur on its chest. It silently sprang up onto the log, flattened its ears and hissed.

Witek took a step back. It was large enough to challenge a lion or tiger. It was no panther either – the ears were not small and rounded like typical big cats, but large, triangular and pointed, almost as if it were a gigantic house cat.

The massive feline leapt from the log and charged. There was no time to hesitate. Witek fired and immediately reloaded.

It was still coming and would be on him in seconds. He fired again, gritting his teeth. There would be no time for another shot.

Then multiple shots rang out as Sienna unloaded her entire clip. Witek threw himself sideways to evade the beast's unstoppable bulk.

Rising to one knee, he turned about, fumbling with the bolt of his weapon, heart thumping in his ears.

The beast had crashed into a pile of large mossy rocks. It bared its teeth but struggled to regain its footing. Witek could see the white patch on its chest was stained red. The cat stood, wobbled, then collapsed. He carefully aimed for where he assumed its heart would be and pulled the trigger. This time the beast did not rise. It shuddered a little, then lay still.

Witek stood, trying to slow his breathing.

"I don't feel great about this," said Sienna. "Such a beautiful animal."

"We had no choice. Just like at the winery. Once again though, we are still alive."

This girl's recklessness was exasperating but Witek appreciated that she would do whatever was necessary when it came to survival.

The wonga wonga vines rustled once more and the hidden figure revealed itself.

Sienna had been correct about weapons — a sheathed blade swung from a belt and long fingers clutched an ornate crossbow. Witek noted it was not loaded and shifted his eyes from the weapon to the hooded face.

The figure regarded them for a while with large eyes boasting irises of a golden yellow hue. Then the hood was lifted and a cloth mask lowered.

Standing before them was no teenager. Nor was he even human. A wide mouth grinned at them from beneath a rather long greyish nose and overlarge ears framed a thin face. The creature's skin elsewhere was of the same odd pallor, making his colourful eyes stand out even more, while his hair was shiny, long, dark brown and worn in neat plaits.

"What is this?" Witek whispered, blinking in disbelief. "A demon? I have not been sleeping. No, I am hallucinating. Someone put drugs in my flask."

"In that case we're both trippin' balls, Witek, because right now I can see, well, some kind of... goblin?"

The creature spoke. "Ha. People of the world. You must classify all and name all."

He spoke with intonations that sounded almost familiar. Perhaps vaguely like French. Witek strained to listen as the being continued speaking.

"Many names you have for us. 'Demon' to some, 'goblin' to many, yes, 'hobgoblin' yes, 'kobold' too. Many names we have for you, people of the world, but I will not offend – ha. Instead, I thank you for your assistance."

Witek gaped. "I cannot accept this is real."

"That outfit," said Sienna. "Some kind of woven fibre? Finely tailored. I've never seen such a thing but it is magnificent."

"Thank you kindly," said the creature, lowering his weapon and fixing golden eyes upon her. "Grandmother made this for me."

This was ridiculous – a mythological creature in rural Australia speaking in plain English. Witek realised he was back at Kirilia – this whole outing another bizarre dream.

"I am Sienna."

The girl thumped him. He was clearly awake.

"Ah, I am Witek."

"I see. 'Sienna of Kirilia' you are then. 'Witek Tree-man of Kirilia' you are then."

"You know about my tree…"

"There is much we see and more we know."

"That marking – the glyphs," said Sienna. "It is your language. You scratch it into trees. Am I right?"

He did not reply but the smile broadened upon his grey face.

"I am honour bound to share my name too. Know that we do not give our names freely to people of the world. I am Briggo, Belden is home. You must know there is no Belden now, just autobahn. I never saw Belden; my family has lived for generations in our home beyond Lynna. Understand?"

"Er… no," Witek managed.

Witek and his family were Catholic though he had lost what faith he had when he lost his friends. Even so, this madness did not fit in with the universe he knew, religious or otherwise.

"Biblical apocalypse," he murmured to Sienna. "Demons in the wake of pestilence. 'Belden' and 'Lynna' must be planes of Hell from whence this imp came."

Sienna touched his arm and spoke. "I am sorry, Briggo. We do not know what you are referring to."

"I do not understand his nonsense about an autobahn," Witek said to Sienna. "Roads in your country are referred to as 'highways' or 'freeways', am I right?"

The creature ignored his comments and studied Sienna before

addressing her.

"You are confused, Sienna. Oh, but you know Lynna. Yes. I see you know."

Witek noticed the way Sienna averted her eyes. There were layers of mystery to this girl, far beyond the business about her identity.

"So Briggo. Are you the only g—" Sienna paused.

"The word 'goblin' does not offend; people of the world have used it for centuries. No, I am not alone. Eldro could take us back beyond Lynna but Eldro is dead and my folk remain in the world. Maybe not for long. Maybe you can help, Sienna."

"Lynna. Is that..." She pointed back up the ravine.

"Yes. Few can travel through from here but when Lynna is stable, anyone can travel the other way, from beyond... with some risk."

"What risk?" asked Sienna.

"Lost in time. Maybe eaten in Lynna. We came to the world with Eldro. Therefore, no risk for us."

Witek's head ached but he forced himself to follow and comprehend the discussion. His mastery of English was better than many of his countrymen but this was baffling.

"Mówisz po polsku?" he ventured.

Briggo looked at him in silence.

"I did not expect you to understand. Have you seen or perhaps met a person who looks a little like me, but female? Maybe passing by this way?"

"Nobody like you, Tree-man."

Witek grimaced. "I see. So, please explain this to me. Are you saying this 'Lynna' is like a doorway or a road from... a place beyond, am I right?"

He refrained from using the word "Hell".

"I know you do not believe, though you begin to understand. Even so, you do not know Lynna, not like Sienna. You are like me."

"So, you say that you and I cannot put our hand into that rock wall, no?"

"Correct. From this side, here in the world, it is impossible for you, human. Impossible for me too."

"So, what lies beyond?" Witek asked.

"I am not honour bound to speak of that, human," said Briggo. "This is forbidden."

"Let me ask a different question. This beast – did it come from beyond Lynna?"

"Oh yes. She did not live near our home. She is from someplace else. A rare kind, a dangerous kind, yes, one who can travel both ways. A beast favoured by some but not my folk.

"This one killed and ate Eldro. Now, we will no longer be hunted and Eldro is avenged. My folk will be pleased. I hope we are fated to never meet another of her kind."

"So, you are saying it was alone," said Witek "We do not need to worry about more of them, no?"

"Correct, Tree-man. No more have travelled here."

"I see. Then why did it come here?"

"She was a hunter and, well, because she could. She was simply expressing her natural instincts to explore new territory and seek prey therein."

Briggo scratched the side of his nose.

Witek sighed. "I am responsible for the security of the people of Kirilia. I need to know if there are other... things in or beyond that place. More big cats. Anything else that could be a threat. You said something about a risk of being eaten while travelling through. Is that where these cats hunt?"

"No. Only here in the world or beyond Lynna. They are very smart cats, yes, very cunning, but normal predators in every other way. Within Lynna, they only travel to or from the other side. Travel fast. Nothing more."

"If not these cats, then what, Briggo?" asked Sienna, her brow furrowed. "What abnormal predators can eat you there – in Lynna itself?"

"I thought you would already… wait, I am sorry. I have spoken far beyond my grateful obligation to you. I cannot say more. Our leaders should speak."

"Very well. How do we arrange such a meeting?" asked Witek. "Where are the others in your group?"

"We are always watching. Our leader will speak when the time is right. We will meet again. Thank you again. Sincerely, thank you."

With that the goblin bowed in a manner that reminded Witek of something from a mediaeval dance and replaced his mask and hood. He turned and dashed away with great agility and speed, leaping from rock to rock as he ascended the hill to the north of the ravine, away from Kirilia.

"Goblin parkour – never thought I'd live to see that," said Sienna, staring at the place where Briggo vanished from sight. "Don't forget the receipts."

"I did not." Witek took out his Marektek and proceeded to photograph the huge dead cat to show Kilo their task was done.

By the time he was satisfied with his evidence, the others

arrived, each of them wide eyed and speechless.

Chad spoke first. "Oh man, please tell me my eyes have been seeing straight."

"They have, dude," said Sienna.

"I'm disappointed you didn't bag me a yowie."

"Forget your yowies, it's not even a panther, nor any cat I know of," said Sameera, running her fingertips over dark fur. "Where on earth could such a beast have come from?"

"Nowhere on earth, sis," said Sienna.

Witek felt eyes upon him.

"I do not know what we are dealing with," he sighed. "I admit Sienna has been right. Things are not normal out here but there will be an explanation."

"Thanks, Witek," said Sienna. "I'll tell you one thing that's real — none of us have to worry anymore about being taken away and mauled."

Witek frowned, remembering Marcelina. He still believed she had spent time in or near the ag zone but had learned nothing of her fate. There was no way to know if this creature was responsible. Brooding would have to wait. He had to ensure his team returned to Kirilia safe and unharmed.

"Our mission is not yet over," he muttered. "We must get back and report. Then we can rest... and try to understand."

————

Later that evening, long after sunset, Witek was free to enjoy a shower. He almost fell asleep on his feet while the water washed the long day's grime from his face. He welcomed this moment of solitude, able to gather his thoughts and look forward to the oblivion of real sleep. Kirilia was a little safer.

While making his way back through the shearers' quarters from the bathroom, he was intercepted by Karmen, standing in the doorway to her room, brushing her long, damp hair. He could smell the conditioner she used – scavenged spoils put to use.

"Feeling fresh?" she said.

"Yes, thank you. Sleepy too. I will collapse on my bed."

"Should we talk a little first?" said Karmen, looking into his eyes.

"It is late. We should both rest. Kilo will have more questions in the morning."

"Yet you found time for a private conversation with Sin—Sienna today. Right in the middle of the mission, you made time for her. OK, fine. I see she is somehow special to you."

"Sienna? No. That was different. I mean, we worked well as a team, at least in the end. But... no. If I could allow myself to become involved with someone, well, I would..."

She looked deeper into his eyes. Karmen's were truly enchanting. No. He could not continue like this. Witek had promised himself he would not let himself become close to another. Never again.

He had not told Sienna the full story. Witek could not bear to lose another he let himself care about. That would end him. He had to ensure he was a machine, effective, reliable and unable to feel anything. Remaining alone was the only way. Safest for all concerned.

Yet today, Witek had been truly challenged. Not just physically. His thoughts, his beliefs, his very understanding of reality. Perhaps that stern promise he had made to himself could be challenged too. Just a little.

Karmen took his hand and whispered in his ear, "*Che, Boludo.*"

He had no idea if it was a term of endearment or an insult. Maybe a bit of both. Whatever. Witek did not resist as Karmen drew him into her bedroom.

23

Phuong

"Watch over your sisters and the kids. Go."

The urgent tone of Rosario Rossi's voice troubled Phuong.

"Come on, stay close," said Giuseppe, running down a hallway.

It was a chaotic scene in the bedrooms. Nonna Rossi was trying to calm everyone. Phuong wasn't sure if her loud voice was a help or a hindrance.

"What's going on? Giuseppe, tell us what's happening," said one of his teary sisters.

"Someone's coming. Dad said stay inside. All of you stay in the back bedrooms. I'll check it out from my room. This way, Foo."

Giuseppe's room had its own small balcony, as did all the east-facing bedrooms.

"We'll watch from here," he said, crouching behind the balustrade.

Phuong stayed low, put the Lite Shot UAV down by her side and looked out.

The sound of an engine was becoming increasingly loud. Something large was coming up the road from Budgieweir.

"Look there," said Phuong.

She pointed down the long straight driveway. An armoured car was parked outside the front gate. Three figures wandered about on the road but were not trespassing on Rossi land.

"Blues," she said. "What do you think they're doing here?"

Then they saw the truck. It was like one Phuong had seen out on the highway hauling supplies back to Canberra, but while its cabin was reinforced with protective armour, it was not hauling a trailer.

The men outside the gate hurried aside as the truck slowed and swung into the driveway, its massive bull-bar smashing the gate aside with ease, toppling a white lion from its brick pillar.

The engine growled as the driver shifted to a lower gear to climb the wide concrete driveway. The men on foot scrambled into the armoured car and followed. To her left, Phuong could see the main balcony, where Rosario and his brothers loaded their weapons. Tina was still barking somewhere out back.

A familiar knot of anxiety twisted Phuong's insides as she spied the distinctive uniforms. The Blues reached the top of the driveway, circled the white fountain in the centre of the cul-de-sac and stopped there. They killed the engines and armed troopers got out, taking positions behind their vehicles. Another man, who had been driving the armoured car, emerged next, leering at the mansion's main balcony.

"Oh, it's him — it's Selvin," Phuong whispered, choking on her words.

"That dog you were talking about? That's him?"

She managed a nod, feeling nauseated.

"Is this how the Rossi family welcomes guests?" shouted Selvin.

Still smiling, his eyes flicked away from Rosario and his

brothers, scanning the mansion.

Phuong shrank lower and froze as his gaze lingered where she and Giuseppe crouched. His eyes alone felt like they were violating her.

"You can lower your weapons. We've just come round for a little chat."

"Then I take it you will be building me a new gate on your way out," Rosario replied, his weapon remaining trained on the Blues.

The air was still, no breeze dispersing the tension between the two parties. Selvin maintained his cocky smirk, unfazed by the Rossi's larger, heavier rifles.

"You of all people can afford a new one. Rosario Rossi: I'd say just about the richest man in the area, with his dear little princesses who get luxury cars when they turn sixteen."

Selvin licked his lips and Phuong cringed. Rosario and his brothers remained silent, not allowing the officer to provoke a reaction.

Undeterred, Selvin continued his rant, his delivery theatrical.

"Do you really think anyone in the valley believed you got all this…" he paused, looking about at the Rossi's trappings with a resentful sneer, "…through honest business deals? A ridiculously successful investment? Come on."

His mockery was met with continued silence. Phuong would not judge the family for their past. How they treated her was all that mattered.

"We know about your little family outing to Brewerton. Just as we know which girl took off and left her assigned worksite without official authorisation."

Phuong felt like she had been shot. Selvin was here for her. She feared the family might hand her over to keep the peace.

"Girl? Brewerton? I know nothing. We haven't been there since you people kicked Mamma out of her home. Must be confusing us with someone else."

"Oh please, Mr Rossi. We have reliable witnesses who support our surveillance. Those luxury vehicles of yours are not exactly inconspicuous.

"Our role is to maintain order within this zone, understand? Our duty – as directed by our government – is to ensure zero tolerance of banditry. We expected threats from outside this ag zone, but theft by our own citizens, that is very disappointing to say the least."

Even from afar, Phuong saw Rosario's face redden.

"Cut the bullshit pig-talk, bouncer. If you really give a fuck about keeping order, your hands should be full. Deal with those scum who burn farms, instead of robbing locals, you bloody hypocrite. I'm sure it's fun pretending to be the big lawman but you're nothing but a jabbering little monkey dressed up as a pig. Fuck off back to Budgie. Don't you have some taxis to check on or something?"

Selvin continued flashing his teeth but Phuong could see the venom in his eyes. She suspected he would not suffer being addressed like this in front of his troopers.

"You," he spat. "You Rossis care about your family, yes? The fugitive. Hand her over and I'll consider not turning that big flash house of yours into dust."

"You have five seconds to get off my land."

Rosario cocked his rifle and fired a round at Selvin's feet.

The Blues ducked in unison.

"You had your chance, Rossi," Selvin shouted, scampering behind his armoured car.

The Rossi men opened fire. Phuong shrank even lower, peering through the balustrade. Selvin was yelling into a radio.

Phuong heard Tony call from out the back. Rosario yelled back a reply. Kids were crying somewhere. Tina was barking. All voices were drowned by something else.

There was an explosion. Windows shattered. Phuong heard more volleys of gunfire and glanced around to see if anyone was injured.

"Dad's been hit."

Phuong saw the red patch on Rosario's shoulder, discolouring his white shirt. The man paid his wound no heed and sprayed several more rounds at the Blues.

Then Phuong was startled by a sudden whirr by her side.

"We gotta use this," Giuseppe yelled into her ear, his fingers jabbing at the control tablet. "How do I get it to…"

The Lite Shot drone was airborne, wheeling up and over the balustrade, before proceeding to circle the garden.

"Wait, Giuseppe. If we do this…"

Then she stopped, exhaled and closed her eyes.

"You know, I just cannot run anymore."

Phuong realised these words were more for herself. She leaned over to the controller and engaged sentry mode.

The pair peered out, watching the UAV zip around with erratic movements. It sought targets, scanning everyone in the vicinity. The moment it had a clear line of fire at the Blues' unprotected rear, Phuong heard its weapon crack. A trooper fell beside Selvin.

"Make that slimeball the priority target," Giuseppe suggested.

"I'll try."

Then a massive aircraft swung into view, passing low over the mansion's rooftop. It was a much larger drone, dwarfing their Lite Shot. As it hovered over the driveway, its own cold artificial "eye" sought targets of its own.

"That's the thing we seen out in the valley," said Giuseppe. "Know what kind it is? Military prototype?"

"Electric-powered assault drone. I read about them being used when the northern Philippine islands were invaded. Bad news for anyone on the ground."

The monstrosity had AdSoS panels all over its dorsal surfaces but she knew these alone were not enough to power a UAV of such size with its heavy payload of rockets. The panels only served to extend its time aloft. Like electric cars, bikes or even the rice skipper, it still required a charging station.

Selvin yelled at someone in the back of the armoured car while the Blues on foot continued exchanging fire with the Rossi men.

"Hit it," Rosario screamed. "Everyone, go for it. Shoot that thing down."

Phuong covered her ears as Giuseppe aimed his rifle at the assault drone and joined his family in volleys of gunfire. She wanted to run but could not think of any place safe to fall back to. She had not even seen half of the mansion's rooms.

Then the rocket drone lurched sideways. Its flight seemed more ungainly, but the UAV remained aloft.

Phuong wondered if there was a way to use their own little drone's AI to target a vulnerable part of the behemoth — like the camera within the nose cone. If only there had been more time to learn every control function.

Over the din, the trooper in the car could not hear Selvin, who ordered him to open the window. Phuong could only see the passenger's silhouette and the glow of a screen in the back.

A message appeared on her own control tablet's screen: "New target detected. Set as priority?"

"If that guy's the controller…"

Phuong hit the word "Confirm" blinking in one corner of the screen. The Lite Shot adjusted its position in the air.

The assault drone wobbled, looking dangerous and unpredictable.

"I think it's armoured," someone screamed.

"Keep firing. Keep firing!" shouted Rosario.

Giuseppe fired several rounds.

Then a rocket streaked forth, a bright flash appearing to Phuong's right, dazzling her vision. A roar and wave of heat swept over the balcony instants later and it shuddered.

As the noise subsided, Phuong heard the sound of the Lite Shot's weapon firing again and she strained to see the action at ground level. Inside the car, the trooper's silhouette was slumped, unmoving.

The words "Seek next target?" appeared on the tablet's screen.

The assault drone spun about and loosed another rocket, which shot down the hill, obliterating a tree beside the driveway. Then another rocket streaked left, into the large garage housing the Rossis' cars. Phuong flattened herself as they were again engulfed by heat.

After several seconds she stood. "We'll all be cooked. Look."

The assault drone was in a lateral spin. The Rossis kept firing. Another rocket shot up into the air, streaking out over the valley.

"It's out of control, Giuseppe."

She heard the wheels of Selvin's armoured car screech. The behemoth was spinning their way, a collision with the mansion inevitable.

Phuong scooped up the Lite Shot controller with one hand and yanked Giuseppe to his feet by his shirt collar with the other.

The pair bolted through the house.

"The backyard," she yelled, not looking back. She could hear Giuseppe shouting behind her, urging his family to run.

Phuong reached the rear balcony and descended the stairs, making for the pool area. She halted at the bottom, contemplating whether to jump in the water or keep on running down the hill.

Phuong never got the chance to decide. She was blinded by another flash and knocked off her feet. She did not know why but she held her breath and covered her face with her hands. She felt herself sliding but did not know which way was up. Someone or something was squeezing her arm. She could not move her legs. They were jammed somehow.

There was a great crashing sound, a terrible rumble that went on and on. Everything was so dark.

Phuong wondered if Giuseppe or any of the Rossis had gotten clear. She waited for someone to drag her back into the light but nobody came.

Then a wet tear trickled down Phuong's cheek as she thought of Duc. How close they had come to being reunited. So close. He would never learn how her actions here just might have helped change the zone for the better.

24

Sienna

"Whiskey Vodka reporting in… Whiskey Vodka reporting in…"

Sienna sniggered. It was Witek, who had set out with Vlad on a reconnaissance trip to Budgieweir in Kilo's uncle's silver Ford Fairlane sedan, which, having been locked away in one of the sheds, still looked good despite having been manufactured decades before Sienna was born. It ran well enough too, after some tinkering under the hood by Vlad, including a battery charge and some kind of workaround for the failing starter motor.

Kilo designated the Ford "Kilo Victor One" implying it was Kirilian vehicle number one. However, Witek and Vlad preferred their own call sign.

Their reconnaissance trip commenced well before dawn, when most people in the zone were likely sleeping. The primary aim was to assess the strength of the Blues.

"Whiskey Vodka, go ahead," said Kilo.

"No budgies with blue feathers in sight, a few dragons in their lairs, a lot of ghosts."

"Thank you, Whiskey Vodka. See you back at the station. Out."

"So, that was to sound like an official communication, right?" said Sienna.

"Correct. We do not know who may be listening."

"And the report?"

"Budgieweir is near-deserted, save for Lucky Dragons personnel, if I understand correctly."

"How did the town get its name anyway? I haven't seen any budgerigars in the zone."

"Budgies lived all around this area back when they built the irrigation scheme. However, I have not seen any wild budgies since I was a kid."

Sienna nodded, yawning. She was unused to such early starts. Karmen was up too, pacing about, while Sameera was finishing an early breakfast with a few new workers from the other farm.

"What matters is their message suggests no sign of any Blues," said Kilo. "We can only hope that they are broken. With luck they no longer have the strength or numbers to behave as they have been."

"What's with the callsigns?" Sameera called over. "I get Witek's 'Whiskey' but not the 'Vodka'… V is 'Victor' if I am not mistaken."

"Correct. However, Vlad insisted."

"So… Kilo?" asked Sienna. "Is there a K-word we're yet to hear?"

Instead of answering, he raised an eyebrow and said, "I can call you 'Sierra' if you wish."

"I'm good, thanks. That's a little too close."

"I apologise," said Kilo, flushing. "Until I spoke it aloud, I did not even consider that it sounds…"

One of the new workers was staring at her over his breakfast.

"It's fine," Sienna said with a sigh. "You know what? It's time to put an end to Sindy Mason. Any Blues left around here should have bigger things to worry about than me. I miss my braids – Mum always did my hair like that when I was little and that's how I'm most comfortable. Sameera, think you can help me with that?"

"Sure sis, but are you 100 per cent certain?" said Sameera, standing to join them.

"I'm over letting some mug shot dictate how I look... or not look. Living a lie is bloody tiring and there's nothing special about me anyway."

Her ability to reach into rock walls did not need to become public knowledge though she was anxious to understand the anomaly.

They followed Kilo to the armoury, where Rocky was enjoying a pungent cigar.

"*Pagi*," said Kilo in greeting.

Sienna noticed the overseer knew some words of the Bahasa Indonesia language but he switched back to English.

"Can you do anything with this?"

Rocky took Kilo's great coat and looked it over, shaking his head. "Maybe can make into something else, yesss."

The garment had saved him from a mauling by one of the dogs at Farm 1469 but was badly torn. Today the overseer was dressed in black, with a hooded cloak draped over his shoulders. His medallion reflected the orange morning light streaming through the doorway.

"That ankh," said Sameera. "Did you get it in Egypt?"

"This? No, an old girlfriend bought it for me in a junk market in Fremantle. That was a long time ago. This lasted much longer than the relationship."

"Why keep it?" asked Sienna.

"I liked the symbolism. My ex said it could represent living a good life, if you followed some sort of code. It did not matter what particular code but the idea was to stick to it as long as you truly believed in it."

"And have you stuck to yours?" Sienna ventured.

"I try to do what I think is right at the time," said Kilo. "I see you have a medallion of your own."

"A gift from Mum. Reminds me I still have family out there somewhere."

Kilo nodded and moved to the doorway.

"Anyway, gear up and prepare to head out. I need to check the med shed then meet with our security team. When I am done, we will pay a visit to this ravine."

Sienna smiled as he vanished from view. It was nice to be believed. The team had shown Kilo the evidence of their successful hunt, but upon reporting the rest, she had expected him to assume they were indulging in the wrong kind of scavenged drugs. Instead, he had listened in silence, then matter-of-factly said he would like to visit the site.

The sound of Kilo's long strides faded. Kirilia's designated infirmary, which already housed a couple of seriously injured people, was stocked with the fruits of the recon team's scavenging runs. Searching household medicine cabinets yielded an assortment of painkillers and other medications, various bandages, even antiseptic.

Sameera began braiding Sienna's hair with rapid skill. Sienna was capable of doing it herself but it would have taken longer.

"So, sis, Whiskey Vodka won't be joining us?"

"No, Sameera. They're checking a couple of other farms on their way back then meeting Nestor about the perimeter upgrades. Guess Kilo considers it safe enough in the hills not to need our whole team. It's just a quick walk up the canyon and we'll come straight back."

"Vlad said Witek is still struggling to get his head around what's out there."

"He'll come round," said Sienna. "Imagine how the real conservative types here would react if Briggo walked in and joined them for lunch."

"I never got a good look at him," said Sameera.

"I feel you'll get your chance soon enough."

Before long, Sienna's hair was done and by the time they were dressed and armed, Kilo returned.

They set out in a ute with 4x4 capability, to better traverse the rutted old stock route north of Kirilia. The key was keeping a slow and steady pace. Kilo took pains to manoeuvre around the deepest ruts, leaving the track altogether where possible to bypass the worst sections.

"Hey, why didn't Karmen come?" asked Chad.

"She is worried about Witek," said Sienna. "She wants to be there when they get back."

"Of course, dumb question. Yeah, sorry, had a late one last night. Few of us took a walk to the west gate and we saw these lights, just kind of flying low."

"What lights?" asked Kilo, his brow creasing above his sunglasses.

"Not sure. The others freaked out a bit, but I said it's just cars or machinery on one of the farms further up the valley. Saw them up this way, pretty far off. We watched them awhile, then they moved away and disappeared."

"Why didn't you report this?" said Kilo.

"We did, man. We told Irish Bob on our way back in. He was on watch and said he'd keep an eye out for anything strange during the night. Guess it was nothing."

"Perhaps not," said Sameera. "Think it might be connected? We know better than to doubt your feelings."

Sienna shrugged. No new threats had come through Lynna, but she could still sense the place that had drawn her attention to these hills from the beginning.

"Maybe it was just a *Min Min* light."

Kilo glanced at her.

"What's a *Min Min?*" asked Chad.

"They're mysterious lights in the Outback. Most of the stories come from the Channel Country in Queensland, way out near Boulia and Winton, but *Min Min* lights have been seen elsewhere, even down this way. Indigenous Australians apparently saw them before colonial times too."

"Should we be worried?" said Riku.

"Some say they were followed or the lights moved parallel to their car. Others tried to approach but couldn't quite get close enough. In the really spooky stories, the people chasing the *Min Min* were never seen or heard from again."

"Well, after that story I will definitely not be sleeping tonight," said Riku. "This canyon is weird enough already."

"No wait, man," said Chad. "I know the kind of thing she's talking about. We have our own homegrown version in West Texas.

The Marfa Lights. Some say they're ghost lights or UFOs but most say they're nothin' but headlights on Highway 67. That's why I wasn't bothered by what we saw last night."

"I am no physicist," said Kilo, "but scientists have explained the phenomenon as distant light bending over the horizon when atmospheric conditions are just right, making the light seem close when its source may be a hundred kilometres away. I have never seen such a thing. Intriguing nevertheless. Sienna, if what you say about this rock wall is true, our physics books may as well be thrown out the window. Let us keep open minds."

Riku jumped out and opened a gate, which was chained but not padlocked, and they pressed on across a flat section with fewer ruts. Then the stock route dipped into a deep gully, which could have posed a challenge if the creek that fed it was flowing. Sienna could see that rarely happened. Beyond it the track improved, until it morphed into a well-maintained gravel road providing access to various short hiking trails in the national park.

Kilo took the ute down a side track when he saw a signpost marked "Mick's Canyon Picnic Area" and they reached a dead end near some picnic tables, a water tank, even a couple of toilets. Kilo reversed into a parking space with precision, which amused Sienna given they would not be sharing the car park with any picnickers.

"You're on watch here, Chad," said Kilo. "Keep one hand on your rifle, the other on that two-way. If you see any danger, use your discretion as to which one to use. I would prefer the radio first. Drive off if there is a threat your weapon cannot neutralise."

"OK man, I'm on it. Take care up there."

"Should somebody stay with Chad and watch his back?" asked Riku.

"I would say 'yes' but on foot we will be more exposed and vulnerable than Chad. It is a short enough walk from the car park. I hiked this trail several times when I was young but do not recall anything too unusual about the rock formation or waterfall. We shall see."

They set off through the picnic area along the well-marked Mick's Canyon Trail, first passing through a pleasant-smelling forest. The trail forked not far beyond the picnic area. The left path was marked "Mick's Lookout" and steps were cut into the hillside. However, they took the right path, following the dry creek bed to the canyon itself.

Kilo was right – in minutes they reached the place familiar to Sienna. The land began rising steeply on each side and ahead were large boulders and a fallen log.

"Up there is the trail we followed all the way from Cooper Hill," Sienna explained.

"Then this is where you made your kill."

Kilo pointed at some obvious bloodstains as he strode by. The corpse was no longer there.

Sienna heard bleating from above and spied a safety fence on an outcrop, behind which piebald feral goats were retreating into the scrub.

"If we are ever desperate for food, keep them in mind," said Kilo as the goats vanished from sight.

"I'd rather be up high with them," said Sameera. "Feels claustrophobic down here."

Kilo marched on past the vine-covered rock pillar in the middle of the gorge and on into the rocky amphitheatre. Sienna hesitated, until she confirmed they were alone.

"Sameera, Riku, wait here and cover us," Kilo instructed.

He strode on to the columnar rock formation then stopped and stared at it.

"Darker than I recall. I see nothing, but I feel…"

Sienna nodded, then reached for the dark stone. It was firm to the touch, unyielding. She withdrew her hand. Then, like last time, she summoned the energy, *her* unique energy, feeling it build in her neck and spine then flow down her right arm.

She realised Kilo was staring at her arm, which bristled with goose bumps.

"You can do that? It seems the fates woven for us were destined to intersect."

Sienna reached forward to push her hand into Lynna. She felt nothing but stone beneath the palm of her hand. Sienna summoned more energy then tried again – in vain.

"It was easy before," she muttered.

"Let me try," said Kilo.

Sienna opened her eyes wide, watching as the overseer concentrated then reached out with both arms, palms forward, fingers spread. She had never met anyone else who could do the goose bumps thing.

Then he whistled to himself. She had heard him whistle the tune a few times before but it was otherwise unfamiliar. He took a deep breath and focused.

Then Kilo's hands disappeared into the rock wall, followed by his forearms, his brow furrowing as he maintained concentration. Then he pulled away, took several steps back and flicked his fingers at the wall. The pitch-black holes he had punched into the rock wall rippled then faded.

"I could not push through," said Sienna.

"There was resistance, but once inside, I felt so much energy," said Kilo. "Other things too, light and dark. Not unlike dreams."

"And nightmares," Sienna murmured.

"So, you know about that too. Yes. It is like all the scary things that terrify you in your sleep are in there. People told me I was afflicted with some kind of sleep paralysis, but it always felt a little too real. Poor sleep has bothered me for as long as I can remember. Never at Kirilia though."

"I sleep well there too."

"Interesting."

Kilo pushed back his sleeve and upturned his right palm, curling his fingers, as if he were clutching a ball of invisible energy, the hairs on his forearm standing on end. He flicked his whole arm at the wall, as if hurling the energy at it. Sienna thought she saw small dark holes pepper the wall for a moment, like water droplets being flicked onto a frying pan being vaporised.

"Kilo, is this how we keep the… the dark things at bay?"

"Perhaps. We have no idea what lies in there – or beyond. We must establish permanent surveillance lest something else come through.

"Allow no one to question your perception, even if they do not understand. By allowing yourself to be drawn here, your team's hunt was successful and Kirilia is safer. Thank you for speaking the truth about this… Lynna."

Sienna followed Kilo back to the others.

"Can… do you think anyone can do… what you just did?" said Riku, his face pale.

"You are welcome to try," said Kilo.

"No, thank you. My hands may become stuck forever."

"What on earth is that thing?" asked Sameera.

"That is Lynna," said Sienna, "and I'm not sure it's part of Earth at all."

"Think this is why the Blues were looking for you, sis?"

Sienna closed her eyes and rubbed her forehead.

"They can't possibly have known. I don't see how –"

Kilo's radio crackled, startling her.

"Hey, y'all coming back now? It's goblin city here."

25

Harrison

Something was coming up the road. Harrison stepped out of the roadside trench, leaned on his shovel, wiped his brow and squinted through his glasses.

"What is that?" said Aditya.

"It's not making much noise so I'd say an electric bike, except for its profile. Looks bigger than a normal bike. Guess both team leaders should know."

Harrison glanced beyond Kirilia's west gate, where the dour big guy tasked with making the perimeter harder to breach stood beside a silver sedan idling on the driveway. He was speaking to the stern leader of the team who had brought everyone over from Farm 1469, who was standing upright through the car's open sunroof, clad in a stolen blue uniform. Harrison wished he could overhear their conversation but they were too far away.

"I think they already see it," said Aditya. "The guards are waving us back."

"Good, I was wondering when we'd get a break," one of the backpackers muttered.

"Yeah, tilling Jon-Jon's turf was easier," said another as he stomped away.

"Hey, I'm not a fan of this work either," said Harrison. "Though I must admit it is nice being free to walk outside a farm's front gate whenever we please. Anyway, I heard their overseer say they're trying to secure some kind of excavator."

"Hurry on, Harrison," said Aditya. "This could be another attack."

"Maybe."

As Aditya rushed to join the others inside Kirilia's boundary fence, Harrison looked at the phalanx of guards flanking the gate, readying their firearms. He turned back to the vehicle, which appeared to be a trike, slowing as it approached. A lone rider was seated upon it. Then Harrison spied the blue uniform.

"Get back here, you mad bloody bastard," one of the gate guards called out. "He's not one of ours."

"Hang on, it's just one guy. Cover me."

Harrison took a deep breath and stepped onto the gravel road, armed with nothing but his shovel. He felt his heart rate rise as he considered the gravity of the gamble he was taking.

The trike was upon him seconds later. The unhelmeted rider made no hostile moves. He just waved his hand sideways and moved as if to steer around Harrison.

"Wait, trooper. Hang on a moment."

Harrison raised his arm, hoping the man was not an impostor disguised as one of the Blues attempting the same kind of ruse the pair in the sedan apparently had employed during their morning outing. The trike did not stop. Doing his best to jog alongside,

Harrison studied the uniform of the ginger-haired rider. It seemed legitimate.

"Corporal, please, a moment. I work for Captain McDonald. I'm trying to return to him in Canberra."

The rider's attention was fixed on the armed group at the gate.

"Good for you, kid."

Harrison inspected the trike crunching along the road beside him. It was a high-tech vehicle but lacked a passenger seat.

Dropping his shovel, he withdrew the paper he kept in the internal pocket of his hoodie. He made sure his back was to the gate as he unfolded it and glanced over his shoulder. On Kirilia's driveway, the silver car was turning around.

"Sienna Jones – she's here," Harrison blurted. "You're looking for this girl, right?"

"I do recall some sketch like that but couldn't care now. This is a failed zone."

"You're leaving?" he panted. "Well, if you're heading off to Canberra, please tell any senior officers that Harrison Fletcher found her and is very much ready to go back too."

The silver car was approaching the gate. Harrison stuffed the paper back into his pocket.

"Sure, kid, but I probably won't see anyone. I'm sticking to the back roads and ain't going to Canberra anyway. I'm done with the Blues. I'm gonna shoot for home, see if anyone's left."

The corporal looked at the gate again and shook his head.

"Get out too, if you can. Otherwise, you lot are on your own. Good luck, kid."

Out of breath, Harrison slumped forward with hands on his

thighs then craned his neck up to watch the trike accelerate away.

The silver sedan roared up then crunched to a stop at his side. The stern team leader leaned out the passenger window. He was gripping a rifle.

"What did that trooper want? He was asking questions, no?"

"Yes," Harrison replied. "Only as to whether it is safe to leave the zone by this road. It seems the Blues have written off this place. I presume you did not see many on your scouting mission this morning, am I right?"

"Hmm. This is true."

"Witek, I should be able to catch him," said the driver. "Hashtag never trust a blue guy. We should take him down while we still can, claim his trike and make sure he tells nobody that we are all out here."

"He just wanted to leave in peace so he can try to find his family," said Harrison.

The stern one, Witek, gazed at the small clouds of raised dust on the road ahead.

"Don't we all?" he muttered, then relaxed back into the passenger seat.

Harrison could no longer make out the trike or rider.

"So, we are not chasing him?" said the driver.

"Not this one, Vlad," said Witek. "Time to return to base."

"Missing someone already?" said Vlad as he shifted the car's transmission into reverse.

Ignoring the comment, Witek unpopped the oversized collar of his uniform in silence.

Harrison scratched his head and turned to walk back.

"Guess I'll go fetch my shovel."

"Hold on," said Witek.

Harrison felt himself flush though he was already hot from labouring while clad in his black hoodie. He glanced around at the road for errant pieces of paper that may have freed themselves.

"That was dangerous, taking a stand, alone on the road like that. I think it was quite brave too. What is your name?"

"Harrison… oh, and I think I have a way of making your reconnaissance outings somewhat safer. You see, I happen to be in possession of a drone."

26

Sienna

It was not the radio in Kilo's hand that bothered Sienna. It was the birds. She could hear the alarm calls of more than one species somewhere in the distance.

Nothing unusual was visible in the vicinity though she kept glancing at the encircling high ground and over her shoulder at the dark rock columns. She still felt the energy of that place, contained and more distant for now.

Kilo's radio hissed and he fiddled with the controls before speaking.

"Chad, what is happening? How many are there? Are you under attack?"

"No, I'm OK, boss. Eight, maybe ten just came out of the woods. Sure, they have weapons, but they're just vibing here in the parking lot, checking me out. I've locked myself in the car."

"Good. Stay there, do not engage. We're coming."

Kilo led the way back down the ravine, jogging at a steady pace wherever the ground was not too treacherous. Soon they reached the forested area.

Riku pointed at the picnic area.

"I know," Kilo whispered. "Make no hostile moves. Stay sharp."

Sienna could see several figures ahead, each clad in a similar outfit, the same kind of woven outer garment Briggo had worn. Bright eyes with large irises of gold, green or blue peered out from beneath hoods. All had the same lithe build.

They were armed. To Sienna, their weapons appeared more like works of art than tools of violence. Many carried spears tipped with long, shining double-edged blades and shafts decorated with etched glyphs. They wore knives on their large belts next to pouches that reminded Sienna of "man bags". A few individuals carried crossbows.

"Over here, travellers."

The voice was female and came from a figure seated on a black pelt atop one of the picnic tables. She was unhooded, her hair worn in numerous plaits, some bleached, others dyed a shade of chocolate brown. Bright-green eyes with long lashes measured Sienna from an olive-skinned face, nodding, before beckoning with a long forefinger that bore a large gold ring.

A grey-faced attendant stood at her side, watching with narrowed golden eyes.

Kilo hesitated, looking in the direction of their vehicle.

"Do not worry about your friend. Briggo is watching over him. Come, travellers. We must speak."

Kilo looked at Sienna and moved forward. She followed, flicking her eyes left and right at the goblins closing in around them. She tensed, ready to draw her handgun, hoping just curiosity drew them close.

"Stop there, humans," said the attendant in a gruff masculine voice.

"The two travellers may approach, Tolden," said the female.

The attendant stepped to one side. Sienna noted he kept both hands on the haft of his spear.

The seated goblin pointed her long forefinger at Kilo.

"You... and you also, traveller."

As her dark eyes locked with eyes of bright green, Sienna wondered what the other was trying to read.

The overseer advanced while Riku and Sameera stood in place, their eyes flicking about at the curious group surrounding them. Sienna shrugged at her companions then hurried after Kilo.

"I am Blanda. Brimla is home. Hail, Kyrios of the Kirilian and hail, Sienna of the Kirilian."

"Hail and welcome to... the Cooper Hill National Park, Blanda and companions," said Kilo. "I trust you have made yourselves comfortable in this place. Well, as much as possible given recent events."

"It is less than ideal," said Blanda, "trapped in the world as we are, with a crude, human cave for shelter. Yet, this place, this tiny remnant of nature, is not wholly unpleasant."

Sienna tried to place Blanda's accent. It was familiar but differed from Briggo's. It almost sounded Mediterranean.

"I see Witek Tree-man is missing. Please, pass on my gratitude for his assistance."

"I will," said Sienna. "So, about Lynna, is it..."

"Travellers, I do not doubt that you have many, many questions. You both know Lynna, but neither of you have been beyond. Am I correct? Do not answer. I know. Let me explain.

"We are not aliens; my folk once lived in the world, just like you.

Humans knew us by various names, in different ages. We have been forgotten, rediscovered, traded with, forgotten, found by other human societies, labelled 'demons' by the ignorant, forced into the wilderness, forgotten again, reborn in human mythology… yet here we are, living and breathing in the world again."

Blanda was right. Sienna's mind swam with innumerable questions.

Kilo could not help but blurt out one himself.

"How… how is it you can speak our language?"

"Even in times of persecution, we were there, watching from shadows, listening, learning. We are not mindless savage imps as tales would have one believe. Education is a virtue. Our languages borrow many words from those of the humans. Our histories speak of times when we lived close to human folk, sometimes with civility. So did the other folk.

"Language and culture were shared between folk, centuries ago, before the last of us left the world. Nobody here speaks your language as fluently as I. Tolden here is fluent in what you may refer to as 'Spanish'. Each of us have our own skills."

Kilo raised his sunglasses to his forehead.

"And you just decided to return to the world? Now?"

Blanda raised her voice and sat upright.

"You think the Age of Return is a casual undertaking? We are honoured to be the generation to experience this, the embodiment of the hopes of generations. Humans have their religions and prophecies. We revered a dream — of the day we would come home, even if our ancestral lands no longer resemble what is described in our histories."

Sienna cleared her throat and did her best to speak in a respectful manner.

"Blanda, I must warn you. Your Age of Return may be ill-timed. A disease has spread through the world and killed most of the population. These are difficult and dangerous times."

After a few moments, Blanda inclined her head.

"Thank you for your concern, traveller. Fear not. The disease of which you speak is lethal only to the humans."

"I understand," said Sienna, "but if you've lived beyond Lynna for so long, there could be other diseases here in the world to which you're not immune. It may be dangerous for you speaking with us up close like this."

Blanda fixed her eyes on Sienna and studied her in silence.

"You are a wise traveller, Sienna of the Kirilian. Thoughtful too. This is appreciated and we should keep this knowledge in mind, in spite of our fortitude. We took the precaution of selecting the most robust among our folk as the first to return to the world.

"However, we were never completely isolated beyond Lynna. Those with the ability to travel have always come back and forth. We took pains to quarantine anyone who returned with signs of illness."

Sienna wondered how an intelligent, cultured species could have faded into the stuff of fairy tales. It was clear Blanda's people had taken great pains to conceal themselves.

"So, you are here simply to come home?" asked Kilo. "Are these your ancestral lands? Indigenous Australians roamed this land for tens of thousands of years. I am no expert but I do not recall your folk being mentioned in any of their legends."

Blanda looked around at the bushland.

"This is not ancestral land. My people had little reason to visit this continent. There are... recent aberrations in Lynna. Eldro did not expect to bring us to this remote corner of the far side of the world. We expected to return to the river valleys where our ancestors prospered for thousands of years, changed though they may be by the industry of humans."

"Aberrations?" said Kilo. "You mean things back there are constantly changing?"

"Great destructive energies unleashed here in the world affected Lynna and the places beyond. The Places of Return now shift on occasion.

"We suspected coming home would be no simple undertaking. These outcomes must be discussed with our leaders. As you know, Eldro, our traveller, was slain and we remain in the world. You can help us, Kyrios of the Kirilian. Yes. I see you know this."

Sienna turned to Kirilia's overseer.

"Kilo... stands for 'Kyrios' then?"

"I believe this is an archaic term of respect, meaning 'lord' or 'master'. Am I correct, Blanda? If so, I thank you, though I am no great lord. I am merely trying to help those at Kirilia, as well as the other good folk in this valley. We are attempting to survive this difficult period, which, as Sienna mentioned, has proven challenging."

"A noble, even lordly. undertaking nevertheless," said Blanda. "The question is what other deeds are you prepared to undertake, traveller?"

"Is there some way I can help? Can I perhaps extend some... Kirilian hospitality? Join us for a meal. I cannot promise our meagre fare will be to your liking. Nor can I predict how every member of our diverse community will react the first time they lay eyes on folk from beyond Lynna."

"Thank you for your kind offer," said Blanda. "However, I must decline. My people are inquisitive but do not know this land. We expect fear and prejudice from human folk and so prefer to remain hidden.

"We are rather partial to goat, by the way, and this land has ample, though I suspect your cooks do not know how to prepare the meat to our liking."

"We may surprise you," said Kilo.

Blanda fixed Kilo with her intense eyes.

"You deflected my question. Will you help with what I really need? You are certainly able, but are you willing to perform deeds far beyond Kirilia?"

Sienna saw Kilo's face twitch as he glanced at the trail to the ravine before speaking.

"Lynna. There are things in there. I felt the dark things. I do not know if I can."

Sienna squirmed. She too felt the terror of what lay within. It was all connected. The "useless superpower" her brother had mocked could be pleasant or horrific, as if the sensation came in equal and opposite flavours of light and darkness.

"You can," said Blanda. "I may not be able to travel like you, or Eldro, or young Sienna. Yet I can still sense what lies within each of you."

"Magic?" Sienna blurted out. "A mystical power we can use to visit some magical fairy land any time we please?"

Blanda laughed.

"The word 'magic' is only used by humans to describe that which is a perfectly normal part of science that they do not yet comprehend. Lynna is perceived as supernatural by those who do not understand a force that is strange and new to them.

"Oh, and if you expect to find a place ruled by wee folk, with insect wings sprouting from their backs and little ears that are pointed like ours, then you will be disappointed."

"What is this then, Blanda?" said Kilo. "Some kind of genetic ability? I never met anyone else who could draw on this energy until now. What are the odds of two of us ending up at Kirilia?"

"I am no scientist," said Blanda. "All I know is that a rare few of my kind are born with the gift of travel — or curse, should you choose to view it that way. You know of what I speak. The dreams. It is the same for you, travellers, is it not? Eldro suffered terribly in his sleep during his youth. In time, he learned how to defend himself."

"What are they?" asked Sienna.

"There is the world and then there are the places beyond Lynna, just as there is wakefulness and deep sleep. Then there are the places bridging the two, like Lynna or dreamy sleep. You and I are creatures of flesh and blood. We naturally exist in the material worlds. Other things naturally exist in those places between: Lynna, dreams, nightmares."

"Entities of light and darkness," said Sienna. "Kilo, those *Min Min* lights Chad saw — they must have come from there. Surely."

Kilo raised his eyebrows then turned back to Blanda.

"Some of these entities are peaceful, others predatory. Sometimes they hunger. Sometimes they reach out into the world, just as the traveller can reach into their domain or pass right through it. Maybe the one you call a *Min Min* is such a thing. Light or dark, they cannot go everywhere. It is known that some places are repellent. Eldro could repel them too, using the right kind of energy."

Sienna shuddered, taking little comfort from the confirmation that all her life she – and Kilo – had suffered something far more sinister than a regular sleep disorder.

"Kirilia – it is repellent," she said. "I felt a good energy there from the beginning."

"You are right," said Kilo. "This is another reason it made sense to go there when the pandemic struck."

"The protection does not extend far. I won't be spending another night in that old farmhouse. You said Eldro repelled them too, Blanda. How?"

"I am not a traveller. Therefore, I do not know how to manipulate energy. Besides, I have shared more than enough knowledge. So, I ask one final time. Will you take us back beyond Lynna?"

"I will not lie to you, Blanda," said Kilo, "I believe I can do this. However, not right now. I have responsibilities here, in the world, as you say. I cannot simply abandon Kirilia. There is much to arrange: food, security, making sure everyone can defend themselves…"

"…and you've just lost an important ally in your political game. Am I right? In the valley there is much we have seen and, well, explosions we have heard. Subtlety and stealth are not strong points for humans."

"Your point is?" said Kilo.

"Perhaps you could use a new ally. If the reports are correct, I understand you are someone prepared to make mutually beneficial arrangements. We can be patient. The hill country hereabouts is well known to us. We are already neighbours. We can watch over the northern approach to Kirilia."

"Perhaps."

Blanda turned to Sienna and stroked the pelt on which she sat.

"You eliminated the predator that travelled through Lynna and hunted us. My folk feel safer in these woodlands now and have been bothered by nothing more. Even so, we will maintain a watch over Lynna. As I said, it is unstable. The way may become easier for others to pass through. We have reason to believe one might have done so already. There is also the risk the path may close and we will be trapped here. I ask you do not keep us waiting too long."

"Very well," said Kilo. "I give you my word I will take you back beyond Lynna, although I cannot confirm when."

"It is agreed then," said Blanda, smiling, her eyes shining.

"Hang on," said Sienna. "What other one has come through? Another big cat? Will more be waiting on the other side, assuming we get through Lynna safely? What other dangers are there? You spoke of 'other folk' – who else is there?"

Blanda raised her eyebrows.

"So, you are volunteering to join us then, Sienna? This is your own decision. Beyond Lynna is just like here in the world. Certainly, there are dangers, there are predators, there are friends and there are enemies. We know how to navigate. Our roads beyond Lynna are more secure than those here in the world."

"Sure," said Sienna, "but these 'others' – you are not the only people who retreated beyond Lynna and are part of this return, are you?"

Blanda leaned back, narrowing her eyes a little.

"There are many different folk, most of whom would not appreciate me speaking about them. They have a right to their privacy. Should you see someone strange and new here, do not approach. We shall deal with such interactions. It is better this way, Sienna, better for all concerned. We have shared our story, this is enough, for now."

"Sorry if I was being pushy. I was thinking more… well, what if a whole horde of angry yowies, dragons, minotaurs, manticores… all decide to come charging through Lynna?"

Blanda chuckled with amusement.

"Minotaurs and manticores? Oh, Sienna of the Kirilian, you are a delight. No. If any bizarre chimeric hybrid creatures actually exist anywhere at all, well, only a human laboratory would produce such unnatural monstrosities. Given the nature of humans to forever dream up new weapons, perhaps I should not joke. Have you ever seen such a being here in the world, Sienna?"

Blanda's face was serious once more.

Sienna shook her head, imagining herself trying to explain to her family she had been speaking with a fantastic creature about beasts of legend. She knew her brother would love this, being a massive gamer.

A whistle, like that of a woodwind instrument, broke the silence. It reminded Sienna of Vlad's koncovka at first but as the notes kept coming, its own distinct trilling sound became more evident.

Blanda leapt to her feet then twirled and grasped a sheathed blade, which had been resting atop the picnic table behind the pelt.

"Stay back, find cover," said Kilo with urgency.

Blanda nodded as her companions formed up around her.

"Something from beyond Lynna?" asked Sienna. "Already?'

"No," Blanda replied. "Humans. The worst kind."

Sienna wondered what kind of humans were regarded as particularly bad. Then she heard the unmistakable sound of trail bikes.

"Feral humans – raiders," Kilo hissed.

Sienna thought of Chad, still alone in the vehicle, and sprinted to the parking area, Sameera and Riku at her heels. Kilo was shouting into his radio.

Chad started the engine. His window was down and he had a smirk on his face. Briggo was in the back tray of the ute with two companions, capering about, holding their weapons aloft.

"Greetings. Ready for battle, friends?" said Briggo.

Kilo appeared, halting upon seeing the ute's additional passengers.

"Hello there, Briggo?" said Kilo. "You do not have to be part of this. If these people are hostile, there will be bloodshed. I cannot let them reach Kirilia."

"Then we stop them," said Briggo. "Chad promised we could ride in the back."

"Made some new friends, dude?" said Sienna.

Chad leaned out the window and winked.

"Could say that."

Kilo hauled himself up into the back of the ute.

"Very well, Briggo," he said. "I will fight at your side. Hang on. These vehicles can throw folk all about the place."

"Why are we so ready to shoot at strangers?" said Riku. "These bikers might be neighbours seeking help."

"None of the friendly farms confirmed any of their people are nearby," said Kilo, tapping his radio. "Even if they are friends, I would rather intercept them here. Chad, drive forward but keep it slow and steady."

Sienna spied a wooded area flanking the track.

"I'm heading over there. If this is an attack, they won't see me till it's too late."

She drew her pistol and jogged ahead.

"Wait, don't run off too far lest we shoot each other by accident," Kilo called after her.

Sienna pretended not to hear and ran on. The scrub nearest the track was not as thick as it had appeared, and she moved deeper into the woods, seeking the optimal place to attack from ambush. A patch of small Australian white cypress pines looked promising so she moved in among the trees and waited.

The motorbikes were closing fast. She caught glimpses of the riders through the foliage. She considered Riku's words but these people sure as heck did not look like friendlies. Those she could see were unhelmeted, a couple even bare-chested. Perfect targets.

Looking back, she could see their ute rolling along the picnic area access track, Riku and Sameera at either side, keeping pace on foot.

The riders were moving fast, some crossing open ground, others weaving through the bushland. Sienna could hear them getting close. It felt like they were circling.

Just as she considered repositioning herself, a trail bike sped around the thicket. The rider had an ugly mess of tattoos but that was all she saw as he vanished into the scrub.

Then she heard Kilo's shotgun fire and some kind of war cry — or perhaps hysterical laughter. Satisfied the riders were a genuine threat, Sienna readied herself.

A rider roared into view, weaving around the small trees straight for her. Their eyes locked. Sienna opened fire.

She got three shots off then spun aside. Too late. The charging trail bike knocked her off her feet as it slid sideways. The rider toppled, rolling away until he came to rest against a small cypress, facing her. Sienna saw the bald man's eyes bulge as blood pooled about his throat and mouth.

Her chest heaved as she confronted the product of her own violence for a moment, then turned away. She regained her feet, whipping her head about, adrenaline pumping.

Another rider circled the thicket then made for her companions on the track. He reared his bike up on one wheel and charged at Riku. Sienna wanted to fire but feared hitting her friend. Then the bike wobbled, the rider falling to one side.

Two more trail bikes charged the ute head on. Sienna paused, trying to choose a clear target.

Then she saw movement on the main gravel stock route road. It was a ute, not unlike their own, southbound. The man in the vehicle's back tray seemed to have a similar appearance to the rider she had just shot.

Thinking of Kirilia, Sienna burst from the thicket, running as fast as she could manage, amazed her legs were unharmed by the collision with the trail bike.

She refrained from shooting, wanting to close the distance for a better chance at unloading her clip through the windscreen. Sienna dodged and weaved around tree trunks, focusing on her breathing. A little further and she would cut them off, with a good firing angle.

She heard Kilo's shotgun again, followed by other gunfire and more gleeful whoops.

Sienna felt confidence surge through her. She imagined she was a predator. This was how the great black cat must have felt when on the hunt, cornering its prey. Stopping the vehicle would be her personal triumph.

The raider vehicle was decorated for war. Graffiti adorned its panels and a severed head sporting red hair was mounted on the bull-bar. The thickset man riding in the back tray was a tempting target but she had to stop the driver.

Sienna raised her pistol and opened fire.

A motor revved. Before she could locate it, something knocked the wind out of her. She spun about, trying to keep her feet. Next came a blow to her head. Sienna did not know which way was up as she fought to see.

As she reeled, disjointed thoughts flashed: family, recklessness, friends, mysteries, foolishness, worlds beyond, travelling, Lynna… the things in Lynna. The things that were coming for her. Now.

Shadows took Sienna before she hit the ground.

Epilogue

Nobody could call this place luxurious but Harrison was not complaining. He licked his lips, savouring the taste of lunch, hoping it lingered awhile.

Not only were there half-decent cooks at Kirilia, there were its amenities: electric power around the clock – even when the grid was down – warm showers, toothpaste and toilet paper.

He knew the consumables would not last. It was inevitable that the dogs would squabble over scraps once resources dwindled and he did not wish to be around for that shit fight. He would have to find another way out before then. Not that leaving would be on the cards anytime soon.

There was no longer any clear indication of Blues in the valley though Harrison hoped one or two stragglers were still out there. His drone would soon reveal the truth. He was pleased that some important people on this farm had received his offer of recon aid with such positivity.

This hillside offered a half-decent view of the area. He did not even need a drone's perspective to chance a glimpse of an armoured car or another electric vehicle somewhere nearby. He only needed one trooper who remained dedicated to the uniform, a reliable contact, a genuine step back to civilisation.

He still held his bargaining chip – information, plenty of juicy intel.

Something *was* moving in the valley and Harrison jumped to his feet. No. Wishful thinking. He must be seeing things. He polished his glasses with the hem of his shirt and put them back on.

It was not his imagination. A convoy was moving in the distance, making for Budgieweir. White trucks, one after the other, in a long line.

Intriguing. New opportunities awaited. He was adaptable. Whatever was going on in the valley, Harrison would devise a way to make it work for him. He always did.

Appendix

Australian Ministry of Home Defence
Convoy Manifest #NR028W

Surname, First Middle/Other	Country of Citizenship	Gender
Alvarez, Ximena Maria	PER	F
Anderson, Jessica Rose	AUS	F
Bachmeyer, Florian Isaak	GER	M
Banda, Amahle Grace	ZIM	F
Cheung, Raymond	AUS	M
Chornovil, Myroslava	UKR	F
Dietrich, Moritz Tobias	GER	M
Dumont, Karin	CAN	F
Edwards, Jazlyn Kylee	AUS	F
Flanagan, Seamus Robert	IRL	M
Fletcher, Harrison James	AUS	M
Flores, Reyna Dela Cruz	PHI	F
Fukuoka, Riku	JPN	M
Greenwood, Amelia	GBR	F
Hardy, Christopher	GBR	M
Hartkopf, Liah Lotte	GER	F
Hartkopf, Maja Theresa	GER	F
Hassan, Ahmed	MDV	M
Ivanovic, Samantha	AUS	F
Jacquemin, Trinette	FRA	F

Johnson, Josie Lee	USA	F
Khan, Ashraf	OMA	M
Koh, Agnes	SGP	F
Lester, Jack	AUS	M
Martinez, Karmen	ARG	F
Mason, Sindy	AUS	F
McIntyre, Bonnie	NZL	F
Nair, Aditya	IND	M
Navarrette Jimenez, Ricardo	ESP	M
Ndebele, Junior John	ZIM	M
Ocampo, Tala Reyes	PHI	F
Owens, Chad William	USA	M
Park, Sally	USA	F
Petrov, Nestor Alexeyevich	RUS	M
Rasmussen, Ann-Sofie	DEN	F
Ryan, Chaylarna Haze	AUS	F
Scott, Kyle Arthur	CAN	M
Sharma, Aradhya	IND	F
Thoresen, Mads Pal	DEN	M
To'o, Iosefa Siaki	SAM	M
Tran, Duc Van	AUS	M
Tran, Phuong Thi	AUS	F
Unnithan, Arjun Pillai	IND	M
Varga, Vladimir	SVK	M
Willems, Sameera	RSA	F
Wolf, Elias Peter	GER	M
Young, Kaylene Janice	AUS	F
Zabrewski, Witold	POL	M

About the author

Kendall Carlsson has a degree in medical science and has worked in research, health promotion, hospitality and farming. Keen interests in ecology, the natural world, sustainability, folklore and traditions have inspired much of Kendall's writing, including *Seven by Seven*, the first book in a new series of post-pandemic speculative fiction.